To

Bes

Pete

Bowing Out

by

Peter Cropper

authorHOUSE®

AuthorHouse™ UK Ltd.
500 Avebury Boulevard
Central Milton Keynes, MK9 2BE
www.authorhouse.co.uk
Phone: 08001974150

© 2009 Peter Cropper. All rights reserved.

No part of this book may be reproduced, stored in a retrieval system, or transmitted by any means without the written permission of the author.

First published by AuthorHouse 01/05/2009

ISBN: 978-1-4389-0060-5 (sc)

Printed in the United States of America
Bloomington, Indiana

This book is printed on acid-free paper.

ACKNOWLEDGEMENTS

I would like to thank the substantial number of people who have helped me in writing "Bowing Out". Mindy Gibbins-Klein, "The Book Midwife", provided invaluable help through her regular consultations, and I must also thank Shirley Caldwell who referred me to Mindy.

Thanks are also due to Maggie Ford of "Spring Rites Productions" whose retreat in rural Derbyshire - aptly called "The Hide" - provided the time and space to make good progress on the novel.

I would also thank my friend Graham Glover, a former policeman, who provided information on bail conditions, and my old friends Andy and Anne Johnson from Carlisle who corrected my misconceptions about what a night out in the Border City is like.

Thanks, of course, are also due to my wife Josephine and daughter Hanne for their unstinting support. Indeed, I should like to thank all family members, particularly sister in law Maria for her help in the field of fashions and furnishings, and my many good friends for their encouragement. I am fortunate to know such a large group of wonderful people.

CHAPTER ONE

Chris found himself pinned against the whiteboard next to the filing cabinet by two of his year ten pupils. "What are these bastards going to do?" he thought. The bastards in question were Michael Anderson and Stuart Boyle. They had always been volatile boys who regarded such requests as "Could you open your books at page seven, please?" to be an insult and an affront to their dignity, but this was the first time that they'd ever turned violent towards a teacher. Framed by these two fearful examples of adolescence stood the shaven headed Jason Farrell, Chris' particular "bête noire" and notorious fifteen year old thug. Chris' crime had been to ask Farrell to turn round in preference to fraternising with Anderson, and now he was about to pay the penalty. Farrell, who occasionally boxed at the local boys' club when he wanted a change from terrorising the streets with his cronies, certainly packed a punch – or, to be precise, two punches. He hit Chris as hard as he had ever hit anyone. The first punch met his cheekbone with such force that it swelled up instantly, while the second one split open his nose and the warm blood spilt liberally down his white shirt.

With some difficulty Chris wrestled clear, raced out of the room and hurtled down the corridor to the staff toilets passing half a dozen younger pupils who were inexplicably hanging round doing nothing. He could swear they were laughing at him. A colleague who came out of his room to investigate the commotion also seemed mildly amused. Still, at least one of his favourite songs, Don McLean's "Castles in the Air"* was playing as he ran, bruised, blooded and humiliated. He could not understand where the music was coming from.

He found himself lying in bed, sweating profusely, for a few seconds too shocked to move. After a short while he groped at the radio alarm and switched it off. Why did he always find it so hard to slide a button across? No wonder his wife became irritated at being woken early.

Quietly, he padded off to the bathroom. He washed off the sweat – the blood had mysteriously already disappeared – and he looked into the mirror. A dishevelled looking man with tousled hair, already sadly greying slightly at the temples, stared back at him. Chris saw a schoolteacher somewhere in his mid thirties who, despite the stresses and strains of a demanding job and the greyness which he could probably remove with something miraculous from a bottle if he chose to do so, looked quite fit and healthy even first thing in the morning. The frequent trips to the gym were proving beneficial.

He had been at Whiteoaks High School for ten years – a long time. As the saying went – you seldom got that for murder these days. Situated about three miles from the city centre between a huge, sprawling industrial area and a notorious council estate, the school had always had the reputation of being "rough". Of course, the school had its share of pleasant children, but perhaps not its fair share and they never seemed to get noticed. Chris had heard of the school – who hadn't? – before he had taken his post there, and he had thought that working there would be a tremendous challenge.

After university, armed with a history degree, he had been unsure of what to do. To give him time to think,

---

*by Don McLean 1981. Universal/ MCA Music Publishing Ltd

Bowing Out

and to make inroads into the debts he had accumulated, he had taken a job in a factory which manufactured cleaning materials. The menial tasks failed to stimulate him, but he was able to disguise his disdain for the work and he made some good mates. Sometimes at the end of the working day they'd go to the pub for a "twilighter", as Chris would call it. Sarah, another product of the university system, then fiancée, now wife, didn't seem to mind.

"You've worked hard all day, you deserve a drink," she used to say. Chris could never quite fathom whether there was irony in her tone.

Nevertheless Chris, Dave Sullivan, Phil Briggs and Jim Roberts became regular visitors to the George. Chris saw nothing wrong in unwinding with a couple of pints.

As Chris stared into the bathroom mirror, his still frowning face stared back. He recalled vividly a particular conversation he had had with his workmates one evening as summer was giving way to autumn. The conversation had been something of a road to Damascus experience for Chris.

"You seem to enjoy working at Blake's," Phil said, after taking a sip of beer. "But I can never really understand why, to be honest. You're a clever bloke – miles cleverer than us, I reckon. Aren't you bored?"

"You know all about 1066, world wars and everything." Dave submitted his application to join the Chris O'Neill fan club. "Yet you're happy to fetch and carry and pack bloody cleaning fluid all day. It makes no sense to me."

"Our Wayne, on the other hand, knows nothing. What they don't teach him at that school!" It was Jim's turn to offer his opinion. "Why don't you do something useful – give the kids your knowledge? I bet you'd get on really well with them. You could talk to them on their level. I reckon you could really relate to them. You're wasting your talent here, mate."

"I couldn't care what happened last week, never mind 100 years ago or whenever the war was," said Phil. He was surprised to find his views had no support. Jim and Dave seemed convinced that education mattered, although the system hadn't really done them any favours. Shouldn't Chris, a bright, personable man, think about transmitting his knowledge and skills?

"Have you seen the time?" Sarah's voice drifted through from the bedroom. Chris had rather lost track of the time. He often cut things fine, and he had certainly mused for too long. "You've got to get a move on, you know. The kids will be …."

"…. hungering and thirsting after knowledge," interrupted Chris, as if they were a well rehearsed double act. It was a favourite expression of his. It had become something of a staff mantra, the irony of which was lost on none of his colleagues.

He dressed quickly and went downstairs for a necessarily rapid breakfast. Sarah arrived soon after, in her dressing gown as usual. Her job in the local greengrocers, ten minutes walk away, necessitated a later departure than Chris'. Sometimes, on his more frustrated mornings, Chris felt dispirited as he began the half hour drive to work just as Sarah was buttering her second slice of toast. Still, that's life, he would think. Bruce Hornsby had hit the nail right on the head with his song: "That's just the way it is, some things will never change."*

Chris had continued to work at Blake's but he did consider very carefully what his workmates had said. To his slight surprise, Phil's ignorance and, what was worse, the cheerful acceptance of his ignorance concerned him. Chris couldn't get what Phil had said that evening out of his mind. How many other people didn't know basic, important information like when the Second World War took place? His excursion into the real world made him think it might be more than he had previously thought. How many people didn't know how well off they were compared to their ancestors? It was important that they knew these things, wasn't it? It was important that lessons could be learned from mistakes made in the past, wasn't it?

---

by Bruce Hornsby and the Range 1986. RCA

Bowing Out

There were plenty of questions to mull over in the slow motion world that was the Blakes warehouse.

Chris came to the inescapable conclusion these issues were important. Six months later he had secured his place at teacher training college. He was to educate the nation's youth of today on the nation's glorious past.

CHAPTER TWO

"Michael"

"Yes, Sir."

"Claire."

"Yes, Sir."

"Vicky."

No reply. "I saw her at the bus stop with Nicola Bennett," piped up a voice from the back. Chris made a mental note to investigate later, if he could remember.

"James Williams"

"Yes, Sir."

"Thank you, everyone," said Chris. "I've one or two important announcements today so listen, please – including you, Kylie." Chris pointed at the little blonde girl holding court near the window and wondered, not for the first time, how anyone aged thirteen could possibly have so much to talk about. Boys? Fashion? He supposed so. Children seemed to grow up far more quickly now than when Chris was a lad. Nefarious activities on the estate the night before? He hoped not, but suspected as much. He'd heard some startling stories about pupils' extra curricular activities.

Still, reflected Chris, he'd been quite fortunate when he had been allocated his form in September – there were worse children than these prowling the corridors of Whiteoaks. In fact, he'd probably be wishing in a few weeks when the academic year ended that he could move up with them even

Bowing Out

though they would inevitably turn into year nine pupils, with all that entailed. Moving up with a form, however, was not Mr. Harris' policy so there was no chance of that.

"Now," continued Chris, "can I remind you that the absolute deadline for payment for your end of year disco is Friday?" The class, now all tuned in to something they found relevant for a change, listened attentively until the end of registration.

Just at the time Chris had been sitting in the staffroom listening to Mr. Harris' start of school day announcements, Sarah drained her second cup of tea. There was still no urgency in her day and there was plenty of time before she needed to begin her stroll to The Fruit Bowl.

Chris would often complain to Sarah about stress at work, but she couldn't really relate to what he was saying. She lit a cigarette to concentrate on the day's first major dilemma – did she really want a third cup or could she wait until her break?

Smoking – this *was* a contentious issue. Chris was against it, absolutely; he was sporting, he regarded it as vital to keep fit and in any case cigarette smoke stank the house out. Sarah often wondered how such a fitness fanatic could justify meeting Pete for frequent alcohol fuelled "academic debriefs" and "note swapping". Surely Chris was not being consistent here? When Sarah put forward her theory that if Chris kept his pleasures then why couldn't she, she was regaled with the argument that while passive smoking definitely exists, passive drinking does not. The conversation cropped up time and again, with very few variations.

"You do realise, don't you, that every cigarette you smoke takes about five minutes off your life *and* does me and anyone else near you untold damage."

"You enjoy a pint. Why can't I enjoy a cigarette?"

"Because the smoke gets everywhere. It gets on your clothes and your hair. It's bad enough on me. At least I don't piss over everyone in the pub."

It would have been fruitless Sarah giving Chris a lecture on how drink can wreck lives, unless she wanted to spark off

Peter Cropper

World War Three. Anyway, whose house was it? It's not as if I smoke heavily, she thought. So sod it.

The postman, on his early walk this week, brought two items of mail. One reassuringly pointed out that the payments for their gas supply were still being made direct from the bank account. Well, why wouldn't they be? Sarah thought that if they sent less needless mail, they could lower their bills. She might write to them, but she would probably get no reply, as that would be considered wasteful. The second was much more interesting. It was a real blast from the past – a postcard from Helen Wilkinson, rebel school chum, who no longer played an active part in Sarah's life. Sarah murmured her surprise and read:

Sarah,

Long time, no hear. Thought I'd let you know I'm still alive. See picture – now in Lakes. Bar work a real laugh! Life loads better without Andy.

Hope you're well.

Helen.

Long time indeed. The card aroused Sarah's interest and some guilt – she really should have tried harder to keep in touch with Helen. They'd been real mates, doing everything together at school and during that glorious summer after they had left. Sarah remembered how they had taken to the road and hitch hiked down south. There was the thrill of embarking on their own adventure as well as the sense of triumph. They had pulled the wool over their parents' eyes by being seen with train timetables at every opportunity. The intention was to make it to Spain but when they discovered just how far that was they diverted and finished up in Torquay. They certainly managed to cram a lot into a short stay on the English Riviera. Sarah struggled to recall the names of the two local lads who had befriended them. She seemed to think Helen's boy was called Lee but, strangely enough, she could not bring to mind the name of her own West Country beau.

She still didn't know whether her parents or Helen's parents had realised what had happened or, if they did know, how on earth she and Helen had managed to get away with it. Perhaps everyone had simply decided that the girls were eighteen and were therefore free to make their own mistakes. Thankfully, any mistakes they had made carried no serious consequences.

They were known in all the key pubs and clubs in their hometown, acting far older than they were, and they provided competition for each other on a Saturday night. Who would wear the most revealing low cut dress this time? Whose make up would be the most eye catching? Who would be the first to be successfully chatted up? It was usually me in all three categories, thought Sarah with a smile, although she conceded that Helen possibly wouldn't agree.

But later, after Sarah had started at university, they'd gone their separate ways. Miles had come between them and they started to move in different circles. Communication became very infrequent before more or less drying up completely. Sarah felt disinclined to come home at weekends – she had moved on, and there was far too much going on in student land – and after Helen had ignored a couple of invitations to visit her, she had stopped asking her. The last time the silence had been broken Helen had told her – again by postcard – that she'd left her job in the bank in Leeds because she'd been denied promotion. Unfairly, the card had said (of course). Sarah had heard on the grapevine about Helen's divorce but wasn't surprised ("Helen," she had said many years ago, "you'd be mad to marry Andy.")

Mind you, thought Sarah, how can you keep in touch with someone who doesn't leave you an address or a phone number? The photograph on today's card, Striding Edge on Helvellyn with two tiny figures about to start the final pull towards the summit, made Sarah smile again because, unless Helen's attitude to serious outdoor pursuits had changed dramatically, there was no way either of the figures could have been her. The card's message gave no clues to Helen's place of work or to where she might be living. Sarah put the card aside, stubbed out her cigarette and dragged herself to her feet. Soon the locals would be clamouring after lettuce, tomatoes and other things healthy and wholesome. She could not, and would not, let them down.

"Do you want me to tell you something amazing?" Chris was digressing, as he was prone to do. A lower school history group which was scheduled to be making sense of, "Divorced, beheaded, died, divorced, beheaded, survived", had replaced his form. Even though the class was on the threshold of their school examinations, Chris seemed able to keep neither himself nor the pupils focused.

Boredom hung in the air. No pupil responded. Uninterested expressions seemed to be everywhere. In response to a sudden outbreak of chatter completely unrelated to the task in hand, Chris called for silence again and then continued. "There are more stars in the sky than grains of sand on the beach. And do you know how you can prove it?"

Again, Chris stood on the shore of a sea of bored faces. He battled on. "You take an enormous bucket, fill it with sand, empty it onto the floor, and count very carefully. Then, you step into a really powerful rocket. …."

Oh, dear. Not too long ago this particular section of Chris' cabaret was guaranteed raucous laughter, rich applause and calls for more. Was it his delivery or the children's attitude which was changing?

It was all quiet today in the cut and thrust world of fruit and veg selling. Apart from the odd moments of curiosity and excitement – why did the tall elderly man need five pounds of mushrooms? – there was not much to report.

"Did you see that programme on the trek to Machu Picchu? The scenery in Peru is amazing, isn't it? Some of those hairpin bends were absolutely unbelievable. Mind you, the driving was more unbelievable. I don't know how the driver managed to keep the bus on the road. But when they got there, it must have been so worthwhile. I'd love to go. Do you think the programme will make more people want to go and that that will have an adverse effect on the site?" Sheila spoke with great gusto. Sarah's colleague in salad was so bloody enthusiastic about everything and sometimes it grated.

"Some of it," said Sarah. "Well, not much, actually – I gave up on it. I thought it was rather boring."

Sarah had the knack of keeping Sheila quiet and thus obtaining the peace and quiet which her increasingly dull lifestyle craved. It was ironic really; by Sheila's standards it seemed a really interesting topic of conversation was taking shape and given Sarah's level of intelligence she should really have snapped up the chance to talk about something like that in some depth. Unfortunately, she couldn't be bothered. Life among the vegetables must have stagnated her more than she'd imagined. It wouldn't be long now until her break.

Sometimes Sarah reflected that this was what it had come to – weighing vegetables and clockwatching. She had lost her way; she was the proud owner of an honours degree in English from a respected, redbrick university, and she acknowledged she should be doing more than this. She knew from what Chris told her that she shouldn't be in a classroom; "I'd probably spend all my time belting the little buggers." She also knew that she shouldn't really be in a greengrocer's – or, at least, that was what convention dictated.

It all depended which way you looked at it. Some days she managed to fight off the boredom and was content to toddle along in her own little world. Other days her serious underachievement and complete lack of direction worried her.

Break. The first milestone of the day had been reached.

Chris' room was handily placed for the staffroom so he was generally one of the first to reach the urn. This time only Sue McGrath from the English Department had beaten him. They exchanged pleasantries, but nothing more. Sue looked as though she had been experiencing a frustrating morning.

"Decent day so far?" asked Chris.

"Yes, OK," said Sue. It was obvious she didn't want to convey any more information.

It said it all, really.

Rather like in an exclusive gentleman's club, each member of staff had his or her own place in the inner sanctum, safely hidden away from the children. Sometimes, strictly for amusement, someone would ruffle a few feathers by moving, but the status quo was generally maintained. Chris wasn't in mischief mode today and he made instinctively for his seat by the window. It could be noisy there near the playground but it was light. The other side of the room was in almost permanent darkness. He awaited the arrival of his best friend who would soon be descending from the heady world of angles, shapes and astonishing formulae which was the Maths Department.

Pete James had joined the staff at Whiteoaks shortly before Chris and it was Pete who seemed to Chris to be the most welcoming as he nervously sat down on his first morning a lifetime ago. The two men quickly became friends. Sport was the main bond that held the friendship together. They would discuss sport, work out together in the gym (time permitting) and Chris sometimes helped Pete with the running of the year ten football team. Chris felt that taking a direct interest in a fifteen year old's sporting activities would probably have a beneficial spin off academically.

He was still reasonably confident that the theory held water, but so far he had seen little evidence of this.

The friends' attitudes towards their teaching careers were rather different. Mr. James was a dynamic, "whiz kid" type who got on famously with pupils and (important) colleagues alike. He gave lie to what Chris sometimes said when he saw job adverts: "There's a school here looking for an enthusiastic, experienced teacher, but that's a contradiction in terms – you can't possibly be both." His approach motivated children and raised standards. He also had a well practised mantra with which he began all lessons - "We are mathematicians, and you can count on us!" – which the children loved to yell at the tops of

Bowing Out

their voices. His promotion to Head of Department at Whiteoaks when Mr. Gilmour retired became inevitable. Mr. O'Neill was rather more laid back – very clever and knowledgeable, yes, but his lessons rarely exploded into life like Mr. James' did. Sometimes he thought his motto might be, "History, there's no future in it." He was much less likely to climb the ladder of success.

The difference in approaches and standing within the school bred no resentment. Chris and Pete always got on well and sometimes they would transfer their association from the staffroom to the Crown, particularly at 3.30 on a Friday. Chris found facing Pete over a pint pot was, with respect, rather more interesting than facing Dave, Phil and Jim. But, of course, there was no such thing as wasted time in a pub.

Pete, as usual, was one of the last to arrive. Probably some eager pupils had found it impossible to tear themselves away from his classroom. Mr. James would have had to explain that he had some urgent business elsewhere involving coffee granules, milk and a teaspoon of sugar. He stopped by the notice board for a few words with Mike Prescott, the youngest member of his department. Mike nodded enthusiastically and smiled. Pete then made a drink and headed for the empty seat next to Chris.

He was ebullient as he sat down. "I can't believe how well those year nines are going. We're miles ahead of schedule. I think there'll be a bucketful of A stars in a couple of years' time. Fantastic commitment."

"My year sevens were on the comatose side of dead." Chris' tone of voice was rueful, perhaps even resigned. "I can't seem to get them going these days at all." Pete thought about how he might inject Chris with some of his enthusiasm. He seemed in need of a bit of a boost. He couldn't just think of a way at that moment so instead he said, "Gym this week?"

"Maybe Thursday," said Chris. "Work's piling up, so I can't say yet."

It was the time for examination marking and report writing and no sooner had one task been completed than

Peter Cropper

the next one demanded attention. Chris was keen for a workout, but he was conscientious and wanted to ensure exams were marked accurately and reports were written as fluently as possible.

Jo Matthews stormed in. She was one very frustrated French teacher. "Bloody year eights," she said to nobody in particular and then, "or, bloody Lee Rogers to be precise. That boy is unteachable. Why is he never absent?"

Tony Patterson looked up from his paper. "He's all right in my lessons, actually," he said.

That's helpful, thought Chris. Jo can take those words of encouragement with her next time she has Rogers' group. He didn't know whether Tony was trying to belittle Jo's efforts or talk himself up. Either way, it wasn't a very useful comment.

"I trust our children have been having fun with Uncle Pete and Uncle Chris." The jolly, loud voice announced the arrival of Steve Lloyd from Craft, Design and Technology. A colleague's mood tended to decide whether Steve's presence was a good thing or not.

"Morning Mr. Lloyd," said Pete. "How's life in CDT?"

"It's absolutely marvellous," gushed Steve. "Design and Realisation – 'formidable', as our Modern Language friends would say. Isn't that right, Mrs. Matthews? We're designing a child's beach toy for the holidays, and soon we'll realise there may not be enough time to make it." Steve beamed at his two colleagues. "The end is nigh, you know," he added dramatically, referring to that magnificent date in July, surely the highlight of every teacher's year.

Chris was once again envious, this time of Steve's bright and breezy approach to teaching. It was all a bit of a laugh to Steve. Chris had had a similar attitude himself once, a long time ago.

The purpose of Steve's visit to the James / O'Neill sector was to discover whether Pete and Chris would be attending Giovanni's for the end of term meal. Livewire Steve saw the organisation of such events as his job. Chris thought it was probably just as well he did as he looked round at some

Bowing Out

very apathetic characters slumped in chairs clutching mugs of coffee and, in most cases, staring into space.

"Partners," said Chris. "Do partners come or not?"

"Only if you think they'd be sad – or mad – enough to want to spend and evening with us," said Steve. Chris decided Sarah was probably neither of those. He would go alone.

"Have you a minute, please, Chris?" Unnoticed, Alistair Johnson, Chris' Head of Department, had sidled up to the group. Balding, and with a moustache which clearly didn't suit him, Alistair looked and acted as though he'd been at Whiteoaks all his life, although he'd actually been there three years fewer than Chris. Chris could perhaps have beaten him at the interview stage for the Head of Department post but he couldn't be bothered presenting himself at the time, and now nobody would ever know. Mr. Johnson was one of those teachers who always looked efficient because he always carried some documentation or other. His methods were traditional, his results excellent at G.C.S.E. His classes tended to be populated predominately by those who were interested in making progress.

"You've not forgotten year ten reports are due this week, have you?" Chris felt slighted by this reminder. His diary was a well regimented and organised document and he knew better than anyone what should happen when (but not necessarily why). He wanted to say, "Do you think I'm thick or just woefully disorganised?" He actually said, "You'll have them Friday, Al – no problem."

"Good," said Alistair. "I know I can rely on my department to keep things running smoothly." That was generally true of Chris, but young Jane Foster, in her first year of teaching, still often looked rather bewildered.

Soon the staffroom took on a Pavlovian appearance – a bell rang, and a group of freethinking adults immediately stood up and walked away. Chris was one of the last through the door. As he walked the short distance to greet his least favourite class, the contents of that dream flashed back at him.

Peter Cropper

In the peace and tranquillity of their green haven, Sheila tried again.

"Mark's got tickets for the Sunday of the Test. Paul's coming down from Lancaster. Australia, isn't it? Or is it New Zealand? Chris likes cricket, doesn't he? Is he going?"

"Chris says England are so crap, you couldn't guarantee the game reaching Sunday," replied Sarah harshly. "And I'm not really bothered which of the tedious Antipodean time wasters is boring us with their visit. I can't stand cricket – can you?"

Poor Sheila. Another put down. She was nice enough, and didn't deserve such short shrift.

The year ten group had finished examinations and the results had been given out and analysed last lesson, if "analysed" wasn't too ambitious a term to use. The pupils were a mixed bag – some were actually making reasonable progress, but others were seriously underachieving. Anderson, Boyle and Farrell hadn't done particularly well this time. As they frequently enjoyed pointing out to Chris, they had not chosen to be there. "Nobody else apart from you would have us, Sir."

The school year would start to peter out soon, but somehow some momentum had to be maintained. Progress with coursework also had to be made. The lessons, thought Chris optimistically, should run themselves.

Firstly there was a small piece of good news to celebrate – Boyle was absent. The Terrible Trio had temporarily been reduced to the Gruesome Twosome. Chris reflected that that awful dream could not be re-enacted – at least not today, anyway.

Chris had heard the average teenager's attention span was twenty seconds but since these pupils and their behaviour could safely be described as below average, he chose to attempt as short an introduction as possible. "The aim now," he said quickly, trying his utmost to sound as positive and dynamic as possible but not really succeeding, "is to press on with coursework. It's simple;

the more you do now, the less pressure there'll be next year. Look back at what you've done, tune yourselves back in, and off you go. The resources are in the usual place. I'll drift around and help as and when I can."

Fifteen seconds. That should do the trick. The pupils would progress, or not. It was their choice.

Predictably, Jenny and Claire set to work with enthusiasm at the front. A cursory glance at their efforts now and again would suffice. They were good girls, who could be trusted. Chris liked them. As the lesson unfolded, some of the others worked fitfully. Greater effort would have been gratifying but on a morning in late June with the sun now streaming through the large windows, Chris reconciled himself to settling for what he saw. At the back, his two friends Michael and Jason did nothing. When Chris tried once or twice to persuade them otherwise he was met with scowls and a bad mannered refusal.

But at least there was no sign of violence and they were doing nothing quietly, muttering to each other. Chris could not hear what they were saying which, he thought, was no bad thing. He quickly reran his dream. He thought of the time honoured advice about sleeping dogs, and decided to act upon it.

The lesson ended, and most pupils had crawled a short way along the path to G.C.S.E. success. The class left for lunch, Chris breathed a sigh of relief and sat down behind his desk. He looked at what Jenny and Claire had done to cheer himself up a bit and then he looked at the work from other classes piled on his desk and reflected upon the need to prioritise. This would require a quick trip to the staffroom for some liquid refreshment and then a return to his empire via an exchange of niceties with the Headmaster.

"Good morning, Chris," said Brian Harris, as he was about to launch himself onto corridor patrol. "Are you well?"

"Not so bad, thank you," replied Chris. "Still enjoying the challenges of the chalk face. And yourself?"

Mr. Harris, no longer a regular at the chalk face, didn't appreciate Chris' brand of irony. The two men enjoyed a professional relationship which was just about acceptable, but nothing more.

Ten minutes paper shuffling, a few scribbled notes and one caffeine injection later, Chris decided that he had devised a suitable route through the pile of work and that year ten reports were on that evening's agenda. He adjourned for his sandwiches.

CHAPTER THREE

Shortly after four o'clock Chris pulled into his drive and smiled to himself. He had decided on a quick departure and he was in the car park before Pete had reached the staffroom. He reflected with some pleasure that he was a day nearer the summer holidays. It was Thursday and there was therefore only one day of the working week to endure.

In the house the vague smell of air freshener was a reminder that Sarah had the luxury of being able to take her lunch break at home whenever she wanted. He reminded himself that today's tea was Sarah's responsibility, and soon the aroma of cooking would replace that sanitised smell that he wasn't keen on. He'd be able to take his cup of coffee into the lounge and absorb himself in the novel he was reading until she arrived. Excellent. This was a fine part of the day; peace and quiet on his own. The lounge caught the sun nicely at this time of day. He also knew for certain that he would eat well. Sarah had her faults but she was an outstanding cook, and she'd probably prepared a casserole during her lunch break and set the oven timer.

A few minutes later, the anticipated delicious aromas began to waft through from the kitchen. The job's not great, thought Chris, but he looked around and thought that domestically he could be a lot worse off. The house was always clean and generally tidy – certainly tidy enough for him. "This'll do me," he said aloud to himself.

After tea had been enjoyed and respective working days had been briefly compared, or rather contrasted, the phone rang. Sarah answered it.

"Chris," she said. "For you. Dave Sullivan."

The voice on the other end of the phone was bright and cheerful. It explained that Dave was in Chris' part of the world and did he fancy a quick one? The Black Horse or the Royal Oak? It was Chris' call.

Chris put the phone down. "Drink with Dave." He announced this as something of a fait accompli. "Any objections, love?"

"No – go ahead," said Sarah. With the remote control close at hand and a copy of Cosmopolitan on the small table, Chris' wife looked well settled. She didn't think it mattered much whether Chris was there or not.

The attractive young lady on the television assured them cheerfully that today's sunshine would not last – she hoped everyone had made the most of it. The clock on the wall showed it was fast approaching seven o'clock.

"Won't be too long," said Chris. "Maybe about an hour. I've some work on later."

He kissed Sarah, left the house and set off to the Black Horse. Sarah relaxed, stretched out and lit her after tea cigarette.

It had been a while since Chris had seen Dave so there were plenty of crucial talking points for the two men.

"I believe City are after that midfielder." Dave set the ball rolling across some familiar ground.

"Which midfielder would that be then?"

"Paul Thompson, I think his name is. I saw him on TV just before the end of last season. He looks like a good player, but I'd have thought a central defender'd be more use to us, wouldn't you?"

"Probably, yes," replied Chris. He wasn't as keen as Dave, who was an avid supporter of the local heroes, but you had to keep abreast of subjects such as this for occasions such as this.

"Mind you," the football pundit continued, "he can play defence at a push, so we could be getting two for the price of one. Buy one, get one free. BOGOF." Dave chuckled at his little witticism.

Chris decided to change the subject. "At this time of year, I'm more interested in holidays. Are you off anywhere this summer, Dave?"

"We've been," said Dave. "Came back about three weeks ago."

"Where did you go?"

"Ibiza."

"Where's your tan then?"

"Faded, I'm afraid. We both had one, though. Have you tried keeping a tan in this part of the world?"

Dave described in excessive detail his liking for Ibiza. "San Antonio's the place," Dave said, but he talked of discos, noise and booze fuelled young Brits so that it sound like the last place on earth that Chris would like to visit.

"Sarah and I are going to Scotland, but keeping a tan after the holiday won't be an issue."

"Why not?"

"Because we'll not be getting one. If we come back brown, it'll be rust." It was Chris' turn now to smile at his own joke.

Dave frowned. "So why are you going somewhere with no sun?"

"Peace, quiet, beautiful scenery…."

"And wet rain," interrupted Dave. He didn't understand.

Chris asked after Jim and Phil, more out of politeness than anything else, but didn't pay much attention to what Dave said. He rested his chin on his hand and played with a beer mat. He could not hide his boredom.

"Chris O'Neill, you're a peeled orange," said Dave. What?

"You've lost your zest," he continued. That was definitely one of Dave's best. It may even have been good enough for Steve Lloyd's repertoire.

"It's school, I suppose," said Chris. "It wears you down constantly. It saps your energy."

"With all those holidays?" said Dave. That old chestnut. The comment was made light heartedly, but Chris had become tired of it over the years.

When Chris said, "If the holidays are so bloody great, why aren't you teaching?", Dave knew his quip had not been well received. Chris knew full well that Dave was nowhere near clever enough to enter the profession, and he recognised his comment had upset his friend.

"Mind you, you don't want to be in teaching," he added quickly, "unless you want to be submerged in ridiculous paperwork. You've also got to like being watched by government spies who sit at the back of your class and whose brief is then to criticise everything you do. What fun OFSTED is."

"OFSTED?"

"The school inspectors. Office for Standards in Education. O-F-S-T-E-D. There's only one "F" in OFSTED." The jokes were flying thick and fast.

To keep the momentum of the evening going, Dave changed the subject and tried to stimulate Chris with more news from Blake's even though it was of no real interest to Chris any more. That conversation quickly ran its course.

"Another one, Chris?"

"I've work to do at home, you know. We can't all knock off at five. But if you're stopping – go on, then. It would be rude not to, wouldn't it? And the new employee here is very pleasing on the eye, don't you think David?"

When Chris arrived home a more optimistic weatherman who promised not torrential rain but sunshine and showers greeted him. They would probably change their minds again a few more times overnight. The meteorological expert's appearance on the TV meant it was nine thirty.

Bowing Out

Chris wasn't drunk but he knew for certain where he had spent the past couple of hours.

Chris greeted his wife a little clumsily as he did when he'd been out for some liquid refreshment. He sat down and glanced at the screen. There seemed to be a fly-on-the-wall documentary starting about a new shopping centre somewhere in the Midlands. Oh God!

"Work," he said, with a determined tone.

"At this time?"

"Work," repeated Chris. He picked up a pile of papers and transferred them to the dining room.

Refreshed by four pints of a new Yorkshire brewery's strong guest ale expertly pulled by the Black Horse's new attraction, Chris wasn't really in the mood for work but he'd felt inspired on the way home. Tonight's exercise wouldn't be time consuming.

He'd recalled a recent staff meeting in which Mr. Harris seemed to have a bee in his bonnet about reports. Chris remembered some of what he'd said.

"I am very lucky to have a very intelligent and literate body of men and women working for me here, and that means our parents are also very lucky because they will be able to receive intelligent and literate reports. Now, in the past, I have had to point out to one or two people that their reports were lacking a bit of substance - no names of course."

He didn't need to name names, because the wriggling in the seats of the more self conscious members of staff gave the game away.

"Clever, pithy one liners are unacceptable." Chris noted with some amusement that Steve Lloyd's face betrayed him. Guilty as charged.

"Now I trust I've made myself clear on that point." Yes, said the rows of solemnly nodding heads. "Any questions on that point?"

There were no questions. "Now, I believe Jim Lewis would like to say a few words." Chris had tuned out of the meeting at that juncture.

Peter Cropper

Chris selected three blank report sheets and filled in the names – Michael Anderson, Stuart Boyle and Jason Farrell. He then paused for a few moments before picking up his pen again.

On Anderson's report, filling the big box allocated for the comprehensive comment, Chris wrote "Insolent, Indolent, Ignorant." in large letters. He wrote the same words on Boyle's report then on Farrell's, but he altered the order of the words each time to keep life interesting and to make each report individual, different and special.

Pen laid down in triumph, Chris looked very pleased with his effort. He rewarded himself with a small tot of one of his favourite malt whiskies from a recently opened bottle in the cupboard.

"Cocoa?" he called through to the living room.

Sarah was in a shopping mall, in front of Debenhams. Three years ago she would have been standing in a green field somewhere near Derby. She was so engrossed that Chris had to call three times to receive the usual response.

CHAPTER FOUR

"Stroll to the Royal Oak?"
"Why not?"
Sarah's reply was well received. There was a chance that a Sunday evening out could rescue the weekend.

Chris had concluded it had not been the best two days. Saturday's plan to go for a long bike ride with Phil incorporating a pub lunch disintegrated when Mrs. Briggs rang at breakfast time to announce her husband's unfortunate illness. Perhaps he'd picked up a bug from a dirty pint glass on Friday evening. Sarah was working at the Fruit Bowl. Left to his own devices, Chris found the becalmed cricket match on the television completely uninteresting and the novel he was reading uninspiring. Any schoolwork he attempted completely failed to grab his attention. He pottered about, lost and bored.

Sunday saw the country washed away in torrential rain. The walk Sarah and Chris had planned was cancelled, and Chris lost his way again. Sunday was painfully similar to Saturday. Missing was the cricket, replaced by the presence of Sarah who seemed to Chris to be constantly in the way although what exactly she was preventing him from doing, he really couldn't say.

The Royal Oak played host to its usual selection of hardened drinkers who had clearly been gathered round the bar since lunchtime, but Chris and Sarah found a quiet corner and the evening passed pleasantly. Inevitably, they talked about what they were going to do in Scotland. Sarah's attitude to the holiday was much the more positive. Chris was disappointed, but not surprised, to hear that his wife shared Dave's sentiments about Chris O'Neill and peeled oranges, even though she couldn't express herself as devastatingly wittily as his former work colleague had done. Chris began to wonder seriously whether teaching had begun to change him, and how he would be able to reverse the decline which was apparently well underway.

On Monday morning, Chris was up first as usual. The calendar cheered him up by showing that they really were on the home straight to the holidays and he went into the kitchen for breakfast in optimistic mood. Sarah came downstairs just in time to organise her toast and to wish Chris a pleasant day at work. The routine was comforting, in a way.

He walked through the school's main entrance and straight into an ambush. Alistair practically leapt out at him from the corridor which led off to the staffroom.

"Chris," he said, visibly annoyed. "A word, please."

"I've hardly landed, Al," said Chris. "Any chance of a brew first, or might it even be possible to put this bag down?"

Alistair was not happy. He followed Chris and cornered him by the urn. When he spoke, it was, for some reason, in hushed whispers. It would have looked fascinating to anyone looking for intrigue first thing on a Monday morning, but the little scenario was ignored by the handful of early arrivals milling round the staffroom.

"What the hell are you doing with these reports?" hissed Chris' superior. "They'll never get through. What did the Head say at that meeting?" He reminded Chris of a pressure cooker being cooled under running water.

Chris was calm. "I presume you mean the excellent reports for Anderson, Boyle and Farrell? They're well written reports. I'm pleased with them. They accurately reflect work, progress and attitude."

"Do you seriously expect me to pass them on?"

Bowing Out

"I passed them to you on Friday, as requested. You have my completed set of year ten reports, on time as ever. It's up to you what you do with them." And then to show how little more mileage Chris considered was left in the conversation, "Did you ever see such a lousy Sunday as yesterday?"

Chris' Monday morning teaching did not extend to lunchtime – he finished with a free period. He had settled down to some marking in his room which he was sure he would complete in time for sandwiches. A knock on his door announced a visitor's arrival.

"Good morning, Mr. Harris."

The large, well built man in charge of Whiteoaks came to stand at Chris' desk. Chris had thought Alistair had been angry earlier, but he had looked positively jovial compared to the way Chris' visitor looked now. He towered menacingly over Chris. Had he picked up Chris' board rubber he would probably either have hit him with it or crumbled it to dust like Goldfinger's little friend Oddjob did with the golf ball.

"You know why I'm here?" inquired Brian Harris.

Chris pretended not to know and to give the question some serious consideration. "Reports?" he suggested.

"Reports," said Brian. "You're an intelligent man, Chris, so I assume you understand the thrust of what I said the other day?"

"Perfectly."

"Then why the hell did you do the exact opposite?"

The headmaster was growing visibly redder. Soon he might burst.

"What I said about those three nuisances summed up everything perfectly. Why say more?"

"Because I want more," roared Brian. "I want literate, comprehensive and interesting reports." He banged out each adjective on Chris' desk with his fist.

"That's what I provide." Chris remained calm. He was not going to give Mr. Harris the satisfaction of seeing him annoyed. In truth, he regarded the matter as so trivial that there was no chance it could possibly make him annoyed. There was more to life than a set of reports.

"Who runs this school?" bellowed Brian. Before Chris had a chance to answer, Brian continued. "My staff will operate as I wish them to. Understand?"

This was not the first time Chris had failed to "operate" properly. There was a problem some years ago when Chris, having been delegated to do so, had refused to take the year nines to visit a stately home a few miles away. Although the building reflected the period they were studying, there wasn't enough there to hold the attention of an average fourteen year old, maintained Chris. He had not backed down even in the face of the headmaster's insistence, and instead he had taken the pupils no further than the school hall to watch the type of video which children of that age should not really be watching. Brian had been incandescent with rage and the whole incident had been stored in his memory banks. He had been hugely unimpressed by the act of defiance and Chris had been put in the picture most efficiently. He always found forgiving very difficult and in this case he could not manage it. Forgetting was out of the question.

The next question was eminently reasonable. "Has it occurred to you that the likes of Michael, Stuart and Jason's parents might well not understand the terminology you've used? They're hardly going to be everyday words for them."

"That's their problem," replied Chris, "and as long as they understand the word 'dictionary', they can solve it."

Brian calmed himself. A blinding rage could be seen as unprofessional. "I take it you won't change the reports?"

"Correct."

"Then I'll have to enclose some sort of a covering letter. I'll make it diplomatic, of course, but unfortunately, it will make it appear that you can't write reports. Your credibility will suffer, so will your professionalism. Is that what you want?"

Chris looked straight at Brian. "You run this school, Headmaster," he said. "You must do as you see fit".

Brian, lacking a suitable reply, left Chris to his marking.

CHAPTER FIVE

The last weeks of the summer term passed exceptionally slowly. The remaining examinations happened, as scheduled, and the class that had enjoyed the interesting diversion about beaches and space rockets did no better, or worse, than Chris would have predicted. As the end approached Chris prepared himself for those occasions when the curriculum was exhausted by bringing out his collection of video recordings of historical programmes collected over the years from the television. He showed these in lessons whether they were relevant to that particular class or not. Because he failed to keep accurate records of who had seen what, some children became excessively familiar with the events leading up to Harold's painful eyeful or the Armada's approach to Plymouth. A temporary lack of departmental technology – it seemed years since the malfunctioning video recorder had been sent for repair - meant that poor Miss Foster didn't have much of a look in on the video front which did trouble Chris, but he told himself that at this stage it was vital to look after number one.

There was no comeback from Brian Harris about the contentious reports – in fact, the head didn't say a word to Chris for the rest of the term, which in itself probably spoke volumes. Chris was going to explain his rebellious actions to the year ten form teachers at the time of the reports being issued but somehow he didn't get round to it and on parents' evening, not surprisingly, neither Farrell nor Boyle was represented, while the Andersons were on holiday.

Finally, the Great Day arrived – the finest occasion in the school calendar. Predictably, it lasted the best part of a week. To show how kind he really was, Chris invited Jane to join her classes with his as the video player whirred incessantly on. Again, London braced itself for the Blitz and once more the unfortunate ones were led to the guillotine in 18th century Paris. Only Jane and a tiny handful of polite children seemed interested.

"You know, I never knew there were such fascinating programmes on TV," she said, as the last group of children filed out, heading for the final assembly of the year. "Could I perhaps borrow some of those videos over the holiday?"

"Of course you can," said Chris. He felt a bit sorry for Jane. Was she short of a home life? She had never said much about what she did outside school. "Don't you fancy switching off totally over summer?"

"Well, I am having a couple of weeks in France with a friend," said Jane. "But otherwise I'll need something to keep me amused."

Chris lent Jane some videos. He wanted to say, "Maybe we could meet for a coffee sometime. Or do you play badminton?" but he checked himself when he imagined what Sarah might say if she were to somehow find out.

Mr. Harris' end of year show ran like clockwork. It was easy to imagine an old, yellowing script kept somewhere in his desk which he glanced at during the last lunch break just to remind himself of his routine. Certainly, the more experienced members of staff could almost have joined in.

"Take care of yourselves," he concluded. "Have fun, but remember, keep safe. We want to see you all back refreshed and ready for work on September 4th." Then he added, "Happy holidays, everyone," and he could almost have been standing on a stage at a holiday camp dressed

Bowing Out

not in his normal conservative grey suit but in a garish stripy jacket with a boater on his head.

September 4th! Chris smiled to himself. It was a lifetime away.

There were some pleasantries in the staffroom after the assembly but Chris chose not to stay long. None of the staff was leaving and, in Chris' view, the staffroom would be mainly populated by the more mature female members of the profession becoming needlessly emotional about the prospect of not seeing each other for the next six weeks even though they would doubtlessly meet up over the holidays, lunching and engaging in idle gossip. Besides, thought Chris, the key personnel will all feature at Giovanni's later.

As he swung his car out of the car park, Chris reflected on the year past – the unresponsive nature of some children and the disobedience and extremely disruptive behaviour of others. Why did the pupils not seem to have any enthusiasm for history any more? Was it his fault? Dave's joke about the orange flashed into his mind. Was his classroom image still good enough?

He drove away from the school and his reverie was interrupted by the sight of three fifteen year olds standing outside the local off licence, flicking vee signs at all and sundry. Chris was sure one was for him. "Have a good summer, lads," he said to himself.

When he arrived home, Chris felt tired and quite irritable. The adrenaline flow had suddenly been switched off. He pressed the answer machine and heard Sarah: "Just checking you won't be around for tea, love. I might go for a drink with Sheila after work. If you're out, as I think you are, we'll probably miss each other." "Of course I'm not around for tea," said Chris to himself. "Doesn't she listen to anything I tell her?" And, "Drink with Sheila? After the grief she gives her? Two faced, or what?"

Feeling nothing like as satisfied as he should on July 21st, Chris stretched out on the sofa for a well earned siesta.

He awoke about forty minutes later. He stretched and concluded he was feeling a little less tired but he had not lost the discontent which had enveloped him before he went to sleep. He glanced at the clock. It was still a while until the scheduled meal but he had arranged to meet Pete and Ray Davidson for an aperitif.

He took a shower hoping it would wash away some of the annoying irritability and searched through his wardrobe for a "casual but smart" outfit. When it was time to go and he realised he wouldn't be seeing Sarah who was probably by now happily settled in the newly opened wine bar not far from the greengrocers, he scribbled a note and left the house.

Driving on this occasion wasn't an option, so Chris walked to the bus stop. It was a lovely evening. The sun had been shining virtually all day and the air was still, soft and warm. The birds were singing loudly as if to laud the start of the wonderful six week period. It would be good to think that the weather pattern was being established for the school holidays. Could it hold for the next few days until Chris and Sarah's trip to Scotland?

Chris occupied himself with thoughts of the forthcoming Scottish holiday during the bus journey. It did him good to make plans for their fortnight "away from it all". He remembered the cottage with its sea and mountain views and the beach virtually at the bottom of the garden. What was the pub situation like? He was surprised that he could not really remember. On some occasions north of the border Chris had been reduced to drinking in hotel bars, ruing the absence of "proper pubs like you can find in England."

He was so preoccupied with this that he nearly missed his stop outside the Feathers – a "proper pub" if ever there was one.

As he walked in he saw that Pete and Ray had claimed a table near the window. There was a pint with Chris' name on it. It should have been a magnificent sight on a glorious July evening. Somehow it wasn't.

Bowing Out

Ray beamed. "Chris. Good to see you. The best night of the year, eh?"

Ray Davidson was Head of Geography and was based in the Humanities block, not far from Chris. He was a little older than Chris, tall but not quite as lean as he used to be. He used to play semi-professional football to a good standard but these days, instead of leading the assault on opposition goals, he tended to lead the assault on crowded bars. Chris and he got on well, by and large.

The bar was not busy. It was the lull between the after work drinkers and those who would visit later.

"Are we expecting anyone else?" asked Chris.

"Ally said he might make an appearance," said Pete. Chris winced. He did not regard his Head of Department as someone to socialise with.

"Mr. Johnson wouldn't join the rabble, would he?" said Ray. "Of course not," Chris hoped Pete would reply.

Instead Pete said, "Well, I'm not sure he'll be joining us professional drinkers here, but he will be dining. Steve talked him into it, and then he finally decided when Jim Lewis said he'd give him a lift."

Jim Lewis! Fantastic, thought Chris. How wonderful to spend an evening with the world's most pompous windbag and biggest intellectual snob in the city. Jim, Head of English, was well read and knowledgeable. He knew it, and he made sure everyone else knew it. In fact, Chris wasn't convinced that Jim didn't spend his time memorising titles in bookshops and libraries so that he could claim his status as the Whiteoaks book king because if he had read everything he had claimed he wouldn't have time to do anything else, such as writing comprehensive and interesting reports.

"Yes," added Pete. "I fancy they'll go straight to Giovanni's."

"I should think so," said Chris. "They'd be well advised to leave the drinking to the professionals. Cheers. To the holidays!" Chris downed half of his pint instantly. Another quick gulp and most of the beer had disappeared. "My round, gentlemen!"

Two hours later, Ray looked at his watch. "Finish the drink you're on, please," he said in his best classroom voice. If he'd used the word "sentence" instead of "drink" he could have been standing in front of a group of enthusiastic, interested twelve year olds.

Chris and Pete obeyed. It was time to adjourn to Giovanni's, but it irked Chris. He'd downed a few pints. He was into his stride. It was a little before quarter to eight and Chris felt as though he could happily stay in the Feathers all night. Crisps and peanuts – or maybe a pickled egg from the big jar on the corner of the bar - could sustain. Did Pete and Ray really fancy filling their faces with pasta or pizza?

By the time Chris had decided it would be worth asking his colleagues if they'd like to revise plans and abandon the meal, they were nearly at the door. Sulkily, like a fourteen year old who clearly isn't going to have his own way, Chris dragged himself to his feet and followed.

The three men walked in silence to Giovanni's. The summer evening was still beautiful. Why hadn't Steve Lloyd shown some initiative and arranged to go to the King's Head at Great Drelsford? They could have taken the bus and then, having enjoyed a few drinks in the garden at the back which looked over the fields to the wooded hills beyond, they could have eaten there. The King's Head served good food. It was probably one of their summer barbecue evenings. Later someone could easily summon up a fleet of taxis to take them back to town.

By the time Chris arrived at the restaurant, he was convinced the venue was wrong. When he and his colleagues went into the private room and saw the assembled gathering standing round in the usual little cliques, Chris was overwhelmed with the sudden feeling that these were the last people with whom he wanted to spend the evening.

Bowing Out

The key moment in the evening arrived. It was time to sit at the table. There were furtive glances everywhere. Who do I definitely not want to sit with?

Sitting with Pete was the safe option, but Chris decided to branch out. He'd had enough of Pete's company in the pub. He would certainly see him again in the near future. So who would he sit next to? He'd given it no thought and suddenly, in a flurry of frenzied activity, everyone started to move.

When the dust had settled, Chris found himself between Sue McGrath and Jim Lewis. He hoped very much they wouldn't talk English Department "shop" across him. He thought he should have given far more advance consideration to a seating plan. Sue he could tolerate, but Jim…?

The meal passed. The food was excellent – it always was at Giovanni's – but Chris' appetite was strangely muted and he picked unenthusiastically at the pasta dish. He was sure the draft lager had been watered down. It was far too warm in the upstairs room which the staff had hired. Had there been a thermometer on the wall, the mercury would have cascaded out of the top.

After the last plates had been cleared and coffees had arrived, Chris tapped an empty glass with a surviving spoon to gain everyone's attention. He rose slowly and a little awkwardly to his feet. Silence fell quickly over the assembled gathering. The facial expressions varied from fascinated to wary according to how well the wearer of the expression knew Chris.

Fuelled by drink, Mr. O'Neill was clearly going to speak.

"Good evening, ladies and gentleman," began Chris. "On this auspicious occasion I'd like, if I may, to pay tribute to some key cogs in the Whiteoaks wheel."

Pete cringed. He hoped his friend wouldn't go too far.

"What would our school be without our wonderful children?" asked Chris. "They are the school, and are they not a constant pleasure to teach? I am particularly impressed with our senior pupils who set such a shining example to the younger ones. On examinations results day, when I very much look forward to seeing you all in the academy of excellence, I hope our year eleven students discover they've got what they deserve – nothing.

But if – or should that be when - this year's results prove to be disappointing, we can look forward to a certain improvement next year as those Oxbridge candidates Anderson, Boyle and Farrell boldly lead the crusade to make our school recognised as the finest educational establishment in our fair city."

Colleagues were uncomfortable with this barrage of irony. Whiteoaks had problem pupils, of course it did, but wasn't it the job of the teachers to nurture and encourage, to help them realise their potential? It couldn't be right to be so devastatingly critical of them, could it?

After a pause for breath, Chris carried on. "But when the dear children go out to play, or at the end of the day when the children's appetite for knowledge has been met, it's great to relax with some of the best colleagues anyone could wish for. It's time someone paid tribute to the Whiteoaks staff. I hope I will be permitted to do that now. Please don't feel embarrassed."

The faces of Chris' audience said it all. Some were tempted to ask Chris to stop, but he had momentum and was very animated. If a colleague stood in his way now, he, or she, would almost certainly come in for some really vitriolic verbal treatment, or maybe worse. It was, on balance, safer to let Chris continue with his speech and hope for some degree of mercy.

"On my left, we have the lovely Sue McGrath," said Chris. Sue considered she had chosen a fetching outfit for the occasion, but, as she herself would concede, she was no oil painting. She was wearing a dark brown Paisley jersey dress with a purple swirling pattern and a bow at the collar which didn't quite go with a pair of American tan tights. The outfit was completed by a pair of sensible brown shoes and next to her chair was a large, efficient handbag. She had tried, but sadly failed, to look modern.

Bowing Out

"I feel I've got to know Miss McGrath well. Only the other day we had an in depth conversation – deep and meaningful it was. I said, 'How's it going?' She said 'OK'. I'd like to get to know you better, Sue, but time's short – forty years from now I may well be dead.

On my right is a marvellous, wonderful person – Mr. James Lewis, ladies and gentlemen. If this man's not read it, then it's not been written yet – it's as simple as that. I feel so intellectually humble in your elevated company, Sir. Please permit me to discuss the finer points of Shakespeare with you over a beer sometime. I could learn so much. Oh, sorry, I forgot – Mrs. Lewis only allows you out on special occasions such as this, doesn't she? And is it true you're very often otherwise occupied playing Mellors to Mrs. Bowman's Lady Chatterley?"

Jim Lewis did not know what to do or what to say. He did and said nothing. That way, he could not possibly be making a mistake. Of course he was friendly with the school secretary, but to be accused of something like that ...

"I had arranged for George Best to be our after dinner speaker," continued Chris. "But when he heard of the appalling standard of Giovanni's beer, he did politely decline. However, we do have, from the world of football, Mr. Ray Davidson. Did you all know that our geography whiz kid who knows the difference between an isobar and an isotherm was once a footballer of some repute?" Ray should have been flattered and he should have looked pleased, but he feared what he might hear next. "Once, he'd score on grounds all over the north. Now, I hear he's so overweight and out of condition he'd have trouble scoring in…"

"Chris," interrupted Pete. "Chris, mate, you're a great speaker, but is this the time or the place?"

"It's after dinner and I'm speaking, so I'm an after dinner speaker," retorted Chris. "Bloody hell, some people with much less talent than me make a career out of it." Then, rather aggressively to his captive audience,

Peter Cropper

"Let's take a vote on it – a bit like Mr. Harris might do, I don't think. Who wants me to stop, then?"

No one spoke.

"Dear Jane," said Chris, looking at his history colleague across the table. "Gentlemen, who among you agrees that Jane would win a 'Miss Whiteoaks staffroom' competition hands down?" Jane blushed. Again, nobody spoke. "Have you ever been driving in the country lanes late at night and seen a startled rabbit trapped in the glare of your headlights? That's Jane, confronted with the prospect of the year eleven class last thing on a Monday. John, is there any lettuce left in the bowl at your end of the table?"

Alistair intervened. "Chris – being so nasty to one of your own department who you work with day in, day out is unforgivable. If you've anything about you, you'll apologise immediately."

Chris smiled pleasantly at Alistair. "Mr. Johnson," he said with mock politeness. "There'll be a fleet of flying pigs booked to take us home before I take any notice of you. With respect," he added scornfully.

He blazed on.

"Excuse me, while I check Pete James' poodle is fine after his meal. Are you OK, Mr. Prescott?" Chris directed his question at Mike Prescott at the other end of the table. "The smiling, nodding Mike. Does he have to sit up and beg if he needs a protractor from Pete's big box of tricks?" Mike could look after himself and he looked ready to challenge Chris physically but the way in which Chris pointed a stray knife at him was quite intimidating. "Down boy," said the after dinner speaker.

"To absent friends," continued Chris. "I propose a toast to Mr. Brian Harris, our wonderful leader. Wir trinken an den Führer." Chris skillfully resurrected the German he had studied to 'A' level standard. "Do you know, he trusts our professional judgment so much, he tells us what to write on reports? He thinks he can comment better than me on the efforts of my pupils in my classroom. Perhaps he's only looking after us. He may take us home next, or at least pick up a lollipop and see us across Brenington Road. On the other hand, he might stop treating us like idiots and let us get on with what we do best while he puts his feet up in his office."

Brian Harris was liked and respected by some staff, and feared by others. Chris wondered if any colleagues would report back, but he very quickly decided he neither knew nor cared.

"And, finally, a toast to my old mate, Mr. Peter James. Pete and I go back a long way. I respect him. Perhaps I envy the relationships he has with his pupils. Have you seen the way the children hang around the maths room at the end of a lesson? They can't tear themselves away. So many questions for the wonderful Sir. But rumour spreads easily. Let's hope it's only mathematical advice that Mr. James is dispensing while the rest of us are pumping ourselves full of caffeine."

Pete stood up. He was as angry as anyone had ever seen him. "That will do," he shouted across the table. "We don't have to take any more of this garbage. Apologise – or get out."

Chris did not appreciate the rebuff. It looked for a moment as if he was going to tip up the whole table in his anger but instead he rejected the clichéd behaviour, spun on his heels, contented himself with simply kicking over his chair and stormed out. Steve Lloyd who, to his amazement, had somehow escaped being named in the tirade, smiled and broke the silence by saying, "As Clive Anderson might have said on television all those years ago – 'whose round is it anyway?'"

Chris left the restaurant in search of a pub for a little solitary drinking and thinking. The heat of the day had finally taken its toll and clouds had built steadily during the time in the restaurant. There was a distant rumble of thunder from the hills beyond the city. It summed up his mood perfectly.

CHAPTER SIX

Chris stirred, turned over and eventually focussed successfully on the radio alarm. There was no need for his bumbling attempts to turn it off this morning. It said 6.08. Mr. O'Neill was, of course, awake considerably earlier than he needed to be. It would even have been too early for a school day. It was clearly a fallacy that alcohol provoked and helped to prolong sleep.

His stomach felt gaseous and overly full. There were vicious little men in his head and each man had a pickaxe which was being swung around very vigorously. He could not recall ever feeling much worse than this after a night out.

He closed his eyes and spun around uncontrollably with the bedroom. The feeling was unpleasant so he opened his eyes again. The feeling was still unpleasant. He felt like a man in a severe physical decline.

Chris thought it probably better to get up and start his first day of freedom. Perhaps a cup of tea and a slice of toast might improve matters. It couldn't make things worse, but he might give the extra fruit jam a miss.

Chris watched transfixed as the kettle boiled and the bread browned in the toaster. He wasn't convinced he'd be able to manage his little breakfast but, when all had been prepared, he took the early morning feast into the dining room and sat at the table, facing the garden. The weather felt oppressive, muggy – perhaps that was why he himself felt so clammy. He recalled the rumbles of thunder he had heard as he wandered towards the White Lion where he'd angrily sunk two or three quick pints before an ultimately successful search for the last bus home. The beer compass had worked again. Had there been a storm in the night? Chris had to pass on that question, but if there had, it hadn't really cleared the air.

As he stared through the window, he began to reflect on the events of the previous evening and he felt cringes of severe embarrassment as he reran the speech in his mind. Of course it had been the drink talking, and Chris was confident his colleagues would realise that. Nevertheless it was unfortunate that the Scottish trip wasn't scheduled for another few days. Usually he liked a week or so after the end of term to deposit his "emotional baggage" as he called it. He liked to spend this time wandering round town, browsing in book shops, enjoying the odd relaxed pint or cup of coffee. The only irritation was the presence of the "back to school" signs which appeared in shops even before the summer term had ended. He used this time to refresh himself before going away, but this year he felt differently. He'd like to set off now, with Sarah nominated as first driver. Well, perhaps not just yet.

His head ached although he was confident that breakfast would stay where it was meant to. The day was already in danger of falling apart in the face of appalling lethargy. How could he stop it? Was Sarah working today?

The kitchen calendar told him his wife was free, so Chris decided to wait patiently for her to rise whereupon they could put forward ideas for rescuing Saturday. As he sat on the sofa musing over the possibilities, he nodded off again.

"Good morning. How's my exhausted pedagogue?"

Chris opened his eyes. He was in his extraordinarily warm sitting room and he'd been sleeping at a strange angle. His neck ached now, keeping his head company.

"Sarah. Hi. What's the time?"

"Ten past ten." Sarah's answer was surprising. Chris still felt clammy and in desperate need of some fresh air.

His movements were sluggish but by eleven o'clock Chris and Sarah were ready for the off.

It was warm enough for T-shirt and shorts but the sky looked unreliable so Chris had stuffed their two cagoules into the small rucksack suitable for shorter walks such as this. The route was a familiar one; at the end of the road, a right turn into Portreath Way and a left into Penzance Close led to the small pathway between the houses which gave onto the open country. Usually Chris thought of Cornish holidays as he wandered through the estate and sometimes he felt he could almost smell the sea air and hear the wheeling gulls, but today he was too mentally jaded to transport himself to the south west peninsula. They ploughed on up the familiar path. Normally he would have noticed the brightly coloured flowers and the fact that the autumn's blackberries were already on the way and he would have had a go at identifying the birdsong, but on this morning Chris only noticed that he was still sweating and his head still ached. The path's incline was gentle indeed, but it felt to Chris as though he was tackling the north face of the Eiger. Sarah walked at Chris' pace for a while but she soon grew impatient and left him behind to stumble along in his own little world which, again, was invaded by unwelcome flashbacks of the previous evening's oration.

Sarah rounded the bend by the white cottage and disappeared from view, but this didn't matter because they both knew the way and eventually Chris would catch his wife up. He turned onto the top road and it wasn't long before he saw her sitting outside the Lamb. On the table in front of her stood an orange juice and a pint of bitter. He knew Sarah would not want a beer at this time of day. His worst fears were confirmed when he saw that it was the juice which had been half drunk.

"Hair of the dog!" said Sarah, excessively brightly. "You know it makes sense!"

Bowing Out

"Thanks a lot," replied Chris, with a pained expression on his face. He looked at his watch which read quarter to twelve and the full pint pot, and retched.

"I trust I've done right getting you that," said Sarah. "You've mentioned many times how great this place is for beer." Chris smiled weakly. Sarah smiled too, somewhat more broadly than her husband.

Chris struggled very slowly through the beer but it wasn't going down well. Its taste, combined with the cigarette smoke wafting across from the other side of the table, was too much to handle. He'd no option but to excuse himself. Sarah sat impassively looking over the fields down to the edge of the city in the distance. The sun was just about winning its battle with the dark clouds and the day promised to get brighter.

Chris returned to the table just as a group of four walkers came over the brow of the hill on the other path, the one that rose out of the woods. As the party drew nearer Chris, to his horror, recognised two of its members. One of them he knew very well.

Jim Lewis, his wife and the other couple looked marvellously relaxed as they approached the pub. Jim was kitted out in everything a typical rambler would be expected to be wearing and he was talking, much to the amusement of his three companions. Everyone burst out laughing when he'd finished his tale. Perhaps it was the story of an idiot who'd decided to make an after dinner speech and who'd also made a total fool of himself.

Chris felt he couldn't justifiably return where he'd just been and as he had no newspaper to hide behind, he strolled to the fence in front of the pub and studied the cattle in the nearby field with enormous interest, reasoning that if he couldn't see Jim, Jim couldn't see him.

His logic was severely flawed, of course, and soon he felt the expected tap on the shoulder.

"Chris!" said Jim.

"Jim! Great to see you on this lovely day. Fit and well?"

"Fine, thanks. Nothing like a walk to blow away the cobwebs."

I would have thought you'd have preferred a walk in the library, thought Chris.

There was a very awkward silence and then Chris spoke. As soon as the three little words had left his mouth he knew he'd said something excessively stupid.

"Enjoy last night?"

"Excellent!" enthused Mr. Lewis. "Great food, great company and what a speech."

Under current circumstances Chris wasn't mentally agile enough to be sure to what extent Mr. Lewis would deal in irony. He should have known better. He said, "Was it OK? Do you think people really liked it? It wasn't O.T.T., was it?" He knew immediately that he shouldn't have asked these wildly optimistic questions and that they were probably naïve in the extreme.

"Chris," said Jim, with a smile on his face, "it was not only nauseating and offensive, it was total crap. You are," and here Jim searched for, and found, the worst expletive he could think of, "a total wanker, Mr. O'Neill. Let's just hope it's been forgotten by September, shall we? Can I leave you with some advice which may help you enjoy your holidays?"

Chris' expression said, "No, you can't, you patronising git," but Jim carried on regardless. "Use this," he said, tapping his head, "before you use this," and he pointed to his mouth. "Now if you'll excuse me, I'm off to join some civilised company, as I've no doubt Sarah would like to as well." With that, Chris was left contemplating the habits of the cows and why some were still sitting down in expectation of rain even though the sun was now starting to shine quite strongly. Jim smiled politely at Mrs. O'Neill and wished her a pleasant day as he passed her and led his companions inside the pub where they stayed despite the improving weather.

"Isn't Jim Lewis a nice bloke?" said Sarah, as Chris finally returned to his seat.

CHAPTER SEVEN

On the following Monday morning as she left for work, Sarah thrust a list into Chris' hand.

"What's this? Nothing strenuous, I hope. I am unwinding, after all."

"A trip to town won't hurt," replied Sarah. "We cannot go to Scotland without these essentials."

Chris glanced at the excessively long list. At the top he read "insect repellent." Granted, he thought. Scottish midges were a particularly virulent strain, as he well knew.

He remembered a trip in his youth when he camped in Glen Nevis with some of his mates after "A" levels. They climbed Ben Nevis in unbelievably good weather and enjoyed wonderful views, but Chris' abiding memory was of the two evenings either side of their mountain expedition when the little buggers descended. You couldn't sit outside, the river bank being particularly out of bounds, and if you dived into the tent for protection they immediately followed. The repellent spray only seemed to wind them up and they then went and fetched all their mates. Two of the lads tried chain smoking to drive the insects away, but that didn't work either. Trips to the pub in Fort William only served to postpone the horror. In the middle of summer on the coast things were likely to be just as bad, if not worse. Oh good.

Peter Cropper

The next item made him laugh out loud. "Sun cream! Sarah, it was last year we went to Portugal. It's basic geography you know – Southern Europe, hot and sunny, Northern Europe miserable and wet." The mention of geography reminded him of Ray's presence at the evening he had been trying, unsuccessfully, to forget. Now what exactly had he said about Mr. Davidson?

"If you could get those things, it would be great," said Sarah wearily. Chris remembered a piece of advice he had been given – never argue with a woman – and he agreed he would go shopping. Never volunteer for a job, but never refuse one – that was another maxim which, Chris thought, usually held good. In the overall scheme of things, a little trip to town wasn't going to change his life.

In Chris' experience, on any given shopping list no matter how long, or, in exceptional cases, short, there is always a quarter of the items that cannot possibly be found, but this morning was the exception that proved the rule. Less than an hour after parking the car – for free! - in the back alley that he swore was known to nobody but him, Chris had bought everything. Mission accomplished! Considering shopping wasn't his forte, he felt very satisfied. He didn't know what amused him more: the fact that Sarah loved shopping, or the fact that she constantly denied that she loved shopping. In triumph he threw the list into a bin and went to the café on Fairfield Street. He exchanged pleasantries with the waitress who recognised him as a regular customer, placed his order and five minutes later was settling down to his cafétière. To celebrate his achievement he had also ordered one of those rather nice caramel slices.

There were only two or three other customers so when the door swung open and a very pretty young lady in a bright pink t- shirt and summery trousers decorated with flowers came in, Chris was recognised immediately. Again, without the protection of a newspaper the feeling of exposure was acute.

Bowing Out

Jane Foster sat down next to Chris and looked very sad.

"I'm not too impressed with being compared to a rabbit," she began.

"Sorry?" The after dinner speaker pretended not to understand, but his act was unconvincing.

"Giovanni's, Friday. I know you'd had a few, Chris, but surely you remember what you said?"

"Oh, yes," said Chris, clicking his fingers in an exaggerated gesture of remembrance. "The speech. Just a bit of fun to liven up the proceedings. I can't imagine anyone took offence – did they?"

"It may have been fun for you, Mr. O'Neill," said Jane. "I thought you were a nicer man than to laugh at other people. I've been struggling – I admit that. So the end of the first year should have been a time for relief and rejoicing at the fact that I now have a long break to recharge my batteries. Instead I have my evening ruined by a colleague who cannot hold his drink and who thinks it's a laugh to take the Mickey out of other people." Her eyes moistened. "I thought we were mates, but now I'm not too sure…."

"Jane," mumbled Chris, head down, "let me buy you a coffee…" but by the time he looked up, Jane was over halfway to the door. He didn't feel it was worth trying to stop her, but he did wish he had her number or her email address so that he could contact her in a day or two and try to repair the damage that way. Jane was good looking, nice and kind, and he felt like a right bastard. He didn't feel like sitting in the café for much longer, so he quickly drained his coffee, settled the bill and left.

In the afternoon, while mowing the lawn, Chris took stock. Jim had been furious and Jane had been little short of devastated. Both his colleagues looked as though they felt that if they never saw him again it would be too soon. However, at least there wouldn't be a problem with Pete James. He and Pete went back a long way. He was slightly surprised Pete had not been in touch before now, so he resolved to ring him after tea.

Peter Cropper

"Hello."

"Jill, it's Chris. Is Pete there?"

There was a slight hesitation. "No, not just now. He'll be back later. I'll get him to ring you."

"Thanks. Are you well?"

"Fine thanks." Jill didn't seem in the mood for conversation.

"And the children?"

"Yes. They're fine too."

"Anyway, if you can get Pete to ring, I'd be obliged."

"I'll tell him you've called. Bye." Jill put the phone down. She'd been unusually aloof, thought Chris.

CHAPTER EIGHT

Thursday morning dawned. It was departure day for Scotland. It had not come a moment too soon.

His dreams that week had featured guest appearances by most of his colleagues. They were all very unhappy. Pete had not returned his call. Chris still hadn't shared the full embarrassment of the previous week with Sarah. He was trying hard to forget it.

He thought that on the whole it was a very good time to be heading north.

Together with breaking up day, the departure for the annual holiday was one of the highlights of the year. There was always a frisson of excitement and a feeling of pleasure in the knowledge that for two weeks some distance was to be put between Chris and Sarah and their everyday domestic problems and stresses. Chris sometimes wondered whether married life was quite as comfortable and pleasant as it used to be. He could sense his own growing dissatisfaction with his job, of course, and he thought that his wife was not as sympathetic to his problems as she once had been. For her part, Sarah also spoke with increasing vitriol about other people, notably Sheila at the shop with whom she spent a lot of time, but also Bob, Chris' brother. Initially Sarah and Bob had got on really well, and when Bob was going out with Linda they'd frequently make up a foursome for nights out in town. As time went on, Bob tended to call less frequently and it had taken Chris - not the world's most observant man - some time to work out why, but now he was sure of the reason. He was, however, less sure of the reason behind Sarah's changing attitude.

Perhaps this year's trip to Scotland could diffuse some of the tension which was gradually, but noticeably, creeping into the marriage.

In order to avoid traffic problems they made an early start, but after half an hour it became clear that it wasn't early enough. Flashing lights on motorway gantries and a police car speeding up the hard shoulder spelt trouble ahead.

"For God's sake," shouted Chris, as they joined the end of the slow moving soon to be stationary queue. "All it takes is one idiot to drive carelessly and we all have to suffer."

"And how is getting annoyed going to help?" replied Sarah.

"Well it's not," conceded Chris. "But, bloody hell – just what was the point of getting up at the crack of dawn?"

"It's my psychic powers," said Sarah. "They're not as strong as they used to be. Once I would have been able to predict this accident, but I don't know what's up with me these days. Perhaps I've reached, you know, that time of life."

Chris always found slow moving traffic annoying, and he was not willing to talk if the queen of sarcasm was unleashing her deadly weapon. He decided to concentrate on silently practising his clutch control skills.

After they had stopped completely he rustled through the rack of cassettes down to his left. Don McLean would have undoubtedly been able to calm the situation had he not been still in the living room. The car's small selection of cassettes belonged to Sarah and the music was hardly to Chris' taste so he opted for silence instead. His passenger preferred otherwise and soon music courtesy of a pop group which didn't seem to hit the headlines any more and which Chris could not name was blaring out. He

Bowing Out

resolved to say nothing and put up with it. After a while he realised that, if truth be told, he was quite enjoying the music. It seemed reminiscent of happier times. The power of nostalgia.

Eventually they passed a couple of cars slightly the worse for wear on the hard shoulder, with two or three dispirited travellers in conversation with a couple of policemen. "Was that it?" said Chris. "All this fuss for that?"

"Would you prefer to see the police scraping bodies off the carriageway? Would that make it feel like the delay had all been worthwhile?"

"Don't be daft," said Chris. "But that's the great British public for you, I suppose. Always keen to have a gloat."

They left the problem behind and picked up speed again.

"How far to the next services?" asked Sarah. "I could do with a stop."

"I need the loo too," replied Chris. "It's not too far, I don't think. You'll just have to hang on."

"I was thinking in terms of another break – the sort I need but you don't."

"Oh, a junkie break," said Chris, pretending to be surprised. "If you're that bloody desperate, open the flaming window and blow the poison out. As long as I don't have to smell all that crap."

"Language, tiger," ventured Sarah.

He was never so conciliatory on the familiar routes back home. Perhaps he was really relaxing into the holiday spirit already; either that or the traffic problems had really got to him. Sarah thought she knew which it was. She lit up. Chris coughed. If he hadn't meant it, he wouldn't have said it.

A few curses later, they pulled into the services. It was a good service area – well manicured lawns, healthy looking trees and a lake where two or three visitors were feeding ducks, coots and moorhens. It had won awards.

Peter Cropper

In the distance the hills rose dramatically. With the weather cooling down as it was, it might not be long before they were snowcapped.

Chris noticed none of this, but his eyes nearly popped out of his head when he saw a price list, and a number of children seemingly intent on creating mayhem reminded him of break time at school. An older boy who disappeared into the amusement arcade looked vaguely familiar. That was an unpleasant moment.

After a lightening of the wallet, Chris and Sarah settled into the area thoughtfully provided for nicotine addicts.

"Very good coffee," opined Sarah.

"I should hope it is at that price. If my lottery numbers had come up last week I'd have bought you a Danish pastry to go with it."

"How's your tea?"

"Warm and wet." It was very good actually, but you couldn't do much wrong with a pot of tea, thought Chris, and at those prices it should be good.

Sarah sighed. "You're not going to whinge and whine all fortnight, are you Chris?"

Chris reflected for a short while. Sarah was quite right. Moaning his way through the holiday would benefit neither of them. Be reasonable. In a blinding flash of altruism he decided that, if only for Sarah's sake, he would make himself relax. She may not work nearly as hard as him – there was no stress involved in weighing tomatoes or deciding from which bunch to select four bananas – but she deserved a break as much as he did. Just because she wasn't using her brain like she should be didn't mean she wasn't entitled to a holiday.

A holiday. Away from it all. Away from whimpering colleagues who had had a sense of humour bypass. Away from the lads at Blake's whose conversation in the pub seldom seemed to vary. And, best of all, away from the kids who, given half a chance, would beat him up because he wanted to tell them about how much more difficult conditions were in Victorian Britain if you weren't well off. His worst nightmare.

Back on the motorway they encountered another delay but Chris put his new attitude to the test. He said nothing – that way he would say nothing wrong. It was one of those mysterious delays which seems to have no cause and, after a short while, the traffic disappeared as if by magic. They were on their way.

Chris put his foot down and they zoomed off. "You know, I really think we've done now with traffic problems." He broke into song: "Ain't no stopping us now, we're on the move."

He turned to Sarah and smiled at her, and she returned his smile with interest. It promised to be a good holiday.

CHAPTER 9

It had been a few years since they had been to the Scottish accommodation.

"You know, I'd nearly forgotten how lovely it is here," said Sarah, as they began the settling in process with the inevitable pot of tea. Chris had to agree, although, despite his service station resolution, the remainder of the journey had left him fractious. As on previous visits he had allowed himself to be misled into thinking that once Glasgow's urban motorway with exits and entrances here, there and everywhere had been negotiated, they were nearly there. The traffic lights on the Great Western Road were all on red. If only he'd known the Erskine Bridge no longer asked its visitors to pay up! A caravan on the slower, winding road along the shore at the top end of Loch Lomond had been "a pain in the bloody arse". Sarah suggested that provided more time to admire the scenery. Chris said that he didn't really go along with that.

The house was small and old. Chris had always thought it was a bit too dark but now he noticed it more. He needed light. Even in summer with the long, light evenings he maintained perversely that he suffered badly from SAD, which, coincidentally, was one of the names his pupils sometimes called him. Their temporary home was plainly but adequately furnished, with one glaring omission.

"No teletext," recalled Chris. There was almost a note of panic in his voice. "I remember now!"

"No cricket scores," said Sarah. "No football news. How will we cope? We'll have to manage somehow."

The house's location was idyllic – that was beyond dispute. There was a garden for those drier Scottish days. It was sheltered from the prevailing westerlies and the protecting screen of trees offered privacy, although nosy neighbours were never going to be a problem. Colourful flowers and a set of garden furniture with an optimistic parasol completed the scene.

"Let's get down to the shore," suggested Chris. He loved to spend time there. It was his place for quiet reflection.

"Shouldn't we go to the supermarket first?"

"That can wait."

It was drizzling, but that came with the territory. Protected by cagoules that were probably in for a busy fortnight, Chris and his wife walked the short distance through the trees beyond the end of the garden to the pristine beach, sandy with no trace of footprints. Rocks at either end provided scope for simple scrambling or the examination of the creatures which made the pools their home. Chris was often happy simply to sit there daydreaming, listening to the sound of the sea.

The beach wasn't private but, remote from the outside world, it might as well have been. The views across the bay to the far peninsula which jutted out impressively into the ocean unfortunately weren't the best today. In the other direction Ben Scratheil had its hat on. Chris had been up there on their last holiday when Sarah had been content to laze at sea level. A track led up through the pine forest with its distinctive smells where the trees creaked eerily in windy weather, before breaking out onto rough moor land where a simple stroll led to the summit cairn.

"No Ben today," sighed Chris. "But maybe you'd like to join me up there some time this trip?"

"Perhaps."

A short while later,

"Chris – supermarket beckons." There wasn't a great deal of point in resisting.

The rain fell a little more steadily as Chris turned the car out of the drive to begin the pilgrimage to the supermarket. It was eight miles – a bit too far for constant to-ing and fro-ing - so the trip had been planned with military precision by Sarah. She had a list as long as her arm.

"Is everything on that list vital?"

"Only if you want to eat and drink, my love," replied the expedition leader. Perhaps if they could be up and down the aisles like lightning there would be time for a wee dram in the hotel on the way back.

A little later, when the food had been packed away and Sarah was weaving her magic in the kitchen, Chris sat in the lounge surrounded by tourist information. He wondered how they had managed to bypass the whisky. "More fool me for letting her drive back," he said to himself.

Listlessly he thumbed through the brochures. A sea life centre – highly rated, and probably very good, but of little or no interest to Chris or Sarah. An old ruined castle – they had been there twice already. A newer castle, ancestral home of the McKinley clan – interesting to look round with its elegant pieces of furniture and magnificent portraits on the walls and with a refuge from the Scottish weather in the form of a tea room, but it was a long drive and they had been there before as well. Forest walks – more like it. They had not all been done either. Chris spread out his Ordnance Survey map and married the information on "this magnificent work of art" with the leaflet details.

Nothing else of interest was unearthed. Forest walks it would be, then. Some dry weather was needed in the morning or whatever would they do?

The weather gods were unkind. Occasional rumbles of thunder and intermittent bursts of lashing rain on the windows brought a fitful night. At times it was like sleeping in a carwash. "But," said Sarah in a period of mutual insomnia, "it will have blown over by morning."

Day dawned, but not bright and fair. Sarah's optimism was misplaced. The rain had abated, although it was still steady and clearly in no mood to make an early departure, and the radio weatherman was unable to offer encouragement – neither for today, nor for the foreseeable future. The sun cream, which Chris had skilfully hunted down a few days earlier, lay forlorn on the dressing table.

One empty teapot and a few mumbled curses later, the sound of crunching gravel outside heralded the arrival of a car.

Sarah opened the door to Hughie Fraser. He must have walked all of five yards from his car to the house but he was very wet. As usual he affected the air of a Scottish laird, but his accent was more English than that of the O'Neills.

"Welcome back," he gushed. "It's been a while."

"Four years," said Sarah. "It's good to be back."

"Brought the weather with you, I see," said Hughie. "It was nice till you arrived." All so predictable.

"So it goes," said Sarah. "Do you think it'll cheer up?"

Hughie pulled a face which suggested hell would freeze over first. Then he added, "By the way, did I tell you gas and electric is now extra? You've probably noticed we've had a couple of meters installed. You'll need 50 pence pieces."

"50 pence a go," said Sarah, after Hughie had left. "It could be worse, although we don't know how long 50 pence gives us."

Chris was unimpressed. "50 pence pieces," he said. "Very apt. You know why they're that shape? So you can get them out of a Scotsman's hand with a spanner."

"He could have told us before we got here, mind you. Did you know about that?"

"No. I don't suppose for one minute we have any?"

Murphy's Law did indeed come into play. Between them they had every coin but.

"We'll need some soon," said Sarah, checking the meters. "Let's go to town, get some, and," she shouldn't have added, "maybe have a little browse in the shops."

"Shops!" said Chris. His face suggested he was somewhere between appalled and panic stricken.

"Can you think of anything better to do on a morning like this?"

"I'd rather walk the corridors with a nail in my shoe discussing Chaucer with Jimmy Lewis," was the curt reply.

Alone in the house, Chris felt dispirited and at a loss. Sarah had only been gone two minutes and already he was wishing he'd gone with her. He could have tested his waterproofs with a potter round the harbour or had a coffee, a read and a change of scene. He thought about ringing her on her mobile to ask her to turn round, but he didn't want to admit defeat. Although he wasn't hungry, he demolished half a packet of chocolate biscuits in no time. He switched on the television. Something only remotely interesting appeared and Chris settled down to watch it, but the programme disappeared abruptly after five minutes. He did not have the wherewithal to bring it back.

He stared at the four walls and the four walls stared back. Mention of Mr Lewis had seen him board a train of thought. Where were his colleagues now?

Pete and Jill were away with the kids soaking up the sun. They loved the hot weather and usually headed off to southern Europe at the earliest opportunity; Pete had even been known to miss end of term drinks on occasion, preferring to link up immediately with his family in order to race off to the airport. This time, for some reason, they had had to delay their departure and, as a change from Spain, they had headed off to Greece. They had heard the people there were friendly and, of course, the weather was guaranteed. Of course, the weather in Scotland is also guaranteed, thought Chris, but it wasn't quite the same thing. Another friend – or was that now an ex-friend? – Steve Lloyd was in France, one of his favourite holiday destinations. He always claimed he knew Languedoc better than he knew Lancashire. He would be having fun – he didn't know any other way. At this very moment he was probably sitting outside a café, fraternising with the locals and amusing himself by practising his schoolboy French. Jane was probably cranking up the video, preparing to watch some history programmes. Chris wondered if she was wearing something attractively summery, as she was in the café, and whether she was wearing her hair up or down today. He could never make his mind up which style he preferred.

And what of his other colleagues whose characters he had so skilfully deconstructed a few days – is that all it was? – ago? None of them was sitting in a remote old house without power in the foulest weather Britain could produce with an accomplice whose idea of fun was trawling round shops.

Chris decided he would join Steve in a cup of coffee.

The kettle didn't respond, of course. Electric kettles tend not to work without power, so Chris blew his own fuse.

"For fuck's sake!" he bellowed. The bedraggled sheep in the next field but one jumped. He must have been annoyed – he only used the "f" word if he was really angry. He had used it in the classroom a couple of times recently, but as it was so much a part of the pupils' everyday language, nobody had noticed. A few seconds later it became apparent that the kettle would probably never boil again as it lay where it had landed in the corner after its maiden flight across the kitchen. He didn't mean to slam the glass door so hard as he stormed into the lounge, and he was alarmed to see the crack running the length of the pane. Hughie Fraser would be unhappy. It could not be dismissed as "one of those things".

Peter Cropper

Chris looked through the window at the garden with the pools of water forming rapidly on the lawn and composed himself. He made a snap decision. He decided he would not tolerate this. Why should he? There must be something better.

Impulsively he went to the bedroom before he had a chance to reflect and change his mind. He took one of the empty bags and stuffed it as quickly as he could with as many clothes as he could. He raided the bathroom for essentials. He checked his wallet, cards, mobile and cheque book. He scooped up some of the loose change from the bedside table. He had all he needed.

He wrote a note to Sarah, trusting Don wouldn't mind if he borrowed some of his lyrics: "I'm bowing out, I need a second chance."* Dramatic, punchy, irrational – it was all of those things. He could not say with any degree of certainty when he would see Sarah again, although he was sure that he would.

---

by Don McLean 1981. Universal/ MCA Music Publishing Ltd

CHAPTER 10

Standing by the side of the road, Chris had only one thought. He told himself he must be picked up before Sarah returned. The countryside was open and treeless and there was no way she wouldn't see him if she were to come back before he had gone. If she did see him, she'd have him, without a doubt. She'd take him into the house, sit him down, and tell him what a very silly boy he'd been. He'd be trapped, and it wasn't fair to keep a free spirit like Chris caged up. He was also unimpressed with soaking he was getting and this made him concerned. He thought that if he were driving and saw a saturated hitcher, the chances of letting him into his nice dry car were not good.

Nevertheless, he remained optimistic. During his student days, he had hitchhiked a lot and he was sure the old magical thumb technique had not deserted him. He had only been standing at the roadside for a few minutes when he found that he could still perfect the hitchhiker's glare known only to the select few – the glare which always forced any driver to scream to a halt. The road wasn't busy, which was not good news on this occasion, but Chris' luck was in and it wasn't long before a new car pulled up. Chris spotted a smart jacket hanging up and a driver dressed immaculately in a white shirt and dark green tie. In sweatshirt, jeans and his veteran cagoule, Chris felt underdressed for the occasion. He was also wet, of course, so he was pleasantly surprised when the driver operated his electric windows and invited him aboard.

"Where to?" asked the businessman / travelling salesman type.

"You tell me," said Chris. "Wherever. I'm on the run," he added dramatically.

"From the police?" The driver said it without the slightest trace of concern in his voice. He was a well built, athletic looking man who considered he could look after himself, particularly in his own little kingdom which was his very swish new motor.

"No – from a lifestyle. Have you ever felt the need to leave everything behind and just get away? I'm riding off into the sunset – not literally in this part of the world, of course."

The driver smiled weakly at the joke. His expression said he had a degree of sympathy for Chris. Perhaps, despite the trappings of affluence, he too was unhappy with his lot. "Jump in," he said. He never once thought that Chris might be lying about the police and that he might be dangerous.

When Sarah returned, Chris was on the road to Scotland's largest city. She saw the note and stood, incredulous, for a few moments. She knew he was fed up, but she never expected this. It was not clear exactly when he had left but that was irrelevant; what was obvious was that he was already on his way somewhere because she had not seen him on her way back from town. Neither was it clear how long he intended to be away, but she was sure he would be back. She reminded herself that she was assured and self contained and she knew she could spend *some* time on her own. But "bowing out" – did that suggest finality? God, I hope not, she thought.

He'll be back, no problem – won't he? She fed the hungry meters, made a coffee, lit a cigarette and felt the trace of a little tear in her eye.

"You said that you're running from a lifestyle," said the well dressed knight of the road. "How do you mean?"

Bowing Out

"I've made a mess," replied Chris. "I've lost all my mates and I'm now stuck for a couple of weeks in a Scottish monsoon in a primitive mud hut," he added, needlessly insulting the accommodation, "with a wife who hates me," he said, greatly exaggerating any problems which existed between him and Sarah. He supposed that by beefing up the scenario he could justify his actions to himself. In fact, he was far from convinced that he knew what he was doing. He had surprised himself. He wasn't normally given to acting on impulse.

"Tell me more. How do you manage to lose all your mates?"

Chris related the story so far, beginning with his declining enthusiasm for teaching and ending with his hasty decision of a short while earlier. The driver listened patiently and didn't say anything but, having let Chris tell his tale, suggested that his actions were a little drastic. "Have you ever known real hardship?" he asked, but when Chris asked him to elaborate, he declined to do so.

A familiar jingle played in Chris' pocket. He responded. Sarah sounded upset, but he would not be blackmailed by tears – he had made his decision. He assured her everything was all right and, yes, he would take care. She must, too. He explained he couldn't possibly return just yet but he would definitely keep in touch. Would Sarah be OK on her own? He really did hope she would, but he did not receive the assurance of a positive reply. He convinced himself that Sarah would be fine and that he held the monopoly on taking drastic action.

"How far are you going?" asked Chris when they reached the outskirts of Glasgow, where the traffic lights on the Great Western Road were still all on red. Presumably they had changed at some stage during Chris' time further north. Up until that point he had been happy simply to let the mystery man take him away, but now, with time pressing on, he realised that he urgently needed a strategy. Chris' new friend had become frustrated with Glasgow's traffic lights. He also presumably did not know that the Erskine Bridge wouldn't have asked him to dig deep.

"I'm going through towards Edinburgh," said the driver, "if I can ever get through this hell hole. I live near there with the wife and two kids. Responsibilities," he added pointedly.

"Drop me in Glasgow, please. Somewhere near the station." Chris had reached some sort of decision. He was heading south, towards more familiar territory.

"I'm not going to the city centre," replied the driver. "If I drop you just before I jump on the motorway? The city centre and the train station are walkable from there."

Sarah tried to phone again but this time Chris' mobile was switched off. Would he return? Was it worth her while hanging on in the cottage for as long as it took for him to come back or might she just as well abandon the holiday and go back home? It seemed quiet on her own, but she reminded herself that she was an independent woman and a survivor. The Gloria Gaynor song might have been written for her. She could decide herself tomorrow or the day after or whenever on what she thought was the best course of action and, in a way, she quite liked that.

Chris checked the trains to England at Glasgow Central and found he had some time to spare which was a good thing because he was hungry. He had heard that in Glasgow deep fried Mars Bars were something of a delicacy but he didn't feel up to such a gastronomic adventure. Instead he walked along one of the city's main streets and found a branch of a well known pizza chain. He tucked into his cheese and tomato with extra toppings with some relish. He then thought he'd better check on Sarah but he was left disappointed as he could do no better than leave a very brief reassuring message on her voicemail. It would have been good to talk to her even though he didn't know quite what he would have said. The battle of the voicemail facilities had clearly been joined.

Bowing Out

He retraced his steps to the station, and at 22.03 the great adventure resumed. The train made its way in the Scottish twilight through the Glaswegian suburbs and towards the Southern Uplands. It grew darker but not pitch black and Chris could see the stark bleakness of the moorlands and the graceful shapes of the smooth, whaleback hills. Only lines of pylons and the occasional farmhouse suggested civilisation. Whenever he had passed through this part of the world he had always thought it might be nice one day to stop and explore but so far he had never done so. The countryside looked wonderfully remote although the occasional headlights on the nearby motorway reminded him he wasn't too far from fellow members of the human race. How he was going to play the next scene when he would find himself in the border city of Carlisle, presumably quite lifeless at half past midnight, Chris was not yet sure.

Sarah was also surrounded by uncertainty as she retired, unexpectedly alone. Should she stay or should she go? As of now, she resolved to sleep on it, if she could.

CHAPTER 11

Carlisle station was practically deserted as Chris made his way across the concourse. His few fellow passengers had left the train with some purpose and had quickly disappeared whereas Chris ambled, looking for all the world like someone who didn't know where he was going or what he was doing. The only people he could see were a bored looking station worker pushing the remnants of the evening's fast food with a very long broom, an apparently homeless man who had settled down for the night next to a branch of WH Smith which had pulled its shutters down a long time ago and a young man with a rucksack who also didn't appear to know what to do next. You and me both, thought Chris.

"So," said Chris to the young man in an attempt to strike up a conversation. "What happens next?"

The man looked blankly at him and shook his head. "No understand," he said. His complexion lacked the pallor readily associated with British people. He looked Southern European. God knows what he must be making of our weather, thought Chris.

Chris looked outside the station. It had stopped raining but there was an unseasonal chill in the air. It was not what you would call a lovely summer's evening.

He wandered outside in search of further signs of life which he found in abundance. Lifeless Carlisle was not. He wasn't sure he'd ever seen a city street so busy in the middle of the day, let alone in the small hours. It was teeming and, what made things worse, he seemed to be the oldest person there. What some of the young Cumbrian ladies were wearing – or nearly wearing – despite the weather made Chris just stop and stare, so much so that one particularly muscle bound male of the species who clearly formed half of a couple with one of the attractive young things gave him a very dirty look. He wasn't the only Charles Atlas lookalike either. The majority of the male population in the busy street looked like powerful farming types with muscles honed from years working in the fields or rounding up sheep on the fells. It seemed that most of the local young farmers had made their way into town in search of some amusement. Some of the lads who had clearly had their fill of finest Cumbrian ale or whatever their poison was on a night out such as this were rather frayed at the edges and they were strutting around most menacingly. They wouldn't have been averse to a bit of trouble if it had come their way. A couple of policemen were patrolling the scene but quite what they would have done if the balloon had gone up, Chris wasn't sure. By the time they had called for reinforcements it could have been complete pandemonium. Chris wasn't sure the lads and lasses would appreciate his gatecrashing the party so he decided to make himself scarce and he retreated to the sanctuary of the railway station.

Was this adventure such a good idea after all? Chris recalled how, on an Inter Rail trip with three student friends years ago, he had spent many hours hanging round stations. They had waited three hours for a ridiculously late train in Milan once but it didn't seem to matter then. They had a very loose schedule to adhere to but if it went wrong it could be changed in an instant. Time was really of no great consequence. When the train had arrived there were young people just like Chris and his friends hanging out of every window. That trip to Lake Garda had been great, sharing experiences with like minded individuals, and when they got to Bardolino they'd teamed up with some girls they had been talking to and everything had been wonderful drinking cheap wine in the Italian sunshine…

His current undertaking, on a dark, damp and cool night in north Cumbria, was rather different and somewhat more serious.

He reached the conclusion very quickly that he was temporarily marooned. The last bus to anywhere had gone, of course, and even if it hadn't he'd be no better off if he took it and found himself stranded in a city suburb or small north Cumbrian town or village. He knew it was a fair walk out to the motorway – and how easy would it be to hitch a lift at this time in any case? He could be stuck at junction 43 all night, or at least until a member of the local constabulary turned up and said, "And where would we be heading for at this time of night, Sir?" Logic suggested he make himself as comfortable as he could to survive the long hours until the morning when he would be able to work out his next move.

Meanwhile, in another part of the same county, Helen Wilkinson, having collected and washed her last empty pint pot of the evening and having driven the short distance home, was also settling down in rather more comfortable surroundings. She didn't live in one of Windermere's larger or more opulent residences, but her house suited her needs very nicely. There was plenty of room for her – a couple with a young daughter had lived there comfortably before – and the location was good, being handy for the town and close to the hills. Not for the first time, she felt very satisfied with her new environment, particularly when she compared it to what had gone before.

In between catching fitful snatches of sleep, the stay in Carlisle station gave Chris more time to think. What were his options?

Option one – take the first train home in the morning. This would be easy and safe, and he would be back in time for lunch. He could try to rebuild some of the fences he

Bowing Out

had torn down at Giovanni's. But, although this would certainly be a challenge, there was no adventure in this idea and it was hardly in keeping with his idea of a great escape. And what if he were to contact his colleagues who had not yet gone away on holiday and they all gave him the cold shoulder? That was possible – they hadn't had that long to forgive and forget. He would brood in the familiar surroundings of his house and wait for Sarah to come home having sacrificed the Scottish holiday. Maybe Sarah had abandoned ship already and was driving home through the night. Maybe she'd even left the cottage as soon as she'd discovered he wasn't there and gone home already. He didn't fancy even the remotest possibility of Sarah waiting for him. "You idiot. What did you do that for?" Maybe option one was not the preferred choice.

Option two – retrace his steps. He could take the first morning train back to Glasgow and then meander his way back north. The second leg of the journey would take some time, because even he couldn't really expect the same incredible good fortune with his thumb technique, but, on the other hand, if he went for the less adventurous option and took the train out of Glasgow's Queen Street station he would be back in the holiday accommodation relatively quickly. But he'd then be back where he was trying to escape from. Where was the benefit in that? If Sarah were there, how would she react if he were to skulk back with his tail between his legs? She'd be pleased to see him at first, of that there was no doubt, but, in all probability, normal service would soon be resumed. "You idiot. What did you do that for?" Maybe this wasn't really an option either.

Option three? It must exist, but Chris couldn't see it just now. He was sure it would all become clear in the morning.

"Good morning, Sir." Of course the policeman woke him just at the point where he was enjoying his period of deepest sleep. He was curious to know why Chris'

Peter Cropper

preferred lodging was a bench at the Citadel railway station.

Chris stated his case. "I arrived on the late train from Glasgow in the wee small hours, and I couldn't think of anywhere else to go. It was like the Wild West outside. I thought I'd be safer in here."

"I imagine you'll be making a move soon, won't you Sir?"

"Yes, of course, I'll be on my way in a minute or two, Officer." The policeman seemed unimpressed but not sufficiently interested in exploring the matter further. Chris didn't look like a member of the criminal fraternity or a clapped out junkie. The policeman walked off past the ticket office, and when he turned to look, Chris was on his feet making some sort of move.

The buffet had recently opened so Chris treated himself to a reasonable but overpriced breakfast and began his deliberations again. Unsurprisingly he was tired and feeling devoid of inspiration but he'd read somewhere that if you thought of nothing in particular and let your subconscious take over, then all would become clear, so he concentrated hard at staring into space.

Martin! The answer suddenly came to him. The theory had worked – and in double quick time!

He'd not seen Martin Cooper for a long time but – here was a bonus – he hadn't therefore offended or upset him in the recent past. In fact, he had never offended him, as far as he was aware. Martin was so easy going that Chris was reasonably sure he could turn up unannounced and – here was the factor that convinced him that Martin was a suitable target - they were definitely of the same mind these days. They were both men on a mission to find something better. However, if he was looking for luxury accommodation he would be disappointed. But he wasn't, and therefore he wouldn't be. He finished his breakfast, picked up his bag and made his way to the ticket office.

"Single to Oxenholme, please." He was about to be on the move again.

Bowing Out

The train took him south. Chris looked left and thought of the question which had once won him the not inconsiderable jackpot in a pub quiz. "Which is the highest mountain in England outside the Lake District?"

"It must be somewhere in the Peak District," his brother Bob who was quizzing with him at the time had suggested. Chris corrected him by pointing out that, in his experience, there were no real peaks in the Peaks, only flat topped boggy wildernesses and charming, tree lined Dales with small rivers in them. "Then why is it called the Peak District?" his team mate had asked. "Good question," Chris had replied.

Chris gave a little thumbs up to Cross Fell, the highest point in the Pennines, the backbone of England.

The train took Chris down the eastern side of the Lake District. He looked to the right this time and he was reminded of the time he and Sarah went walking above Haweswater, a little way to the west of where he was now. There had been a drought - or at least, Cumbria's best effort at a drought – and, sitting in the sunshine and looking down on the lake which was greatly reduced in size, Chris had told the story of the village and how it had been "drowned" at the behest of the big city corporation. Sarah had listened with great enthusiasm. They had not been going out long back then in the halcyon days of studenthood and the long summer "vacs" and Sarah hung on Chris' every word. But times change…

Back in Scotland, it was breakfast time. Sarah picked listlessly at a couple of pieces of toast. She had not slept well and the feeling of tiredness was exaggerated by the damp and cloudy weather – good for Chris' old friends the Scottish midges, not so good for English visitors. There was no sign of sunshine on the horizon, so Sarah decided to let the weather make her decision for her. It was miserable, she was miserable, and so it was probably best for her to cut her losses and abandon ship. Chris could be irritating, infuriating even, but there was no doubt that she missed him and she thought it better to miss him in the comfort of her own home.

Besides, he might even be there. If he was, she was sure she could help him sort out whatever was on his mind – or, at least, she would commit to trying her best to do so. "Sarah, my head's in the bin," he'd say. "Help me fish it out." She would, of course, as any good wife would.

She packed her bags and threw the clothes Chris had left behind into a separate holdall. The feeling was unpleasant and sad - a bit like that which she had encountered when she was helping to clear her Nan's house after she had died. She took a couple of deep breaths and dealt with the emotion as best she could. The house didn't need cleaning. They'd not been there long enough to make it dirty. She flung the bags into the boot of the car.

She wondered briefly whether she should ask Hughie for a refund and, having decided against it, she left the key on the inside of the door where she was sure it would be safe and drove off quickly. Maybe she'd write to Hughie when she got home to explain the situation, but that wasn't uppermost in her mind just now.

On the platform at Oxenholme, it was once again time for Chris to gather his thoughts. Martin. Where exactly was he?

He had known Martin for a relatively short time, but in that time they had become good friends. Originally he was a friend of a friend and Chris had met him because he was in the group which used to play five a side football at the leisure centre, so he had seen him on most Monday evenings for a while. Martin was very clever, but one of those people who is totally unfocused and constantly restless, and he flitted from project to project like a butterfly, never realising his potential. He was one of life's wanderers. It was not really much of a surprise when he announced he was leaving for a life in the country; he had no ties and had grown tired of the city. Rising crime and pollution levels particularly disturbed him. He had

Bowing Out

always longed for the quiet rural life away from the noisy city and he was going to enjoy it.

Chris had heard from him, but the information didn't give too much away about his whereabouts. Martin's first brief letter said he'd made friends with someone who owned a caravan somewhere in Grizedale Forest and his new friend was willing to rent out the van. It wasn't the height of luxury, but it would serve Martin's purpose. The second, and final, communication said that Martin had found a job with the Forestry Commission. He was working outside in the fresh air and was very happy to do that from now on. Martin, never one to follow convention very much, had not included his address. There was obviously no strong hint that Chris should pay him a visit, but no discouragement either, and Chris was sure they could carry on their friendship where they had left off. It was definitely worth a try. He was right to go for it. He had nothing to lose.

So Chris made his decision and he left Oxenholme station and wandered down the hill towards Kendal, the town it served.

CHAPTER 12

Even after all this time, Helen Wilkinson could sometimes scarcely believe her good fortune.

Once she had been trapped in a bank, seeing the same tired faces every day, performing the same routine tasks and listening to the constant malevolent gossip in the lunch hour. She was as good a worker as anyone there but she was the only one who seemed able to notice this. Five times a week she would undertake the same drive from her home on the eastern edge of the city through the predictable traffic jams, the only excitement being not knowing how easy it would be to find a parking space. Then, of course, there was the thrill of doing it all again later in the day in reverse – direction, not gear, of course. Weekends were all much of a muchness; perhaps a Saturday evening in the pub (always the same one) with Andy, maybe the odd meal out (but always in the same restaurant), sometimes Sunday lunch at Andy's parents but seldom, if ever, any element of unpredictability. Dying love, aggravated by the boredom, was also in the mix. Then her husband had wondered why she had to leave.

"We can fix this; I know we can, Helen. I can change. I will change."

"No. It's time we both moved on."

That was the gist of the conversations Helen and Andy had time after time about the state of the marriage and its future prospects. There was no real anger; Andy showed

Bowing Out

desperation, while Helen went more with resignation. She had always tried hard to go along with Andy's optimism but she had never succeeded, so in the end she had bowed to what she thought was the inevitable and given up.

What did she have now? Independence. No career, but a job with very little responsibility which provided the chance to meet interesting characters. No two days were ever the same. A nice little house. A view at the back, not of someone else's house over a garden fence, but of the wooded hills. Friendly neighbours who she actually saw and spoke to on a regular basis, especially in the summer months. No tedious commuting. No boring weekends.

No contest.

"You know," she often said to Fran who worked in the bakery at the end of the road, "I don't know why I didn't do this a long time before I did. Is there anywhere better than this to live?"

"I don't know," said Fran. She couldn't say. She had never lived anywhere else.

Later, after coffee, croissants, butter and jam and a period of intense relaxation with this week's copy of her favourite magazine, she fired up her little runabout and set off out of town and through the lanes to the Black Horse. The countryside was lovely any time but today, in the bright sunshine, it looked particularly wonderful. Perhaps the forestry worker – the interesting, Bohemian looking guy - would be in for a pint or two. "Let's hope he is," Helen said to herself. She had made friends with quite a few of the local men, but nobody special had emerged from the crowd. Maybe this new man, who, for some reason, had recently switched his allegiance from another watering hole, would be different.

It was downhill to town and it wouldn't take long for a strong walker such as Chris, so he resolved to exercise his legs rather than his thumb. Even with his baggage he was able to hurry through the suburbs. His obvious target was the town centre, because, he imagined, there he would surely find some means to take him closer to

Martin. He was soon crossing the river and heading up the main street with its traffic, crawling as usual. Out of all these vehicles, one must be going my way, he thought. It's just a matter of finding the right one.

By the time he'd reached the town hall, Kendal's impressive collection of cars, buses, coaches and lorries had fallen victim to the perils of the one way system and the minor collision which had happened out of sight round the corner, and everything had come to a complete standstill. This gave Chris time to scrutinise every lorry's name and home base and he spotted one owned by a firm in Barrow in Furness. That was in the right general direction, so he seized his chance and knocked on the door of the driver's cab.

"Going home?" The driver looked startled.

"Any chance of a lift?" added Chris, "assuming you're on your way back to base."

"Aye, why not?" said the driver. Someone hammering on his cab was unusual but it didn't faze him. He was not a particularly big man, but his time playing amateur rugby league in the Furness area had taught him how to look after himself. In any event, he agreed with the view of the policeman in Carlisle and the businessman in the Highlands that Chris didn't look to be a threat. He'd dealt with far fiercer men than this on rugby pitches at places like Millom and Askam.

"I'm Chris," said Mr O'Neill, as he made himself at home. He hadn't introduced himself to his last friend on the road and had later thought he possibly should have done. When you are wandering round and everything is uncertain you never know how useful strangers might become.

"John."

There was plenty of time for as much familiarisation as Chris thought necessary as John and his new companion inched their way along Kendal's streets and then finally broke free from the Auld Grey Town's shackles. Chris had found someone with transport in the part of the world he was interested in. A good contact, perhaps.

Bowing Out

He reeled off what he thought were relevant questions. He'd read somewhere that people always liked to be asked questions and that no sound was sweeter to anyone than his or her own name.

How long have you been doing this, John? Where's the farthest you've ever been sent, John? I've heard the cabs in these things are like well appointed bedrooms. How comfortable is it kipping down in here, John? I bet you can tell some great stories, John. What would you say is your favourite all time experience? Is it true you guys have a woman in every port, so to speak, eh John?

John was a man of few words and he answered briefly out of politeness and to pass the time. He'd picked up plenty of hitchers during his wanderings and he liked to help people to get from A to B, but they were all mere ships in the night. There was no reason to think that this bloke – Chris, did he say his name was? – was any different, although he was more talkative than most. He didn't feel inclined to return his passenger's questions so Chris told his story unprompted which John listened to up to a point, but it was now an even longer tale than the Scotsman had had to endure and it taxed the trucker's attention span.

The story came to an end and the cab fell quiet, giving Chris time again to consider his options. He didn't know exactly where he was heading. If he stayed with John, of course, he'd be in Barrow. Then what? If he asked John to drop him on the main road to the south of Grizedale, would he have time to get into the forest under his own steam and find the caravan or would he end up blundering round in the dark before settling down under a pile of damp leaves? Time was not on his side and the latter possibility seemed by far the more likely. The thought was not very appealing. Not surprisingly, he was beginning to feel rather tired. Hunger was also playing its hand, so he made a choice.

"Can you drop me off in Ulverston please, John?"

"Ulverston? Surely, having come this far, you don't want to miss the delights of Barrow? My home town has

Peter Cropper

a lot to offer, you know. Submarines, shipyards, a rugby team that's sadly seen better days, a football team that certainly has, and more seagulls than you can shake a stick at on Walney Island, if you like that sort of thing. It's the pride of the Lake District Peninsulas. Great pubs, too." John had suddenly become animated and for a minute, Chris fancied John might be about to offer to show him one such establishment and buy him a drink or two, but he didn't. Chris thought about jumping in with a similar offer himself, but he, too, stopped short. Something – probably the fact that he thought that really there was nothing to be gained by doing so - told him not to.

"Ulverston'll do nicely thanks."

"As you wish."

And so, just as the fish and chip shop in the main street was about to open its doors to the hearty Furness appetites, Chris found himself in Ulverston's market place, yet again being forced to contemplate his next move.

It's a hell of a long way home, thought Sarah, as the miles slipped by ever so slowly. She was competent enough behind the wheel but she wasn't used to driving long distances in a car on her own. Chris always did the lion's share of the driving and she'd been happy to let him, but now she was not sure that that had been a good move. A bit more experience at this type of thing would come in handy. She hadn't even reached the top end of Loch Lomond yet and already she was beginning to feel tired. She wondered what on earth she would do if she were unfortunate enough to break down in this inhospitable landscape. Would there be a signal out here for her mobile? She didn't dare look. People said you should take a break every two hours. "Tiredness kills. Take a break." Sarah couldn't believe how people could ever have the stamina or the constitution to go two hours without stopping, especially on a road like this which demanded total concentration.

Bowing Out

She passed a lonely, optimistic hitchhiker and she thought of her husband. There were fewer hitchers these days, she thought, almost certainly because it wasn't as safe as it used to be. That made her worry about Chris. She pulled in at Tyndrum to take a break and talk to Chris. She was relieved to find she did have a signal and she rang Chris' mobile, but it was the bloody voicemail again.

The road through Glencoe and over Rannoch Moor had been taxing, so Tyndrum, a small oasis in the wilderness at the southern end of the Scottish Highlands, was something of a godsend. Sarah broke her journey for a well earned cup of tea and she allowed herself to be tempted by something from the day's first batch of cakes. She felt a mixture of independence and solitude. It was something to which she was not accustomed.

As he sat down and awaited the jumbo sized haddock with chips, peas, bread and butter and tea and all at a reasonable price, Chris thought he'd pass the time with a quick check on vital equipment. All was there, but his mobile had been switched off for ages. He discovered plenty of messages, the tones of which had increasing degrees of desperation about them.

"Chris, love, it's me. Where the hell are you? I'm worried sick. Give us a bell, please."

"Chris, what did you do last night? Where did you sleep? It wasn't half lonely here without you. I just need to know you're all right."

"Please phone and put me in the picture. That's the least you can do. You want some space and time – I can see that. But I do need to know you're safe."

"Please ring." Tears this time.

Chris rang. He spoke to Sarah live, although he had selfishly hoped the voicemail would have made things easier for him. He did feel better then, however. He had been a sod not to phone, but that was then and this was now and at least Sarah now knew he was fine, and he knew that she was fine and she had arrived home safely. Sarah told him it had been a tough journey, and that she

Peter Cropper

admired Chris' stamina and the way he could drive such long distances without apparently feeling tired. Yes, he would definitely leave his phone switched on. Where was he? He'd rather not say just yet, but she wasn't to worry about him. She could ring him whenever she wanted to, within reason.

CHAPTER 13

The pub at the top of the market square had a single room, so Chris took it. He had had enough of roughing it the night before, and, in any case, he wasn't short of money. He was a fully paid up member of the teaching profession and, as such, a comfortable bed was the very least he deserved.

The man he was talking to at the bar seemed to have a lot in common with Chris.

Tim taught in a school in Barrow – "if you can call it teaching." He was a linguist. "Have you any idea how hard it is persuading kids up here of the importance of a foreign language?" he asked Chris in an animated fashion. Chris conceded he had no idea. "France. Spain. Most of our kids, stuck here at the end of Britain's longest cul de sac, don't even know where the rest of England is."

"It sounds as though you're not keen on being up here?"

"Don't get me wrong – teaching languages to young Barrovians is a nonsense, but this time of year it's great. August – I think you'll agree, it's the most wonderful word in the English language. All day every day to get out and about and enjoy this wonderful part of the world. Sometimes the sun even shines but, even if it doesn't, it's lovely just the same. And with a bit of local knowledge, you can get to places the tourists miss. I could potter round the Furness for ever. That's why I came up here in the first place." Tim's accent suggested he came from somewhere in the south of England. Memories of childhood trips to the Lakes had drawn him there in later life.

"And you have the knowledge, I'll bet," said Chris. It made Tim sound like a London taxi driver.

"Oh, yes."

Chris thought he'd be a bit bold. "I bet you know Grizedale Forest. That's round here, isn't it? I've heard it's a lovely spot, but I've never been myself. You'll know how to get there on public transport, I expect." To the best of Chris' knowledge the Ulverston to Grizedale bus ran infrequently, if at all. "Is there a decent bus service from here? Or would a train be a better bet?" Chris knew that this was out of the question since the days of Dr Beeching and his swingeing axe but he thought that he would play the ignorance card and see where it took him.

It was a long shot but it whistled past the stranded goalkeeper into the top corner, and a short while later Chris had booked a morning lift with his new friend Tim with the local knowledge.

These Cumbrians – or were they still Lancastrians? – could certainly conjure up a breakfast. It even passed the ultimate test – there was black pudding sitting next to the Cumberland sausage which curved round most of the edge of the plate. The sun was shining as the country finally showed signs of drying out. It was pleasantly warm as Chris sat near the window and watched the market town spring into life. All was looking good as Chris ordered more toast and a fresh pot to build himself up for the excitement to come.

At 10.30 precisely Tim pulled up outside the pub where Chris was waiting, his ubiquitous bag by his side.

"All aboard for the great Grizedale adventure."

"Good morning. Impeccable timing, Sir." Chris began with a fulsome compliment.

"Well, said Tim, "show me a competent teacher who cannot keep good time. Five minutes recap, ten minutes to introduce the new material, some oral practice…"

"Exactement," agreed Chris. "Tell me where we're going and what we'll find when we get there," he added, excitement in his voice. He thought that by sounding enthusiastic he could encourage the enthusiasm in Tim, thus ensuring that the expedition kept going for as long as was necessary.

Tim was no longer a teacher; he now became one of the Cumbrian tourist board's finest and most knowledgeable employees, and he poured forth on the delights of the Furness region of the County Palatine of Lancashire. He did know the area, of that there was no doubt, even if he did go on a bit.

Soon they had left the main road, Barrow's lifeline with the outside world, and they were on the lanes which meandered delightfully past fields of sheep and through woods, the countryside always gently undulating. Footpaths appearing frequently to the left and right promised delightful walks through the trees. Occasionally a farmhouse or a bed and breakfast was passed, and even an odd hamlet, but there was little sign of substantial life. On the one hand, Martin's caravan might stand out if it were anywhere near a road, but, on the other hand, it could be difficult to find anyone to ask about its whereabouts if it were hidden away. But the uncertainty – that only served to make it more exciting, didn't it?

"How far exactly would Sir like to go with Tim's Tours?"

"Until we find a caravan which looks like the sort of place where a drop out would live," Chris wanted to say, but he thought that might sound a bit daft. On the other hand, he wasn't sure how to give a better answer to the perfectly reasonable question. Here he was in Grizedale as, presumably, was Martin. All they needed to do was link up, but at this moment it seemed rather like trying to find a needle in a haystack – or, perhaps, one particular pine cone in the whole forest.

Peter Cropper

"If you can drop me in the next village, that'd be great. I'll have a potter round and get a feel of the place."

"Then what will you do?"

"Oh, I'll be fine," said Chris. "I'm sure I'll be able to find somewhere to stay. I'm quite used to holidaying off the cuff on my own."

Ten minutes later, the two men parted. "I've enjoyed your company," said Tim. "You're a good bloke and we've a lot on common." He took a piece of paper out of the glove compartment and scribbled down some figures. "Here's my number in Ulverston. Give us a shout if you fancy a pint sometime."

Chris stuffed the piece of paper into his wallet. It could prove useful. "Thanks for that. And thanks for your company and the lift. If I don't see you before – Happy New School Year."

"To you, too," came the doleful reply.

Chris treated himself to a wry smile.

Back at the O'Neill residence the sun had not yet made an appearance and the dull weather matched Sarah's mood. After constantly encouraging herself as the motorway miles dragged by that she would get home under her own steam, she had managed it. It had not been easy, but, lubricated by several refreshment stops and fortified by a nap at a service area when she knew it would have been dangerous to drive on and that she just had to pull off the road, she had succeeded. It just showed what you could do if you had to. At least driving all that way on her own had made her tired enough to sleep well, despite the frequent intakes of caffeine.

But now, in the morning with a full day at home stretching before her, she really was unsure what to do. She wasn't due back in work, of course. She could turn up to the Fruit Bowl but that would involve fielding all sorts of awkward questions from Sheila. However, there was no getting away from it - it was either that or stay at home and talk to..? Sarah suddenly realised how much time she spent with Chris when she wasn't working and how few people she could call upon for company at a moment's notice. In fact, she couldn't think of anyone who might be available as an immediate shoulder to cry on, and that depressed her greatly.

Helen Wilkinson wasn't far away, relatively speaking – compared with the huge distance that Sarah had covered the previous day, she lived just up the road – but the thought of setting off again so soon simply didn't appeal. "And besides," Sarah reminded herself, "the silly cow hasn't told me exactly where she is, has she?" That annoyed her greatly, and made her feel depressed.

She left another message on Chris' voicemail. "I'm back home now. I wish you were, too." Then, having snapped her phone shut, she cursed him very loudly because he had failed to keep his promise about keeping his phone switched on.

Tim's car disappeared round the bend and Chris heard it pull away from the village. When it had gone, all that was left, apart from birdsong and the distant hum of a tractor, was the sound of silence. It was the type of rural peace that Chris normally loved but now, just when he needed some human contact to help him gather in a few clues, there was none to be seen.

It was a typical village. The old church was perhaps Norman, or possibly it had been built a little later. Chris was no architecture student, and he hadn't a clue, but it was a grand building, sturdily constructed to withstand anything the elements could produce. There were some cottages scattered round, but little else in the immediate vicinity. He couldn't stand outside Heather Cottage for the rest of his life wondering what to do, so he picked up his bag and opted for a little exploration.

The village shop offered the first chance of gleaning useful information. Chris breezed in. "Good morning," he ventured. "Can you help me? You don't happen to know a guy called Martin, do you? Martin Cooper. Lives in a caravan."

"Where?"

Peter Cropper

"Somewhere in Grizedale Forest, as far as I know." Chris immediately recognised the unhelpfulness of his answer.

"It's a big place. What does this guy look like?"

"About my age. Medium height. Brown hair." Chris made him sound as if he could be any one of thousands of English males. He didn't find it easy describing people at the best of times. Here he was trying to describe someone he'd not seen in years. He was probably wide of the mark in any case. For all Chris knew, Martin was now bearded and suitably wild looking with unkempt hair.

The lady in the shop didn't find the description helpful, and so Chris did not find the lady helpful.

The next contestant was an old man who came strolling round the corner with his faithful collie. He too failed to reach the final of the "Locate Mr Cooper" competition, and the game show promptly ran out of players.

The church clock informed everyone that it was midday and the pub doors flew open as if operated by the striking mechanism. The urgency in opening up all seemed a bit needless as there was hardly a clamour among the locals for refreshment but there would be at least one person in the pub Chris could ask.

The typical country pub in the typical village had the tranquil morning-after-the-night-before air that Chris had always liked. The smell of polish and air freshener lingered having won the battle against the stale tobacco smoke, and the stools were neatly positioned against the tables where new beer mats had been placed with seemingly fanatical regard to symmetry. The ashtrays had all been emptied and there was an empty coffee cup next to a newspaper on the bar, but otherwise all was immaculate. The pub was ready for the rush, but it was not going to happen in the immediate future.

The pumps were lined up for inspection. Chris noticed the pub sold two of his favourite beers, but it was only twelve o'clock, and he had no idea what sort of demands the day ahead would place on him. A pint or

Bowing Out

two now could render him useless for the rest of the day, and it struck him that he didn't have time to waste.

"Good morning. Or should I say afternoon? Do you serve coffee?"

"Certainly, Sir. Cup or cafetiere?" It was a very formal exchange, somehow out of keeping with the whole area.

Chris took his tray to one of the tables near to the bar so he was in conversation range. He wanted to press the barmaid for information. He pressed the plunger and thought quickly. He needed to find out how well the barmaid knew the local area.

"The weather's picking up at last." Chris went for a very safe, very English opening gambit.

"Not before time," replied the lady behind the bar. She was not stunningly beautiful, but there was definitely something attractive about her. "And what's more," she added, "it's settling down for a few days. Or so they tell us."

Good. Searching for needles in haystacks, or pine cones in forests, could be rotten in the pouring rain.

"Do you live round here?" Chris winced as soon as he'd said it. It sounded like a desperately corny chat up line, but if Claire saw it that way she was too well mannered to say so.

"I don't live in the village," she replied, "but I am relatively local. Twenty minutes in the car, or a little more in the rush hour – that's to say, if a local farmer is moving his sheep or his cows across the road from field to field."

"That's rush hour up here, is it?" asked Chris with a smile.

"It is," replied Claire. "Congested city streets, motorways turned into car parks – that's not the way we do things round here."

"You do know how lucky you are, don't you?"

"Oh yes I do." It was Claire's turn to smile now.

"And how long have you worked here?"

"A couple of months. I was meant to be taking over from another lass, but she changed her mind and decided to stay. Luckily for me, the landlord kept me on over the summer. It's hard to believe," she said looking round, "but we do get busy in here from time to time."

"Plenty locals?"

"Well, yes," said Claire. "Locals, tourists – we do all right really. This place is pretty much the hub of the area. There are only really a couple of other pubs within striking distance."

Possible other sources of information, thought Chris.

The pub's popularity was good news. The chances were that someone in here would know Martin or, if he really hit the jackpot, Martin himself would come striding through the door at any time...

It was time for the 64,000-dollar question. "You don't happen to know a guy called Martin Cooper, do you?" asked Chris.

"To be honest, I don't know many of the locals myself," replied Claire. "I very often seem to be on the graveyard slot," she added, lowering her voice in case her employer was in earshot. "But if you come in this evening, my colleague will probably have a better idea. Helen seems to know everyone round here."

"Thanks for that," said Chris. Silence descended as he worked his way through his cafetiere of Columbian.

CHAPTER 14

Exactly what was she supposed to do for the next fortnight of her life?

Sarah sat and stared at the garden and thought, and the more she thought, the more depressed she became. This was her holiday which she had saved for and which she was looking forward to, and now it had gone. It was all Chris' stupid bloody fault. Or was it? There was nothing to have prevented her from staying in Scotland on her own, except that was it - she would have been on her own and what would she have done? Now she was at home on her own and what was she going to do?

"I can't stand being on my own!" she bawled rather pathetically at nobody in particular, perfectly encapsulating the real nature of the problem.

The garden was looking untidy. This was something she could focus her attention on. For two weeks? She didn't think so. The sun was breaking through now, but, in her current frame of mind, she persuaded herself that it wouldn't be too long before it would start to rain again.

She made a half pot of tea – there was no point in filling it up as she usually did - and vowed to make a couple of calls after her tea break. She'd given up on phoning Chris. She hoped Jane and Lisa would be around.

Coffee finished, Chris considered his next move. There wasn't a lot of point staying in the pub although the more he looked at Claire standing nonchalantly behind the bar, the more attractive she became. His seat was comfortable and he was still full of his full English, but he did have to consider such matters as food and accommodation in the Grizedale area. There was absolutely no point in going back to Ulverston, good though his billet there had been. It would not make the best base for his search.

It was, indeed, a good job he was a fully paid up member of the teaching profession with a healthy bank balance.

He enquired about accommodation at the pub but there were only two rooms and Claire's inspection of the diary brought disappointing news.

"You could stay at mine, if you like." That was what Chris would have liked to hear, but, of course, there was no chance of that. Instead, Claire said, "There are a couple of places at the far end of the village that you could try. They're both fine, as far as I know."

"I'd better make a move then. Nice talking to you. See you again, I hope."

"Goodbye," said Claire, without a flicker of emotion.

Low Rigg guesthouse was pleasantly located at the end of the village with a view across gently sloping fields to the forest beyond. It stood in its own grounds, mature trees being a noteworthy feature. The garden path was bordered with delightfully perfumed flowers and the perfectly manicured lawn with the bench in the middle looked most inviting. If the interior matches the exterior, this place would make an excellent short term base, Chris decided.

He was in luck; Mrs Jackson could offer accommodation. For how long did he want it? Mrs Jackson's guess was as good as Chris'. He estimated two nights. Now that would be a challenge – two days to locate Martin Cooper, and, as a bonus, maybe two days to woo the attractive Claire? He asked Mrs Jackson the inevitable question - you know, the one about Martin Cooper - but she could not help. Chris put his bag down in the corner of the simple but adequately furnished and spotlessly clean bedroom and, again, wondered exactly what he was going to do next. As there would surely be nobody wandering about in the middle of the afternoon, he retired to the garden to enjoy the now surprisingly warm sunshine and to wait until the village sprang to life in the early evening.

"Jane's away for a few days, I'm afraid." That was not what Sarah wanted to hear. Kevin seemed amazed to have had a call from Sarah. Jane never spoke about her these days. He thought Sarah was lost and gone forever, and he'd never felt suitably inspired to make enquiries about her himself. Kevin and Sarah had never really got on especially well, but Kevin knew how to be civil on the phone.

She tried Lisa a couple of times, but all she got was the answer phone. That was just like trying to talk to Chris. The message gave no indication when she would be back – it could be five minutes or five hours or, if she were like her other friend, five days.

Sarah reflected. She was getting good at that. Her husband was away and incommunicado. She could try ringing him again but the chances of the phone being switched on were slim and she now had the overwhelming feeling that it would be better to give Chris some space and time. But how much space and time did he need? This future business would be so much better if it were not racked with so much uncertainty. The two friends she hoped to rustle up locally were unavailable. She had ruled out an unexpected return to the Fruit Bowl. Much as she disliked the idea of another session on the road, she felt she would have to try to find Helen or she would go mad. She was the only real contact she had left, unless she headed off to the Deep South to her parents, but that would be an even longer journey and the thought of the barrage of questions she would have to face when she got there was too awful to contemplate.

Peter Cropper

The first task was to locate Andy Wilkinson. He would surely know where Helen was. He would be hiding in an old address book somewhere. She embarked on a long expedition through the dining room drawers.

Chris strolled into the pub. After a pleasant session of reading and catching up on some sleep in the suntrap of a garden, he'd showered and changed and he felt suitably refreshed, as well as being confident that the search for Martin Cooper wouldn't be a long one. It was a strange confidence that he could not really explain. This time there were two barmaids for him to admire.

"Good evening, ladies." He embellished his charm with a broad grin. The winning smile, which Chris believed had impressed so many ladies in the past, was returned. Claire and her colleague knew how to be polite to their customers.

The pub had more visitors this time – there could hardly have been fewer. The four young men in the corner were cyclists, a fact given away by their uniform. They were vivid in their brightly coloured clothes and they wore that special footwear that cyclists wear. The necessary helmets were waiting patiently in a regimented row by the table. Was it not possible or permissible to ride a bike in the country if you weren't dressed like that? The young family at another table had enjoyed their day. The two girls were placid and well behaved; one was buried in a book, while the younger one seemed content to weigh up the surroundings. Every now and again she related details about what she could see to her doll with the curly blonde hair. Dad looked happy and relaxed as he nursed his freshly pulled pint and began to examine the menu while mum was deep in tourist literature planning the next day's itinerary. The two men at the bar were locals. Their ruddy complexions and old clothes showed that they worked outside most days, and they spoke with an accent such that Chris had to strain to understand what they were saying.

Bowing Out

It was hard to justify two bar staff although Chris wasn't complaining. He still felt rather drawn to Claire while her colleague was not much less attractive. The new girl looked vaguely familiar, although he couldn't for the life of him imagine where he would have seen her before.

Surrounded by a pile of old letters, last year's diary and a few unused Christmas cards, Sarah triumphantly pulled out an old address book which had not seen the light of day for some time. Turning to the W section, she found the appropriate entry. It had been a very long time since she had rung that number, and she could do no more than presume that Andy still lived there. She had nothing else to go on.

"Welcome to BT answer 1571…." Sarah began to wonder whether anyone had a phone that they were willing to answer. The trouble with this type of answering machine was that you could never be sure that you had reached the right number. She could only hope it was Andy's phone she had contacted. She decided against leaving a message. She would try again later, but for now she would leave the pile of papers on the floor – there was nobody there to ask her to do otherwise – and go out somewhere. Anywhere that didn't involve staring at four walls. She couldn't think of anywhere more suitable than the supermarket, even though she had driven home with a car load of food which they had intended to enjoy while in Scotland. She could buy some food for the freezer – and some meals for one?

"Don't think like that," Sarah told herself quickly as she locked the door behind her.

Chris chatted to Helen. No, she hadn't lived in the Lakes all her life. Yes, she was a city girl really, or at least she used to be, but who could possibly prefer battling through the traffic on a daily basis in order to spend the day in an office to this sort of life?

Chris appraised her carefully. She wasn't quite as pretty as Claire but there was a certain something in her smile. Where she did score over Claire was in her more pleasant personality which was immediately apparent. Her fingers were ring less, and she contrasted with Claire who was dripping in jewels. He could *not* get rid of the idea that he knew her from somewhere.

"Have you worked here long?" It sounded only marginally less corny than "Do you come here often?" but it was a functional question, designed to discover Helen's chances in the "hunt Cooper" test.

"A couple of years," replied Helen. This was an encouraging answer. Martin must have drunk in the pub sometime in the last two years. In fact, based on his previous liking for a pint or two, he'd probably drunk in the pub in the last two days, but, then again, if he were a regular, was it not strange that Claire didn't know him? On the other hand, perhaps Martin had changed and gone self sufficient. By this stage he could well be a hermit, living off natural spring water, wild berries and the fat of the land. Even as they spoke he might be stalking deer or up to his knees fishing in a river somewhere.

"So you know quite a few of the people who live here then?"

"Oh, yes. There's not many people round here. This pub's like Crewe station. Virtually everyone passes through at some stage or other."

The 64,000 dollars were still up for grabs. "I think an old mate of mine lives somewhere round here. Martin Cooper. Do you know him?"

"That's not a name I recognise, I'm afraid. Sorry."

The younger of the two locals at the bar turned to Chris. "I couldn't help overhearing you," Chris imagined he probably said. (He did.) "Martin Cooper, you say? I know Martin. I've worked with him in the forest."

Chris concentrated hard on what the man was saying and then concluded he'd struck gold. "How well do you know him? Do you know whereabouts he lives?"

Bowing Out

"I don't know him that well. He's quite a secretive bloke really. He tends to keep himself to himself. He lives in a caravan, I believe, somewhere in the middle of nowhere up a track."

His older companion chipped in. "Aye, I know vaguely where he lives. Do you know the derelict cottage just past the pond?"

Chris didn't, but he did have his Ordnance Survey map which he pulled quickly out of his pocket. He was well prepared and optimistic; he had it with him for just such an eventuality. "Could you do me a huge favour and show me whereabouts his caravan is please?"

Chris spread the map out on a nearby table. The older man gave Chris an excellent idea of the caravan's location. "To the best of my knowledge there's no other sign of life up there, so even though I can't say for sure exactly where it is, if you find a caravan, then you've found Martin. The caravan is bound to be in sight. Nobody would take the trouble to pull it off the track over the rough ground into the forest itself." It all looked very promising. Martin's residence didn't look to be that far from the village but without the help of the two men it could have taken forever to find. "Let me buy you two gentlemen a pint," said Chris. "It's the least I can do."

CHAPTER 15

And so Sarah's miserable day crept very slowly towards its conclusion.

She had wandered up and down the supermarket aisles, becoming more and more upset as it dawned on her that any food shopping that she now did *would* be for one. It had been a long time since she had been shopping for one and it wasn't something she wanted to start to do again even though it would only be for a short period of time – wouldn't it?

When she returned home the house seemed twice as empty as when she had left it. It was depressing. She went straight to the phone, picked it up and pressed the redial button.

"Hello." A little milestone had been reached. Someone had answered a phone. It was the type of event which might merit a mention on the local news later. She never thought such a short, simple word could be so welcome.

"Andy Wilkinson?"

There was a short pause while Andy tried without success to identify the caller. "That's me. Who is it, please?"

"Sarah. Sarah O'Neill. Helen's friend from a long time ago."

There was another silence during which Sarah tried to work out just what Andy was thinking. She didn't know whether Helen had ever told him what Sarah thought of him. "If only I'd listened to Sarah," Helen might have said during an altercation with Andy. "She was right all along. She said we were never made for each other." If that were the case, ringing Andy for help and advice now would be a complete waste of time, unless he was very much the forgiving type. After what seemed an eternity, Andy spoke.

"Sarah. Nice to hear from you. It's been ages. What are you up to?"

The tone of his voice was neutral. It wasn't exactly enthusiastic but neither did it suggest animosity. Perhaps, like Sarah, he was just glad of having someone to talk to.

Sarah was also very non committal in her response. She didn't feel like sharing her immediate problems with Andy so she told him all was well and that she was happy enough dealing in fruit and veg. She said that she had a strong desire to get back in touch with Helen. Could Andy provide any information on her whereabouts?

"We don't keep in touch really," said Andy. "Neither of us could really see the point. No kids, and all that. We just wished each other a nice life and she rode off into the distance, never to be seen again."

"So you've no address even?"

"Like I said, I've never needed it. She went to the Lake District. That's about all I know. South Lakes, I think. I do know she said she'd head to Windermere for starters because that's where most of the people are. Where she went after that, God only knows."

That wasn't too promising. It didn't look as if this contact would get her very far. Perhaps she would have to wait for Jane and Lisa after all.

No she wouldn't! If she sat around any longer waiting for human contact she would drive herself mad. There was absolutely no reason not to seek out Helen. After all, she was on holiday. It would become a sort of working holiday, that's all – a working holiday with an interesting challenge.

"I've some time off at the moment," she continued down the phone, "and I really would like to see Helen again. I think I'll go to Cumbria and try to find her."

"I'd have thought you'd be away with Chris," said Andy, "or, at least, wanting to spend time with him at home. Are we not in the middle of one of his endless school holidays?"

Sarah played confidently at this tricky delivery with a very straight bat. "He's actually away for a few days with a couple of his work colleagues, walking in Snowdonia. And even if he wasn't, he wouldn't mind me going off on my own. Time spent apart can freshen up a relationship for both parties." She immediately wished she hadn't said that, but it was too late now. "He knows I've been wanting to get in touch with Helen for ages now." She couldn't decide whether she was trying to reassure herself or whether she was indulging in some particularly striking irony or, indeed, both.

There was another slight pause. "Sarah, it's been good to hear from you. Leave me your number. I've got to go now, but I'll ring you back soon." As if, thought Sarah. It's probably his new wife or a girlfriend dragging him off the phone. What was I doing ever imagining that I'd get any help from Andy after all this time? And why would he want to ring back later if he's no further information to impart?

Nevertheless, she gave Andy her number. There was no reason not to. She wondered if he had bothered to write it down.

At about the same time that Chris was embarking on his third pint with his new and helpful friends having convinced himself that linking up with Martin the following day would be an easy task, Sarah's phone rang again. "That's Lisa's ring," she said to herself. It wasn't the first time that day she had caught herself talking to nobody in particular.

"Sarah. It's Andy." When he'd said he would ring again, he had meant it.

Bowing Out

"Hi. What is it?" Sarah hoped she didn't sound too curt. She was pleased to hear from him again and curious as to what he might have to say.

"Sarah, you know when you said you fancied trekking off to the Lakes to try to find Helen? I'm due some time off work. Would you mind if I came with you?"

CHAPTER 16

Monday morning dawned. It was the start of the working week, and Chris and Sarah had work to do, but not work as most people know it. They were two people on exciting and interesting missions.

Sarah woke a little later than she would have liked. She had lots to do. She should really have set the alarm but she had been weary when she went to bed. Andy had arranged to pick her up at ten o'clock and she hadn't packed yet. Nor did she know how much she would need. She went downstairs for breakfast and the blinking of the red light on the answer machine caught her eye. It was Chris, and the message, as well as confirming he was fine, said that he was in his favourite location and things were going really well. He sounded very bright and cheerful, and a little under the influence.

"His favourite location." That could only mean he, too, was in the Lakes. Chris loved to spend his leisure time in two places – the Lakes, and the far southern tip of Cornwall where he would walk along the cliff tops and remark with irritating frequency how great it was to feel the wind in your hair. Sarah smiled sadly as she recalled how thrilled Chris had been when they had bought a house on an estate where the roads were all named after Cornish towns and villages. "That can only mean this must be the right place for us," he had said. Sarah was sure he would not have had time to reach Cornwall so she

Bowing Out

persuaded herself that her husband was in the same sort of area as that to which she would soon be heading.

Things were starting to go her way. She wasn't moved to sing "Oh, what a beautiful morning", but she felt confident. She was off to seek out Helen but instead of the anticipated solo slog up the motorway she had a chauffeur lined up. There was also the chance – albeit it was an outside chance – that she might find Chris and, despite the way in which he had treated her, of course she still wanted to see him. They were both long shots – the National Park is a big place - but she felt optimistic that she would find at least one of her quarries. After breakfast she set about her tasks with some relish. This would be a good distraction to stop her from dwelling on such things as what Chris had said about their new address all those years ago, and she didn't want Andy to find her upset.

Chris sat down to an appetising Low Rigg breakfast. Mrs Jackson put the busy plate in front of him and enquired about his plans for the day. Chris took a sip of tea and said he was looking forward to a wonderfully rewarding day in the forest.

"Are you a walker then? Or do you have one of those new modern bike things that can go absolutely anywhere?"

"You mean a mountain bike, Mrs Jackson. No - I'm looking for my mate. Do you remember, the guy I asked you about?" Mrs Jackson's memory wasn't all it used to be. "And I'm sure I've now got all the information I need to find him."

"Good hunting, then," said Chris' landlady as she toddled off over the dark blue, shag pile carpet back to the kitchen. Chris was left alone with his full English. The only sound was the rhythmic ticking of the clock in the hallway and the birdsong from the garden. There was nothing at Mrs Jackson's to commemorate anyone dying of excitement. Chris, like his wife, felt as though everything was falling into place. Even the sunshine was holding.

Ten o'clock came and went and nothing happened at the O'Neill residence. At first Sarah welcomed Andy's lack of punctuality because, despite a lot of frenzied activity, she wasn't ready, but by the time the clock reached half past she was straining at the leash and growing impatient. Marvellous. Was there anyone left who you could rely on?

One quick cup of coffee later she stormed to the phone, rang Andy's number and got no reply. That at least suggested to her that he was probably on his way. If only she had his mobile number. "But," she said to herself, "I'll give him the benefit of the doubt. There's not much else I can do."

An hour and a bit behind schedule, Andy rang the doorbell. Sarah quickly shed her annoyance, put on her best beaming smile and opened the door. Andy looked at her apologetically.

"Andy. Great to see you."

"Likewise. You're looking well."

"Thank you. So are you."

He had aged only a little in the time since they had last met. He had a bit less hair now and what he had was cut shorter, but overall the years had treated him kindly. Perhaps his conservative lifestyle had helped. He had hardly changed his way of life since Helen's departure. He had taken no chances but, as a result, had not really moved on. That was the reason he was now so willing to help Sarah. He regarded an exciting quest to track down his ex wife with another woman as taking a giant step out of his comfort zone in which, he had suddenly decided, he had spent long enough.

"Step in."

"Thanks. Sorry I'm late. Traffic." He unashamedly used the standard excuse which any driver could use in most parts of England without fear of being contradicted.

"Tea? Coffee?"

"Tea would be great, thank you." He was curious to look at the house. It was evocative of another era. While Sarah prepared the drinks in the kitchen he sat quietly in

Bowing Out

the living room which seemed to have all the trappings of domestic bliss. He saw a couple of photographs of Chris and Sarah. In one of them they were smartly dressed and smiling. It looked as though they were attending someone's wedding. The other photograph showed them relaxed and happy against a backcloth of a lake and a pine clad mountain slope. The scene, Andy supposed, was in Austria or Switzerland.

There were a couple of Sarah's magazines on the coffee table and, next to that, a postcard of somewhere hot. Andy turned it over to find it was from someone in the Greek islands but he turned it back when he heard Sarah coming out of the kitchen with the tea tray. Sitting there where he had sat with his ex wife all that time ago made him wonder whether he would like to do all that again. If they could find Helen it might not be too long until the four of them were sitting together again in the lounge, or sharing a couple of bottles of wine on a summer's evening in the garden. Plodding Andy, the realist tending to pessimism, surprised himself with his new found optimism. He had definitely taken the right steps – two heads would be better than one in the search, and on the front of the other head was a pretty face, which was an obvious bonus.

Sarah put the tray down on the coffee table. "Biscuits?"

"Go on then. Yes please. We'll need to build up our strength for the challenges ahead."

Sarah returned from the kitchen and pleasantries were exchanged but conversation wasn't easy and Andy couldn't stop looking at his watch. He, too, was anxious to be off. Sarah noticed this with some annoyance, because, if they had fallen behind schedule, it was Andy's fault.

"You've not come here to drink tea in our living room, have you Andy?"

"No. We can hit the road just as soon as you want."

Chris sat on the bench outside Low Rigg and studied the map. X marked the spot. The route didn't seem complicated. He needed to go all the way through the village which wouldn't take long, walk a couple of miles at most along the road, and then turn right up the track. He backed himself to find Martin's caravan within the hour.

The village was quiet; the few weekend trippers had gone and the locals were nowhere to be seen. Yesterday's cyclists would be back on familiar territory now, at work, doing whatever they did in their mundane existences. They would be clock watching already with only their expedition next weekend to look forward to. Their week would drag, and then their time in the saddle on the open road would fly past, because that's how life worked. The young family was presumably still on holiday, possibly following a waymarked trail in the forest or enjoying a sail on a lake, but the holiday wouldn't last forever. They, too, would be back in their normal routines before they wanted to be, but Chris had the potential to make any changes from here on permanent. It was wonderful to be free of all his responsibilities and yet, he reminded himself, if all else failed he could simply go home and start again in September. He might have to wear sackcloth for a while in the staffroom but he could do that. He had the skin of a rhinoceros. He felt very pleased with himself. He was in a no lose situation.

He left the village behind and found himself out in the country. Was this the track? Chris looked at the map, gauged how far he had gone since leaving civilisation and decided it probably wasn't. It didn't seem substantial enough and he hadn't yet passed the wood on the left. He also hadn't noticed the stream which, according to the oracle, he needed to cross, so he decided to press on.

A few minutes later he was confident he had found what he was looking for. This was a wider, well trodden track and it gave the impression of going somewhere. It had a lot in common with Chris. He turned off the lane and estimated that, if the locals' information was reliable, he would reach his target in about twenty minutes' brisk walking.

Bowing Out

"What's made you want to track Helen down after all this time?"

It was a good question, and Sarah looked at the cows in the passing fields, as if they could provide a reasonable answer. Perhaps it was time to tell the truth about her and Chris. Putting Andy in the picture about their domestic situation would surely have no long term repercussions. It would be like unburdening yourself to a stranger which was sometimes a good thing to do.

While she was thinking, Andy grew tired of waiting for the answer and added a second question. "How long do we have to find her? What I mean by that is, when is Chris due back from Wales? You see, I noticed you didn't phone Chris or leave him a note, so presumably you're expecting to find Helen pretty quickly. Either that, or Chris is planning to take a long time to climb Snowdon."

"I rang Chris last night to tell him about my plans," said Sarah, but her acting skills deserted her, and she sounded far from convincing. The shrewd Andy didn't fall for it.

"He's gone, hasn't he?" It was an inspired guess.

"He's gone to Snowdon, like I said." Andy could tell Sarah was annoyed.

Nevertheless, he was not to be deflected. "He's gone, hasn't he?" he repeated, bravely.

"Yes, he's gone." Sarah response was quieter now. The answer was a little ambiguous, but they both knew exactly what it meant. She spoke in hushed tones as if she were speaking reverently in a cathedral.

"Is that why you contacted me?"

Sarah was suddenly animated. "What do you mean? Out of desperation for a man?"

It was Andy's turn to be quiet.

"I contacted you because I knew you'd know where Helen was. Or at least, I thought you would. Helen was the only person I could think of to talk to and that was the only thing that would stop me going bananas in an empty house. Happy with that?" She was more annoyed now. "Drive on. Thank you."

The locals knew their way round. They were probably familiar with every leaf on every branch on every tree in the woods and, thanks to their directions, Chris found himself at the caravan in which, he presumed, lived Martin. There was no other, he had been reliably informed. He knocked on the door, and waited. There was no reply.

He looked through the window to look, firstly, for evidence of human habitation and, secondly, for compelling evidence that it was Martin who was living there. On the table was a coffee mug and a plate covered with crumbs and on the floor next to a couple of pairs of shoes a paperback lay open with its cover face up. Chris strained to make out its title and failed but then realised that in any case he didn't know Martin's taste in reading. In fact, come to think of it, he no longer knew much about Martin apart from his abilities as a footballer, and yet he was searching for him as if he were to be some sort of saviour. A red t-shirt, jostling for position with a rucksack, lay on the long seat by the window. Clearly someone was there, although not just at this moment. Another knock on the door predictably brought the same lack of response.

Chris was really following the scouts' doctrine these days. He felt he was prepared for anything. He took a pad and a pen from his bag and scribbled a note saying who he was - obviously - and where he was staying. He explained when he next expected to be in the pub - namely, that evening - and he provided his mobile number. Having secured the note as best he could to the van, he set off back towards the village. Either by his making a return visit to the van or by Martin reacting to what he read, they would inevitably link up before very long.

CHAPTER 17

"So – where do we start?"

Shortly after passing the sign which welcomed them to the National Park, Andy had spotted a farm shop and tea room, announced he was thirsty and pulled into the car park. It was the sort of place where Chris and Sarah liked to stop on holiday with its mountains of fresh produce, steaming pots of tea and a tempting range of home made cakes. It was the sort of place where they would buy enough fresh fruit and veg to feed a small army and then Chris would grumble at how much they had spent. "It's certainly more expensive than the Fruit Bowl," Sarah would invariably add, but then, in the café, the exorbitant prices would be forgotten as they made holiday plans. It was always an exciting time, the start of the holiday. She smiled wistfully at the memory. Early optimism that Chris would be located quite easily had evaporated and she felt as though that little scenario might never be repeated.

Sarah didn't reply. "A penny for them?" Andy added.

"Sorry. Miles away," replied Sarah.

Where indeed did they start? Although they were certainly physically closer to Helen and probably closer to Chris than when they had set out, it didn't feel that way.

"Well, here we are," said Andy, using his considerable skills in stating the bloody obvious. "But where is she?"

Sarah seemed woefully bereft of inspiration. At that moment Cumbria seemed about as big as the United States. She sipped her tea and again failed to summon up any form of suitable reply.

Chris arrived back at the Black Horse but decided not to go in. It was mid afternoon, and he reasoned that Martin was not likely to be there. It would be all too easy to go in to look at the female scenery and pass the time, but at this rate he'd turn into an alcoholic. So instead he decided he'd…

He'd what? He realised he'd put all his eggs in one basket. He had persuaded himself he had to find Martin and that nothing else mattered. He had also convinced himself that it would be a relatively straightforward task. But what if his and Martin's paths never crossed? What if they met up and found they had too little in common, or even found that they couldn't stand each other?

What was he to do now, at this precise moment in time? The weather was still fine enough to take advantage of Mrs Jackson's garden but he felt as though he'd spent too much time there already, he'd nearly finished his book and he didn't feel like driving to the nearest bookshop at the moment. He let himself into his room, stretched out on the bed even though he didn't feel tired and, staring at the ceiling, he wondered unsuccessfully what to do next.

"It must be your round for coffee," said Andy as they settled into the busy café with its distinctive blue and yellow décor. Andy and Sarah had made further progress and they had arrived in Windermere, the bustling tourist centre of south Lakeland. It was busy, but then again it could not be otherwise as the schools had just broken up. To reach the café Sarah and Andy had had to dodge families operating in slow motion, prams, buggies and elderly couples, all of whom seemed intent on getting in

Bowing Out

their way. The decision to go to Windermere was based on factors such as its status as the largest tourist centre in the area making it a logical starting point and Andy's recollection that Helen had stated that Windermere was her intended destination. Of course, that was ages ago, Andy helpfully pointed out. "She could be anywhere now. In fact, come to think of it, how do we know she's still in the Lakes?"

"I got that card recently," Sarah replied impatiently. "I told you that before." (Had she?).

"When did you say you got that?"

"A couple of weeks ago, maybe. That's what put me on her trail, remember?"

Andy felt more encouraged. "The chances of her having left in the last fortnight are slim, I suppose. We should find her quite easily."

"Yes, all we have to do is scour every pub and hotel in Cumbria and, knowing my luck, she'll be in the last one we get to."

"I hope you like Jennings ale," said Andy. "If you don't now, you'll develop a taste for it."

By some miracle, Andy's remark actually made Sarah smile. The waitress, who had crept up unnoticed, was pleased to see such an obviously happy couple.

As they drank their coffee and nibbled at scones with jam and cream, Andy said, "When does the search begin? And, assuming it might take some time, are there not accommodation implications? What type of accommodation are we looking for?"

Sarah, normally such a pragmatic person, had chosen not to give these issues much thought and she felt overwhelmed by the latter two of these three questions. Andy decided he would have to take the lead as Sarah simply sat there looking bewildered. He looked at the clock on the café wall and continued, "I think we need to start looking when we've done here particularly as," – and he shot Sarah a rather enigmatic look – "I imagine we'll need a couple of singles, won't we?"

Will we? They both thought exactly the same thing.

Chris persuaded himself that Martin would be in the pub that evening. It was his only strategy, and so Chris was there at six o'clock. This was the time the pub started serving food. He wasn't very hungry, largely because he had eaten an enormous breakfast and he hadn't expended much energy during the day, but having a meal would give him something to do now.

He studied the menu and chose curry, and after positioning himself near the window he entertained himself by wondering whether, at this precise moment, someone in Calcutta was trying the delights of Cumberland sausage. Then he realised it was past most people's bed time in India, and, even though this wasn't the most amusing thought that had ever entered his head, he laughed.

"Happy?"

It was the barmaid – not the one he'd first met, the one who looked like she'd returned from a recent visit to the jeweller's, but the other one. She had crept up unnoticed.

"Very much so, thank you. I've had an excellent day in this wonderful part of the world."

"You don't mind if I join you for a few minutes, do you?"

Chris said he would enjoy some company.

"Have you been looking for that guy you were asking about?"

"Yes, that's right. I walked to the woods and followed directions that a couple of locals gave me. I found a caravan which is obviously lived in, but no one was there. I just fastened a note as securely as I could and then came back. I was rather hoping he might read the note and meet me here, but he's not arrived yet."

"No," agreed Helen, "but it is still early." The pub was deserted apart from an old man in the corner. It might have been the man Chris had seen with the dog the previous day but he couldn't be sure. There was no dog with him this time. He was sitting quietly, and reading what Chris assumed to be the local paper as he must have done so many times before.

"You're quite sure you don't know this guy I'm looking for?"

"Positive." Helen sounded a little impatient – a little tired of the repeated reference to Martin. She wished she hadn't raised the subject. She was more interested in finding out a little more about Chris who was still plagued by the feeling that he'd seen Helen before, so she changed tack.

"What have you done today apart from searching for your old mate?"

"Mooched about – you know. It looks nice round here but I'm not too familiar with this part of the world so I don't really know where to go. It'd be useful to have someone around to show me one or two of the sights. Someone maybe with time on his hands during the day."

"Or her hands?" suggested Helen. A brief lull in the conversation followed. The other customer slowly rose to his feet and made his way to the bar. Helen followed him, took up her position behind the bar and served him the packet of crisps which would perfectly complement his half drunk pint.

Chris looked closely at Helen. Who is she?

The man returned to his seat and resumed his study of all the local news that was fit to print. Helen came out from behind the bar again and sat back down beside her new friend. The pub was silent apart from the occasional sound of newspaper pages being turned.

"I reckon it's time we knew each other's names. I'm Chris."

"Helen." This was the information that solved the mystery. Helen, Helen, Helen.

The penny dropped.

"Do you know someone called Sarah O'Neill?"

Helen looked surprised. It had been a long time since she had heard anyone mention that name and, before sending the recent postcard, a long time since she had given her old friend much thought.

"I used to knock around a lot with Sarah O'Neill at school but then we didn't keep in touch as much as we might have done." She looked closely at Chris. "I have seen her more recently than that, though, and," she added, realisation suddenly dawning, "I've seen you before as well, haven't I? Chris O'Neill. You're Sarah's husband, aren't you?"

"I am. I thought I recognised you. It's good to meet you again after all this time."

Helen looked Chris up and down. He'd caught the sun a little while wandering from B and B to pub to caravan and back and in his t-shirt and denims he looked rather handsome. She was surprised now that she hadn't recognised him earlier. "It's good to see you as well," she agreed.

Andy and Sarah left the café and considered their next move – or, at least, Andy did. Sarah was busy considering what had happened to her recently. Less than one week ago she was packing the bags and looking forward to her annual holiday with her husband. Now she was about to book into accommodation - possibly into a double room - with her friend's ex-husband. It was bizarre.

"I realise it's the start of the school holidays, and it's obviously busy, but if we can't find accommodation here, we'll never find accommodation anywhere," said Andy. "It will make an excellent base for our search. All we need to do is trawl about and book somewhere we fancy."

Sarah felt a little unnerved by Andy's zeal. He was obviously keen to book somewhere, but whether this was exclusively to search for Helen or whether he was also keen to be booked in with her, she couldn't tell. She suspected it might be, at best, a combination of the two or, at worst, the latter, and she didn't feel very comfortable with this.

Andy had surprised himself. Staid, and a plodder at the office, he had previously cherished his routine. Not so

Bowing Out

long ago he would never have found himself in a position like this. This was a big change for him. He liked it. Outside the comfort zone was the place to be.

"Have you ever stayed here in Windermere before?" asked Andy. Sarah was too bemused to reply.

"I think I know the best part of town to go to," Andy continued and he led Sarah to a network of side streets which contained predominantly bed and breakfasts and guest houses. Sarah, now feeling completely helpless, followed meekly. She tried to open her mouth to suggest booking into separate establishments, but no words were forthcoming.

"Which of these do you fancy?" Andy was giving her a choice, which was nice. Signs announcing a lack of vacancies ruled some places out instantly, but there was still a surprisingly large choice for the time of year. Sarah felt she wanted to absolve herself from all responsibility and she said rather timidly, "you make the choice, Andy. I think you're better at this type of thing than I am." Andy felt good.

A few minutes later they were booked in. Andy had found a clean, non smoking establishment with an en suite double room available at a most reasonable price. Perfect.

One or two locals came in at regular intervals which meant Helen had to go to the bar and serve them. None of them looked like Martin which was a disappointment, but because business was not brisk Chris and Helen had a lot of opportunity to chat. Things went well. They had a lot in common, apart from knowing the couple who were about to spend a night together a few miles away. They both enjoyed walking and Helen told Chris about the myriad of waymarked trails in the forest.

"Walkers tend to rush through to the bigger fells and leave this part of the Lakes alone," she explained. "But if it's peace and quiet on unloseable paths that you want, this is the place."

"You sound like you know them well."

"Well, when I'm on the evening shift here, like I am this week, I've plenty time during the day and if the weather's fine, walking is the thing I like to do best." She smiled at Chris. "The forecast's good for tomorrow."

CHAPTER 18

Andy strolled confidently into the dining room and took his place at the breakfast table. He nodded a "good morning" to the couple with the fruit juice by the window and he greeted the family which was just finishing eating at the bigger table in the corner next to the Welsh dresser. He sat down and investigated his new surroundings.

The house was typical of the many old Victorian town houses which had been transformed into tourist accommodation. The dining room was decorated in pale blue anaglypta wallpaper punctuated with photographs of local mountain and lake scenes. The carpet didn't complement the colour scheme on the walls particularly well. The room seemed to be overflowing with ornaments which had perhaps been handed down from generation to generation, or maybe they were the result of frequent trips to local antique shops. There was some kitsch in there, but Andy supposed that some of the pieces might be quite valuable. There was a comfortable, old fashioned, relaxing – if cluttered - feel to the place.

Mrs Walsh, an efficient, business like yet at the same time friendly landlady who took a great pride in her well run establishment, bustled over. "Would you like to order, or will you wait for your wife?"

"I'll wait, if you don't mind," beamed Andy. "Even now, after all this time, I can never guess which parts of a full English she'll fancy. So unpredictable, like most women."

"Help yourself to juice, if you like. Can I bring tea or coffee while you're waiting?"

What would Sarah prefer to drink?

"One pot of tea and one pot of coffee, please." It was a clever selection. Andy didn't mind which he had, so Sarah could make the choice.

"Mrs Wilkinson", meanwhile, had slipped out of the front door into the garden. She had to go outside, because this bed and breakfast was designed strictly for the healthy. She positioned herself far enough away from the house so as not to intrude. She took in a lungful of smoke, the better to think.

Nobody a week ago could have predicted the previous night's events. What should have happened was that Sarah and Chris O'Neill should have cuddled up on the old settee after enjoying a spectacular Scottish sunset on that beach which they regarded as their own. What did happen was that she shared a double bed with the ex husband of her best friend from school.

That was bad enough. Did anything else happen? She had noticed Andy took great interest in proceedings from behind the book he was pretending to read as Sarah hurriedly made her way from the dressing table to the shower to the dressing table, and, a little later, she was certain he was not really asleep as she nervously slipped into bed. It took her a long time to convince herself it would be all right to go to sleep, but even her impressive track record for insomnia would not allow her to stay awake all night.

Andy waited patiently at table for Sarah. There was no rush even though, in theory at least, today's aim was to visit as many watering holes in Cumbria as possible in the hope of reaching their goal. It had been a while since he had shared his bed with a woman, let alone a woman as attractive as Sarah. She had not said much this morning. Andy thought Sarah was tense, so he needed to think of some activities which would help her relax.

Bowing Out

At the same time as the happy couple breakfasted in Windermere, Chris also was eating in a pleasant dining room and a positive frame of mind. That Helen was a really nice lass, with a winning smile which seemed to feature more frequently as the evening wore on. It was quite lucky that she enjoyed walking and had agreed to join him for some fresh air the following morning otherwise he would have gone to the caravan, probably found it empty, and been left wondering what to do again.

"Mrs Jackson, you've excelled yourself. Yesterday's breakfast was merely very good, but this reaches hitherto unachieved heights of brilliance."

"Pardon?"

Chris tried again. "Your breakfast is quite probably the best I've ever tasted anywhere." He was feeling cheerful and optimistic and prone to handing out compliments.

Mrs Jackson smiled very broadly at Chris. She knew her cooking was good but it didn't often receive such fulsome praise. Most of her guests murmured a cursory "thank you" as she brought the plates and took them away again. They then said not much more as they settled their bill on leaving although she had had very nice comments in her visitors' book as well as some repeat business, so she reckoned she must be doing something right.

"That's very nice of you."

Chris smiled back. "It's very true, Mrs Jackson."

After a short pause, Mrs Jackson asked, "And what are you doing today? Have you found your friend yet?"

"I've not found my old friend but I think I've found a new one. I was talking to her last night in the pub. She works there, so you might know her. Helen, she's called."

"Yes, I think I do know her," replied Mrs Jackson tonelessly.

Eleven o'clock-ish at the visitor centre, Helen had said. Chris was there at ten to, so he had a bit of time to kill. There was a shop to look round with books of local interest, and leaflets and maps to study, but he was

Peter Cropper

restless and not interested in browsing. He wandered over to check the arrangements for cycle hire for possible future reference, but that didn't fill much time either. He felt a strange mixture of excitement and apprehension and found himself pacing up and down the courtyard, nervously looking at his watch. Anyone observing him would have thought he was waiting for an important interview rather than an innocent meeting with a fellow rambler. Eleven o'clock came and went.

Just after Chris' watch told him it was twenty past, he heard, "Hi. Sorry I'm late."

Helen had swapped the attractive clothes of the previous evening for her walking outfit, but she still looked good, if overdressed for the occasion. She looked as if she were intending to attempt one of the great Alpine challenges rather than a gentle stroll on south Cumbria's wooded hillsides, but Chris refrained from commenting. Instead, he said, "Helen. Lovely to see you. I've been looking forward to this from the moment I woke up. Where exactly are we going? I'm in your capable hands."

"In my capable hands! That sounds exciting. But I'm not sure exactly where to start."

Chris thought that sounded strange. The previous evening Helen had given the impression that she knew many of the walks in the area. Now she was suggesting she didn't know the way out of the car park.

He supposed that he had better take charge. "Am I right in thinking there are various coloured waymarked paths in the forest?"

"Yes, I think you're right," said Helen. She looked absolutely clueless.

They wandered over to the shop and Chris picked up a leaflet.

"The lady must choose," said Chris, "Pick a colour."

"You did say you'd be staying tonight as well, didn't you?" asked Mrs Walsh as she cleared away the breakfast plates.

Bowing Out

"That's right," said Andy. "We've come to look up some old friends who we've rather lost touch with. We're not too sure where they live so there'll be a bit of detective work for us. We just don't know how long it's going to take."

"That sounds exciting," said Mrs Walsh. "Do they live in Windermere or surrounding area? If they do, I suppose you could look them up in the phone book. Use mine if you like. Have you noticed, though, that whenever you look someone up in the phone book, they're always ex directory?" What a suitable and sensible thing for Mrs Walsh to say.

"Indeed," said Andy. "All part of life's rich pageant. It's one of life's mysteries. It's rather like when you go out for the day and leave the washing up, there always seems to be more there when you get back." Sarah smiled to herself, because she and Chris found that, too. Mrs Walsh didn't react. In her line of business, days out didn't come round too often.

Instead she brought the directory and Andy appeared very much as if he were looking for an old friend's number. Sarah watched the spectacle with interest and said nothing. On the one hand, she was a bit shocked by his conniving. She was sure that the Andy of old whom she remembered would never have been able to pull off a stunt like that, so you had to admire his new resourcefulness and ability to bluff his way through. Perhaps he had taken up amateur dramatics.

As she looked at him carefully perusing the entries, Sarah had to concede that actually he wasn't bad looking. He wasn't as pleasing to the eye as Chris, but all the same…

"As predicted," said Andy, "they aren't in. I don't suppose," he added, keeping up the pretence, "that you know them? Phil and Rachel Marshall. About our age. Phil's a car mechanic by trade. Perhaps he's fixed your car at some stage? And I think Rachel works in a chemist shop – or at least, she has done in the past. Whether she still does now, I'm not too sure." Andy was clearly enjoying embellishing the pretence. Sarah thought he was admirably convincing.

Mrs Walsh reacted as Andy hoped she would. "They aren't names I recognise. I'll ask around my friends if I can remember and see what I can find out for you."

"Thanks very much," said Andy. "That's very kind of you." You do that, he thought, but I'm willing to bet you draw a blank.

Nice one, thought Sarah. You've definitely got a bit more about you than I'd imagined. This new insight into Andy's character made Sarah think that spending some time with him might prove at worst interesting, at best…?

"That was a brilliant piece of acting," said Sarah as she and Andy set off towards the town. It was one of the few things she had said that morning and Andy was pleased to hear her speak. He found women who didn't speak unnerving.

"Thank you." He didn't really know what else to say.

Sarah continued. "Have you ever thought of going on stage? You ought to be treading the boards somewhere with that ability."

"That's very kind of you," smiled Andy. He thought Sarah was genuinely impressed with his efforts, but he couldn't be sure. Still, there was probably something to build on. The next task was to devise an interesting day for them both. Simply going from pub to pub wouldn't do it, although he thought it might be a good idea at some stage to go through the motions at least.

"When does our search for our friends Phil and Rachel begin?"

Andy grinned. It was good that Sarah was happy to join him in his pretence, but she would have found it much less annoying if he had given her an answer.

"So what are we going to do? Drink more bloody coffee?" A note of irritation appeared in Sarah's voice which reminded Andy that it wouldn't be all plain sailing.

Bowing Out

He would have to tread a little carefully. It confirmed that he needed to think of something a little more interesting to keep his fellow detective entertained.

The weather was still behaving itself and this opened up all sorts of possibilities. Andy considered them quickly and came up with a suggestion.

"A boat trip?"

Sarah thought for a short while then shrugged her shoulders. She had no better suggestion. "If you like. Where's the water?"

"The lake's about a mile that way. All downhill, though."

"In these shoes?" Andy looked at Sarah's footwear and couldn't for the life of him see why she couldn't walk a mile (or maybe a little more, if the truth be told) on tarmac in them. He deferred. Softly softly catchy monkey.

Sarah looked down at her feet as if she were convincing herself that what she had said was true. Andy glanced the other way and saw the tourist bus bound for the lake in the distance. "What we need is an open topped bus on such a grand morning as this to whisk us off to our destination. Good heavens," he added a moment or two later. "Look what's here. Now that can only be fate."

Sarah's expression suggested she was a little less impressed with this ruse than she had been with Andy's previous role plays, but she allowed him to step back and assist her onto the bus, a little like a gentleman would.

They got off the bus at the lake which was a mid morning hive of activity. A wide cross section of the British tourist population was there, from elderly couples who had been coming for years and who could recall quieter times to small children in buggies who were probably making a first visit and a baby in a backpack who certainly was. In between were young couples strolling hand in hand by the water and middle aged couples, some of whom had children in tow. One very well behaved family could have been that which Chris had previously seen in the pub in Grizedale. Some people had made an early start at the ice cream parlour while others had brought along scraps of bread, much to the delight of the ducks, coots and swans which were in constant attendance.

"You've got to watch those guys," said Andy, pointing at one of Her Majesty's graceful white birds. "They can break your leg. Or is it your arm? And how come, despite frequent warnings about this, that nobody knows anybody who this has happened to?"

"Would that be another of life's mysteries?" wondered Sarah.

Andy smiled. That was the type of remark he liked to hear. He thought it showed that Sarah was relaxing into the day.

By the booking office for the boat trips was plenty of information and a good choice of lake excursions. Red cruise, yellow cruise or blue cruise? They all looked attractive propositions. Andy was keen for Sarah to relax further and he was determined to look after his charming companion.

"It's your shout, Sarah. Pick a colour."

CHAPTER 19

Helen's selected colour was green. "Green's always been my favourite colour," she said, "so that's the one I'm going for."

"'Silurian Trail '," read out Chris, "'nine miles. Strenuous'. I'm not being funny, but are you quite sure you're up for something like that?" It was certainly within Chris' capabilities but he suspected it might be slow going in parts on rough and boggy terrain and he didn't know how much stamina Helen had. He also couldn't lose sight of the fact that later he needed time to try to link up with Martin. Comfortable as he was in the accommodation at Mrs Jackson's, he clearly could not stay there indefinitely.

Helen looked sheepish, as if she were a little girl who had followed up her discovery that green was her favourite colour by doing something really really silly.

"Mm, nine miles," she said. "I can't imagine you'd have much difficulty with that but I'm a bit out of practice at this walking lark." She didn't seem to know what she should do. "I could maybe manage it, but I'm not really sure."

"Shall we think again?" asked Chris.

"Good idea."

There were seven other trails from which to choose, four of which started at the visitor centre. "What do you make of the white one?" said Chris after a short deliberation. He had picked something not too long and not too short. The plan was that it would be a challenge for Helen, perhaps, and a decent leg stretch for him.

Helen read the information. "It goes to Grizedale Tarn. A walk in the woods with a small lake thrown in for good measure. It sounds good to me. Shall we give it a whirl?"

Sarah had plumped for red, not because it was her favourite colour, but because she considered it the most appealing of the cruises on offer. "It takes in the northern section of the lake which will give us the best mountain views. The Langdale Pikes should look good today. We'll also have the option of a stop off at Ambleside, although it is a bit of a walk from the pier at Waterhead to the centre."

Andy was impressed. He looked again at the information to decide how much knowledge Sarah had just gleaned and how much she already had. Sarah was pretty well clued up about this part of the world. He found it hard to imagine that Helen would be so knowledgeable about somewhere away from her familiar surroundings.

"Red looks good to me," he said, "and there's not long to wait." They sat quite closely together on a bench and watched one of the swans trying to persuade a young man from the Far East to part with his snack.

"Of course, this is all a product of the railway age," said Andy. "I think the railway arrived about the middle of the 1850s. Before that, this would have been a tiny lakeside village with not much happening."

Was he trying to convince them both that Sarah didn't know more about the area than he did? Sarah felt as though he was trying to trump her ace but, on the other hand, she did like the fact that he had a bit of life in him these days and that he had begun to show more interest in things. Maybe if he had shown a little more interest in life when he was with Helen he wouldn't now be sitting by the lake with Mrs O'Neill waiting to embark on their great nautical adventure.

*Bowing **Out***

The posts indicating the way led Chris and Helen across the road and into the trees where the path went slightly uphill as it started to pull away from civilisation. They passed the wooden musical instruments where a couple of children were taking it in turns to bang out something vaguely resembling music on the xylophone, and then the path curved away and crossed the stream before heading off into the depths of the forest. The sound of the young musicians' tuneless composition faded before finally being absorbed by the trees and the foliage.

Chris was unfamiliar with this part of the Lakes and, as Helen had predicted, the forest was surprisingly quiet given it was holiday time. Perhaps it would have been busier at the weekend, but today any visitors to Lakeland must have ventured no further than the regular tourist honeypots.

Conversation was fitful, failing to flow as well as it had done the previous evening. Chris was puzzled by Helen's almost complete lack of confidence. She seemed shy and withdrawn and this contrasted sharply with her attitude the previous day when Chris had considered her quite an extrovert. He tried to draw her out, with such questions as:

"Can you tell one pine tree from another? Scots Pine, Douglas Fir – what's the difference?" and

"A friend of mine can tell birds apart by their song. He doesn't even have to see them. I find that amazing. Have you learned to do that during your time here?"

It was hard work. Helen didn't ignore the questions but her answers were brief so that they could not be used as a basis for in depth conversation. She seemed to be concentrating very hard on keeping her footing.

The posts veered off left and led up a slope through a thicker section of trees. "Is this the right way?" asked Helen.

Don't you know? thought Chris. Surely you've been this way before at some stage? But he didn't comment on her lack of knowledge. Instead he said, "We must put our trust in the posts. If they say it's this way, then it's this way."

Helen pressed on grimly. She didn't look to be enjoying this section of the walk very much. It was nothing more than relatively steep, and the ground just a little damp, so Chris was surprised at the way Helen's legs shot from underneath her, given the obvious quality of her footwear.

Helen rolled over a couple of times – whether naturally, or for dramatic effect, Chris could not be sure - and she came to rest a little further down the slope away from the path against a small tree.

Chris scrambled down to where Helen was lying. She had fallen only a matter of a few feet and she had rolled and then hit the tree quite gently. She hadn't hit any rocks en route. Chris' first consideration was whether she had hit her head, and he was sure she hadn't. He hoped very much that she wasn't badly hurt.

"Helen! Are you all right?"

She looked up at him like a frightened puppy. She was wailing hysterically out of all proportion to what had just happened to her. "I think so," she said eventually in a little voice between giant sobs.

"Try to stand up if you can," Chris suggested when she had become a little calmer.

"I'll probably be able to, with your help," she sniffled. "But I've hurt my foot." She held out her hand and Chris helped her to her feet.

"Which foot is it that's hurting?" asked Chris.

Helen didn't reply.

"Can you put your weight on your feet?"

Again, Helen said nothing but she hobbled around a little. Chris found it hard to decide how much discomfort Helen was really in and how much of it was designed to draw attention to her plight.

"Will you be able to carry on, or do we need to summon help?"

Helen thought it might be exciting to see a mountain rescue team battering its way through the trees towards her brushing aside any branches which were foolish enough to get in the way, but then she looked at Chris and changed her mind. "I think I'll be able to carry on with your help," she said, hesitantly. "It's probably just a bit of bruising." Would you like to check? she then thought.

I'll have a close look if you like, thought Chris.

She put her arm through Chris' and the walk resumed. Helen limped but declared she thought she could probably carry on but, if Chris didn't mind, could she keep tight hold of him to make sure that she didn't fall over again?

They carried on slowly, and their posts led them into a lighter and clearer part of the forest where the track was firmer and conditions underfoot were easier. Chris thought Helen might let go after a short while but she didn't and he didn't ask her to do so. In the first place, she could still be shaken up and in need of some support, but also, it was rather nice to have a young lady on your arm while enjoying a forest walk.

"Mountains," said Helen, as some of the peaks from nearer to the centre of the Lake District came into view. "They're grand, aren't they? I like them in winter when they're covered in snow. Have you seen them like that?"

"Oh, yes," replied Chris. "They somehow look higher, more majestic and more challenging when under a covering of snow." He thought he sounded a little strange, more like a guide book than a typical English man who, according to type, was supposed to be phlegmatic. It wasn't the type of phraseology he would use under normal circumstances, but perhaps that was because walking arm in arm with a woman who wasn't your wife did not constitute normal circumstances.

"Some visitors are real experts and can name the mountains, but to me they all look the same. I bet you can name them, Chris. What's that really big one over there, to the left of that wood and the white cottage we can see in the distance?"

Chris felt flattered so he named the mountain just for Helen. He may or may not have named it correctly, but that didn't really matter to either of them.

"And how high is that one?"

"In feet or metres?" asked Chris, the better to impress.

"Do you know both?"

Chris gave what he considered a feasible answer, in both feet and metres. Helen looked at him in admiration. "And have you been up it?"

A long time ago, when Chris was in the sixth form, he had embarked on a youth hostelling trip in these parts. He and his two mates Mike and Dan had spent a memorable week of glorious walking in atypical sunny weather. They had conquered a good number of peaks after which they had enjoyed long, convivial and seemingly endless evenings in the local pubs. He couldn't remember ever having had better weather than that since in Cumbria, not even when he and Sarah were privileged enough to see the bottom of Haweswater. While he could not be certain, it was a fair bet that he had climbed the mountain in question, so he told Helen he had. He said he'd managed to reach the top quickly. He didn't add that that was in his younger and fitter days.

"In that case, I hope you aren't finding this walk disappointingly easy," said Helen. "Wouldn't you rather be up the big hills than down here with me?"

"I just like walking," said Chris. "All types – hills, woods, coast. Flat, steep. And I especially enjoy walks with charming female company."

Helen smiled coyly. "That's a nice thing to say." It may have been Chris' imagination, but he felt that Helen held on to him just a little more tightly as they continued towards the tarn.

The good ship "Tern" pulled into view and then tied up at the pier. It was, according to the timetable, a few minutes late, but nobody seemed to mind. Everyone there was on holiday and the sun was shining pleasantly.

Bowing Out

There were no commuters anxiously waiting for the 7.58 to Waterloo, work slaves fearful of the reaction they may receive if they walked in a few minutes late unable to meet the boss's stony glare with a Reggie Perrin type repost which would either result in a rare smile from the superior, or possibly the sack.

"Tern," said Sarah. "That's one of those attractive white seabirds with the dark brown head, isn't it? Not to be confused with black headed gulls."

"That's right," replied Andy. "They sometimes call them 'sea swallows' because of their forked tails." Sarah didn't know that, and it was difficult for Andy to judge whether she appreciated receiving the extra nugget of information.

"Are you a twitcher then? Where's your Barbour, bushy beard and binoculars which would need to be surgically removed from round your neck?"

Andy was on the ball. He could sense the thrust and parry and Sarah's apparent need to score points off him. He felt that he wanted to bring it to a close. They were supposed to be a team in pursuit of a common goal so cooperation, not competition, should be the name of the game. It could be a long, hard quest. But, on the other hand, if Sarah were the type of lady who thrived on such banter, he should perhaps keep it going.

"No, I wouldn't say I was a keen birdwatcher," said Andy, having worked out that something along these neutral lines was the most suitable reply. "I learned a bit from my mates at school so I suppose bits and pieces of knowledge have stuck, but I'm no expert."

He escorted Sarah to the water's edge, then stood back to allow her to board first. She was shapely and because her t-shirt was a little on the short side, there was that glimpse of flesh between the bottom of it and the tightly fitting blue jeans. Andy liked that.

They settled down for the cruise and Sarah instinctively went for her handbag before stopping herself. She would resist the temptation for now. She was in the fresh Cumbrian air and had probably been smoking rather more than was good for her lately. She knew Chris' views on her habit but wasn't sure what Andy felt although, judging by his positive reaction when he found a non smoking guest house, she guessed that he, too, was not in favour. So, she thought, by doing without I'm doing myself a favour and I'm reducing the risk of alienating Andy. It would also be one in the eye for Chris who frequently claimed she had no willpower. "You see, I don't need them," she would have said to her husband, had he been there. Of course, he wasn't there, thought Sarah. But Andy was. It was a shame Chris was not there to see her great achievement but, never mind, Andy was shaping up to be a reasonable replacement.

The boat set off towards the northern end of the lake. For a while neither of them said anything, both being content to admire the scenery. Then:

"How long do you reckon this trip will take in total?"

"Do you mean today, or the whole thing?" said Andy.

"First things first. Today," answered Sarah.

"I suppose that depends on how long we spend in Ambleside, if indeed we go there at all," came the reply. It set Andy thinking. If the day went well – and it had certainly been fine so far - it would be good to spin it out as much as possible but, on the other hand, he hadn't lost sight of the fact that Sarah was keen to find Helen, as indeed was he – he thought.

The path snaked on and progress continued to be slower than Chris would have liked. He thought Helen's injuries would have eased and that she would have found walking a little more straightforward by now, but that didn't seem to be the case. This suggested to Chris that either she had done some real damage, in which case it might be sensible to return to Helen's car as soon as possible, or that she was exaggerating the severity of the fall for some reason. He suspected it might be the latter, because she had not fallen that far. He glanced down as

Bowing Out

surreptitiously as he could to see if there was any swelling but the boots prevented him from seeing anything.

"How's the injury?" he asked. "Is it getting any better?"

"A bit, I think," said Helen. "I think that, with your continued support, we'll get round the course."

"Are you sure? I was wondering if there was a short cut we could take back to the visitor centre. I'm not sure we shouldn't get that foot of yours looked at."

"It's lovely of you to show such concern," simpered Helen. "But if you'd be so good as to carry on helping me as well as you've done so far, then I'm sure we'll be fine."

And of course, thought Chris, if I asked you about a short cut back, I don't imagine you'd have the faintest idea where to find one.

The track carried on. It was all very pleasant but Chris began to feel that once you'd seen one tall majestic pine rising from a clump of bracken, you'd seen them all, especially given the long time he had to inspect every tree. He enjoyed the smell more than the scenery – that distinctive pine smell. He imagined it would be like this in the endless forests of Scandinavia, and he was transported back to an Austrian holiday where the aromas were exaggerated owing to the warm, pure mountain air. Finally the tarn appeared through the trees. It was tucked away a little off the path. Unobservant people in a hurry might have walked straight past it.

Helen heaved a great sigh of relief and sat down on a log at the water's edge. "Chris," she said, "maybe it would be an idea if you could look at my ankle for me. If I take my boot and sock off, could you check it for any swelling?"

"OK," said Chris and he knelt down in front of Helen. She seemed to enjoy peeling off her footwear. "I can't see much in the way of swelling down there – just a bit of bruising. It doesn't look too serious to me."

"I hope you're right," said Helen. "Would you mind feeling round the ankle to see how badly it is swollen?

You probably are right, but it would be good to be reassured."

Chris inspected Helen's ankle. Helen enjoyed it so much that she felt moved to throw her arms round Chris' neck and give him a kiss when she struggled to her feet again. She held Chris tightly with a strength which belied her serious injury and he would have found it difficult to release himself even if he had wanted to.

"To Ambleside, or not to Ambleside - that is the question," said Andy as the boat approached Waterhead with its pier, refreshments, water birds and collection of small hotels.

"I don't fancy going straight back," said Sarah. "If we do, the whole expedition won't have taken much more than an hour. Are you all right with that?" she added.

"Fine," said Andy. "I suppose it boils down to how much time we want to spend searching for Helen as opposed to how much time we want to spend relaxing as if we were holidaymakers," he added, surprising himself with his boldness.

"And your view on that?"

"Firstly, on a purely practical level, most bars are still not open. But also, to be perfectly honest with you, I've got rather used to spending time without Helen. It'll be interesting to see her, obviously, but if I don't, then what have I lost? I wasn't with her when I got up this morning, and if I'm not with her when I go to bed tonight, or any other night come to that, then so what?"

Sarah thought carefully about Andy had just said. He'd said, "interesting", not "great" or "lovely". He apparently thought he was simply on his holidays and he seemed very content with the company he was keeping.

And what of herself? What if they didn't manage to find Helen? Would it really matter?

Just then, as the boat prepared to moor at the lakeshore, she thought that it probably didn't matter a great deal to her either.

CHAPTER 20

"Bloody hell," said Ray Davidson, with feeling. "That went fast."

It was every teacher's favourite day of the year in early September, and the staff at Whiteoaks sat in their usual groups waiting for Mr Harris' staff meeting. As usual, the children weren't due in school until later, which gave the teachers a chance to listen to the Head's plans for the forthcoming term. As usual, the meeting failed to start on time.

There was a buzz of conversation as colleagues swapped stories about their activities of the past few weeks. Pete James was sitting between Ray and Steve Lloyd and they were comparing notes about their summer holidays. Yes, all had gone well. Pete said they'd made a great choice in Greece. "Spain is good," he said. "You know I'm a big fan of Spain. But it's right what they say – familiarity breeds contempt. And over the past few years the lager swilling, union jack shorts wearing brigade has been coming more and more to the fore."

"Is it true you were fed up of bumping into Anderson, Boyle and Farrell when you were in Spain, and that's why you changed venue?" asked Ray.

The three men laughed. "No, I've never seen them there," replied Pete. "But, bear in mind, those three lads have exams this year so they will be reformed characters.

I think you'll see them turning into model students." The three men laughed again.

Not to be outdone, Steve poured forth about France. He spoke at length and in great detail about the villages and the countryside. He had been to the coast this time, which was something he didn't normally do, and he'd loved it there as well. Excessive detail, thought his two colleagues, but they let him carry on. They could see he was enjoying himself. Steve did paint a good picture and they could almost have been in Languedoc with him, but the realisation that they were in fact in the staffroom on a gloomy September morning made the holidays seem like ancient history.

"And where did you go?" Steve asked Ray.

"Edinburgh," Ray replied. He had had a good few days there. He was very impressed with the castle, he climbed Arthur's Seat and he investigated some of the city's pubs while his wife enjoyed the Princes Street shops, but he felt he had been rather outdone by the tales of European adventures so he chose not to elaborate.

"You didn't bump into Chris while you were in Scotland, did you?" asked Pete. "And by the way – where the hell is he? Has anyone seen him over summer?"

"Have you not, Pete?" asked Steve, surprised.

"Well, no. Why do you think I've just asked?"

"Well, you're his best mate round here. If you've not been in touch with him, I can't imagine anybody else has."

By the time Mr Harris belatedly opened the meeting, all members of Whiteoaks staff were present and correct, bar one.

"Welcome back to you all," said Brian Harris. This was his well rehearsed September rhetoric. "I hope you had a good holiday and are feeling refreshed and ready for the exciting and interesting challenges which this new school year will undoubtedly present." The staff smiled weakly in unison.

Brian Harris continued. "Unfortunately, Chris O'Neill is missing and will be for the foreseeable future.

Bowing Out

He has some personal issues which he needs to address. He's asked me to say no more, but he does wish you well and hopes to return as soon as he can. I've contacted the supply people and a history specialist is due in next week to take over Chris' timetable until he comes back." The history man couldn't make the start of term because he was on holiday. "Until such time, there'll be cover implications, I'm afraid." The staff looked thrilled.

One or two of the staff, memories of Giovanni's still fresh, exchanged knowing looks. The general consensus was that Chris wasn't brave enough to face his July audience although, as Pete said after the meeting, "I wouldn't have thought Chris would have a problem with us, even allowing for the rubbish he spouted. That episode was six weeks ago, after all, and he's fairly thick skinned."

"Well," said Steve, "the fact remains that we'll have to battle on without him. Do you think we'll be able to cope, Al?"

Mr Harris knew Mr O'Neill wouldn't be joining the other runners at the starting gate for the Christmas Handicap because he had received a sick note explaining Chris' forthcoming absence. It had been obtained from Doctor Brooker, one of the younger doctors in the practice, and Chris had come down from Cumbria to pick it up. This time, however, neither railway nor thumb was required. When you are sharing your life and your accommodation with your new lover and some stability has been reintroduced, such methods are not needed.

At the end of the Grizedale Tarn ramble, Helen could not have been more grateful if she had tried. They had retired to the café at the visitor centre and settled into a quiet corner. Tea and Cumberland ham sandwiches were ordered. Helen was walking better at this stage, but she still had a noticeable limp as she made her way past the counter to her seat.

Chris was her hero – he had saved her life. If he hadn't have been there she would have died of exposure in that terrible forest. She didn't know how to thank him. Perhaps she could put him up for a few days when funds to stay at Mrs Jackson's had run out. How long was he proposing to stay at the bed and breakfast? she wondered.

Chris told Helen he had booked in for one more night. Of course, he didn't know how long it was going to take to locate Martin Cooper, neither did he know what he would do if he failed in his quest. There was something else he didn't know – would Martin be willing to put him up? If he were willing, how long could he expect to be allowed to stay in a caravan? When he thought about it, there were lots of things he didn't know. The more he thought about it, the more he came to the conclusion that the decision to locate Martin might have been a fanciful, non starter of a plan.

What he did know was that he wasn't ready to return home and it was clear that Helen was perfectly willing to accommodate him for a while. He also knew Helen had a car and she had mentioned she was worried that driving on her bad foot might lead to serious permanent damage. Sarah had the O'Neill mobile and Chris didn't want to be immobile for too much longer. Helen had pointed out very fastidiously that the terms of her insurance meant anyone was allowed to drive her car with her permission, but, of course, only special people could expect to receive that permission.

The offer of a base in Windermere with an attractive lady with a car was too good to resist, but because the idea of commuting from Windermere to Whiteoaks on a daily basis was not feasible, Chris had to come up with something – hence the trip to Doctor Brooker. He could leave the way open for a return to school and at the same time still be paid for spending time with his new lady in his new location.

It took some practice, but rehearsals went well. The doctor was inexperienced and perhaps a little naïve, but

Bowing Out

it would still have to be a good show. Chris had seen one or two fallers over the years at Whiteoaks and he cast his mind back to what they did, what they said and how they reacted. He looked at a leaflet in the waiting room concerning depression and, to his delight but not surprise (his research had left no stone unturned), it all fitted in well with what he was about to say. He had thought of plausible school scenarios and he now had to convince the doctor that he couldn't face them, that they had been such a constant worry over the summer that they had wrecked his holiday and that, if he returned to school, it would tip him over the edge. "In fact," he explained in the surgery, "there is just no way I could return. I swear I'd rather top myself."

Doctor Brooker followed common practice. "How would you do that, do you think?"

"An overdose. Quick, painless – going to sleep and not waking up. No problem."

He left the surgery in triumph with a prescription and a sick note. Doctor Brooker insisted Chris came back the following week, which was a minor irritation but a small price to pay. He had got what he wanted. "That's great," said Helen. "We can spend loads of time together when I'm not working."

It sounded wonderful.

Chris liked his new surroundings. It was a dream come true to be based in the Lakes, and he found Helen's house very pleasant. It was not as big as the house he was used to but it lacked none of the basics and he could live without such devices as the dishwasher which he had at home. He could never fully understand why he and Sarah had invested in one when there were only the two of them there, but he had to admit they had had their use out of it. Now it was back to seeing if a certain brand of washing up liquid really was kind to hands.

"At home." Chris wondered what that meant now. Was it the house he and Sarah left to go on holiday to Scotland and to which he had (not yet?) returned, or was it Helen's house with the view of the low fells rising attractively out of Windermere? He supposed that only time would tell. Chris thought of Sarah, wondered how she was doing and, rather against his better judgement, he rang her mobile. He had to leave a brief message on voicemail.

CHAPTER 21

During their time in Cumbria Andy led Sarah into pubs with which he was familiar and he asked if any of the staff knew Helen Wilkinson. He neither displayed much enthusiasm nor did he receive any encouragement. Sarah was surprised how few pubs they visited. She had been expecting a more thorough search, and she found it difficult to believe at times that Andy was not simply going through the motions. He seemed more interested in being a tourist. He knew some of the more out of the way locations and he took Sarah to places she hadn't seen before. She thought she knew the Lakes well, but compared to Andy she hardly seemed to know the district at all.

She and Chris had passed the sign to Kentmere many times but they had always been racing towards the central Lakes and they had never taken the time to turn off and investigate. Andy took her there, up the road which became narrower and narrower until it seemed to Sarah that it would disappear altogether. They reached the head of the valley where they were surrounded by mountains.

"I don't think Helen will be hiding up here," Sarah said.

"Neither do I, but it's a lovely place, isn't it. Do you fancy walking up that fell? We can return in a big loop and finish up coming back along that track."

Andy patiently led the way. He never complained about being held back even though Sarah could tell he would have liked to go faster.

Sarah felt more at ease on the lower fells beyond Tarn Hows. She had been to the lake itself before with Chris, but Andy led her up onto less frequented ground. "I think you'll like this walk," he said. "It's easy and quiet and we can return in a circle to our starting point." It was a pleasant walk, but Helen wasn't there. Clearly she hadn't chosen to do it that day.

Sarah relaxed into her time with Andy. She was having her holiday – unexpected location, unexpected company, but these were mere technicalities. The only concern she had was financial. She could not be sure she would get the money back they had paid for the Scottish cottage – she didn't know Hughie Fraser well but she wasn't confident – and her job at the greengrocers was not particularly well paid. It was at times like this she wished she had used her intelligence a bit more. "You will get a job commensurate with your ability when you finish university, won't you Sarah?" her father had said. Sarah had nodded – and now look at her. She and Chris had always agreed that they should have separate bank accounts although whether she would have used part of Chris' money to fund what was becoming an enjoyable break for her without him if they had decided to run a joint account, she wasn't sure. Perhaps it was just as well that the temptation wasn't there. Although she felt some annoyance towards him, there was no point crying over spilt milk or bearing a grudge against him and what he had done because neither of those reactions would move the situation on. She had read somewhere that being resentful used up energy that could be far more gainfully employed elsewhere. She could be remarkably philosophical and level headed at times.

Sarah and Andy had a conversation over Cumberland ham sandwiches one afternoon.

Bowing Out

"Andy, we're not making much headway, are we? Do you think we're spending a bit too much time seeing nice places and not enough time attending to the matters in hand?"

Andy spread the mustard liberally over his ham. "Aren't you enjoying yourself?"

"I am, Andy, but to be honest – how long are we going to be in the B and B?"

"Don't you like it?"

"I do, yes, it's excellent. Good choice. The thing is, to be honest, I'm not sure how much longer I can afford to stay there – financially, I mean. And then we've got to eat in the evening. It all adds up, particularly," she added with a smile, "when you also take into account the amount of coffee we get through during the day."

Andy returned her smile. "You're right, of course," he replied. After a moment's thought he replied, "Why don't you let me settle the bill for us both when we're done?"

Sarah looked on in amazement. "I can't let you do that."

"Why not?" Why not, indeed? Andy had offered so he must want to, and I can't afford it, thought Sarah.

It didn't take her long to agree to Andy's suggestion. She produced her nicest smile and beamed at Andy over the teapot and china cups. "That's a lovely offer, and providing you permit me to treat you to a couple of meals out, I should be delighted to accept." It sounded like the formal acceptance of a Victorian marriage proposal. It was a long way from that, but nevertheless a most appropriate way to respond to a lovely gesture.

Sarah felt good. She felt relaxed. Andy must think something of her. She smiled again, topped up both their cups and noticed, not for the first time since they had arrived in the Lakes, that she didn't feel the urge to reach automatically into her handbag to pull out cigarettes.

They decided to give it a week.

After the seven days were up, they both agreed the chances of finding Helen were slim, especially as they had not chosen to intensify their efforts. What seemed to matter more was that they had had a good time and that they had enjoyed each other's company so much. They both admitted privately that searching for Helen was merely a sideshow.

As arranged, Andy paid the bill. He let Sarah buy a couple of meals, but, true to his word, he took it upon himself to pay the rest. Sarah thought it must have cost a fortune, but when she tried to object and offered to make a further contribution it became very apparent that Andy would have none of her protestations, so she left it alone.

The car journey back to the O'Neill residence was tinged not only with some sadness but also with uncertainty as Sarah began to turn her attention to what or who she might find there – or not. She ran two possible scenarios in her head.

In the first scenario, Sarah walks in to an empty house – a nothingness. After Andy has left to continue his journey home the house immediately seems twice as empty, if that is possible. There is no indication as to where Chris is or how long she will have to wait for his return, and so she has no idea how long she will be living on her own.

In scenario number two, Chris is waiting. He is unhappy – it could not be any other way. Sarah has failed to put him in the picture. "For God's sake, Sarah," he yells, "why did you not tell me where you were?" He then sees Andy trying to blend into the background. "Do I assume you've been with him all this time? I know him from somewhere, don't I? How the hell did he come into the picture? Well, there's no need to explain because this is where he goes out of the picture. Piss off home, you." Andy, smaller than Chris, does what he is told.

Sarah did not care for either of the scenarios so she tried to think of some others. She couldn't. So, she thought, either it's going to be unpleasant the minute I walk through the door or unpleasant a few minutes after I walk through the door. She was not happy and very much wished their "working break" had not come to an end. If

Bowing Out

only she could have paid for a further week, but then that would have simply postponed the inevitable.

They pulled up at the house. It was an ordinary summer afternoon. There were a couple of children riding up and down the road on bikes but, apart from that, nobody was about. The local work slaves hadn't returned home yet. There was no outward sign of life at the O'Neill residence, but neither was there anything to confirm that the house was empty.

"Is Chris there?" asked Andy.

How the hell should I know, thought Sarah, but she didn't show her irritation. "I don't know," she said, "but, if he is, he might not be over pleased to see you. Why don't you wait in the car or perhaps better still have a trip to the Mason's Arms and I'll ring you on your mobile to let you know what's happening?"

"Not a bad idea," agreed Andy. "It's all gone a bit tense. A drink might calm the nerves." He immediately wished he'd not said that. He sounded selfish. What about Sarah's feelings? "Can you remind me how to get there?"

"Down there, first left, then second right. It's about 200 yards on the right hand side."

Andy drove off leaving Sarah alone at the front door.

You think you're nervous, Andy Wilkinson, she thought.

Sarah opened the door and the alarm sounded. She punched in the numbered code and silenced the familiar bleeping sound. It didn't need Einstein to work out that the house was empty. Either Chris was back in residence and had gone out, or he'd not yet returned.

She toured the house looking for clues. The kitchen was a good place to start. She pushed the door open, nervous at what she might find.

There were no dirty plates, dishes, knives and forks, neither was there any clean crockery or cutlery lying around. The kitchen looked just the same as when they had left. This was fairly compelling evidence. She could not imagine Chris, living on his own, both organising the washing up and then putting everything away in the right place, but she needed a little more proof that he had not returned.

She opened the fridge door. Nothing had been added to or taken from the small supply of food which had been left there at the start of the holiday. A glance in the kitchen cupboard revealed the same thing.

She went through the lounge which looked distinctly unlived in and then up to the bedroom. There was nothing out of place. Chris' shoes were not spreadeagled across the floor. The bed had probably not been slept in; it would not have been so neat if it had been occupied. She became fully convinced that Chris had not been home.

She'd seen enough and went to ring Andy when she noticed the answer machine winking at her. There were half a dozen messages, the most relevant of which said,

"Sarah, love, it's me. I'm just ringing because I don't want you to worry. I can't come home yet – I need some space. I don't really want to tell you exactly where I am, but I'm fine. I've got a base and I'm doing some thinking. I'm sure I'll be back, but probably not yet. You take care. I'll see you."

Sarah rang Andy. "Coast is clear. When you've finished your pint, fancy joining me in a bite to eat? I'm sure I can rustle up something."

Sarah found enough in the cupboard and the freezer to concoct a simple but tasty meal. With the setting sun shining through the window and the bottle of wine Andy had brought back from the off licence, it was a pleasant occasion. Certainly Sarah had been anticipating facing something far more unsavoury than this.

"Lovely meal," said Andy as he pushed his clean plate to one side. "I don't think there are many women who could produce something so tasty on limited resources having just returned from holiday. I don't recall Helen ever having done that."

Bowing Out

"Thank you," said Sarah. "It's the least I can do. It's nice to be complimented, and good to know I compare favourably with Helen."

"Sorry. There was no need for me to mention her."

"Don't worry." Sarah smiled. "Thanks, Andy. I have enjoyed that break even if it wasn't mission accomplished."

"So did I," said Andy. "It turned into a really good holiday. But I suppose I'd better be thinking about getting off. Back to it in the morning, I suppose. The chaps at work will have been missing me," he added.

"Do you think anyone else will have been missing you?" ventured Sarah.

"Hardly."

Andy changed his mind. He didn't leave until the next morning because he was wary of breathalyser possibilities, and because Sarah made it very clear that she wanted to express just how much she had enjoyed his company and how much she would like to spend some more time with him. She was right – cooking a meal was the least she could do. As she went to sleep, Sarah thought it surprising that what happened between them late that evening hadn't happened sooner.

CHAPTER 22

It was quiet in the house, but Sarah didn't mind. She felt refreshed and ready for her scheduled return to work. Sheila would ask about the holiday, of course, so she would have to decide whether to tell her about a spurious fortnight in Scotland or whether to tell her the truth. Sheila would look in wide eyed amazement if Sarah chose the latter option. Sarah's decision, which could wait for the time being, would, of course, depend on to what extent she wanted to keep her business from everyone else in the immediate vicinity.

She had a couple of days to herself but instead of the future seeming bleak and inhospitable, she found she had quite a positive outlook. She was hopeful she would see Andy again soon, and Chris might return sooner or later. If he does, thought Sarah, it will be on my terms. If he doesn't, he doesn't. It was amazing how philosophical she was becoming in these uncertain days.

She put her new found confidence to the test and rang Hughie Fraser. She didn't know him that well, and once she would have had to pluck up all her courage with the help of a couple of cigarettes before ringing. Now she went straight to the phone and punched in his number.

"What happened to you? I got the key back with a note to say you were leaving, and you simply vanished. Was there something wrong with the cottage?"

Bowing Out

Sarah sounded assured. "No, the cottage was as good as ever. I'd recommend it to anyone. It's just that Chris and I were overtaken by events and had to leave suddenly." It was true, but Hughie was not given more precise information.

"Nothing serious, I hope."

"Everything's OK now." Again, Sarah went into no detail but, as far as she was concerned, told no lies. Her husband had disappeared, yet everything was fine in her eyes. She knew really that didn't add up, but she ploughed on. "But things have been rough, to be honest," she continued in a plaintive tone, "and I don't feel as though we've had much of a break. We'd book another one if I had the money, but things are a bit tight right now, and so we wouldn't be able to go till Chris' Christmas break when prices will be sky high and I wouldn't be able to get any time off from the shop. I know it's a bit unusual and perhaps a bit improper to ask, but could you see your way to perhaps giving us a small refund on the cottage?"

Sarah could hardly believe what she'd said. There were no ums or errs. So brazen. Such confidence.

Equally incredible was the arrival of a letter with a Scottish postmark a few days later. Hughie's letter was handwritten and had the personal touch. He said he was sorry to hear of the problems and, while he was unable to reimburse the cost of the whole fortnight, he hoped the enclosed cheque would help to ease the difficulties and obvious disappointment. He looked forward to seeing her again and he hoped she would choose his accommodation again if she fancied Scotland for a future holiday. It was a good PR stunt, but whether Sarah would return there with all its memories was too early to say.

The cheque was for a larger amount than Sarah had hoped for. She thought that in reality she should send a portion to Chris, but what could you do with these people who didn't leave an address? Perhaps she would use it to treat Andy to a couple of nights away before very long.

Peter Cropper

With Hughie's letter came another crucial piece of snail mail. It was ironic; if you believed everything you heard and read, nobody was using the post any more, and soon nobody would be able to even if they wanted to because there would be no post offices anywhere, but Sarah's postman was being kept busy with all manner of vital correspondence. If he hadn't brought that postcard...

The handwritten envelope gave the game away straight away, of course. She kept her cool, opened it calmly and read the contents.

Dear Sarah,

I hope you've settled in back home now. I apologise for ruining the holiday like that. Something just snapped, I suppose, and I had to get out. With the car you had the facility to drive home, and you've still got it to run around in. I don't think I'll be needing it any more.

I'll cut to the chase. There's no easy way to say this, but I'm not sure I'll be back. You're probably wondering where I'm living. In fact, I'm in the south Lakes. I have been very lucky, because I met a lady, we hit it off and I moved in. I'm spending some time with her.

I could come home – and "never say never", as the saying goes - but where would be the sense in that? You see, Sarah, I don't think there's anything down for us anymore. All being well, we've both got long lives ahead of us, and it would be criminal to live a lie when we could both be so much happier. I know I've found happiness and I'm sure you will, too. You're very attractive with a good personality, but you and I aren't right for each other so what's the point in carrying on?

I wish you well - I really do. I hope you meet someone who makes you as happy as the new lady makes me.

Chris

Bowing Out

Chris didn't mention who he had moved in with – he didn't want to rub Sarah's nose in it. It would have done nobody any good. He was prompted to write the letter because, not only had he found somewhere to live, but he had also found himself a job. This made him feel a new and very real sense of permanence surrounding his new environment. Money wasn't an issue thanks to Doctor Brooker's help but he felt he needed something to occupy himself – something to give his new life a sense of purpose. He was looking for something flexible and part time that he could do as and when to fit round the free time he was intending to enjoy with Helen. He couldn't sit round reading and pottering round all day, every day particularly if, as he hoped, he was there for the long haul.

That was the thinking behind his visit to Low Rigg. He knocked on the door and waited while Mrs Jackson toddled her way through from the back of the house.

"Hello, Mrs Jackson," he said politely. "Do you remember me?"

"Of course I do," replied Mrs Jackson. "I'm not senile," she felt like adding, but instead she said, "You stayed here not so long ago. You wrote a lovely comment in my visitors' book. I really appreciated that."

Mrs Jackson did seem on the ball.

"No problem," said Chris. "I only wrote what I saw. It was just a refection of the lovely time I had here."

Mrs Jackson smiled. "But nobody's praised the garden before like that."

"Well someone should have because it's a magnificent garden," said Chris. "How on earth do you maintain it as well as running this brilliant B and B?"

"I don't," replied Mrs Jackson. "A young lad from a farm a few miles away comes to do it."

"That's handy," said Chris, hiding his disappointment.

"Well, it is, but he's found a job in London and he'll be on the move soon. Great for him, not so brilliant for me. There's no way I can do that gardening at my age."

Peter Cropper

Chris could scarcely believe his good fortune. A job opportunity which was just what he was looking for had fallen right into his lap, and he had already curried his employer's favour.

Chris burned off the non existent competition and stormed through the interview. He was offered the post of Low Rigg's head gardener and accepted without hesitation. There was no contract, no formalities – just a gentleman's / lady's agreement that he would come to do the essential maintenance when he could.

"But you must let me know when you're coming," said Mrs Jackson, "otherwise, if I'm out, who is going to put the kettle on?"

"That sounds great," said Chris. "Will there be any chance of that delicious cake I believe you do to soak the tea up?"

Mrs Jackson smiled again. Her earlier suspicions were confirmed - her new man was a bit of a charmer. He was a polite young man, the likes of which you didn't meet too often these days. She couldn't work out how he knew about her baking skills of which she was so proud, but that didn't matter. She was so pleased with the new arrangements, as was Chris when he discovered how much he would be paid.

CHAPTER 23

Sarah reread the letter, and reread it again. To her surprise, she wasn't surprised. She then tried to gauge her reactions, but she didn't find that easy. A number of questions demanded answers.

Did she feel upset? Yes, of course she did. That was a stupid question. The letter did hint at finality but, on the other hand, Chris had left open the possibility of a return which assumed that she would have him back. Would she?

Was she relieved? Relief did come into it. She now knew for certain Chris' whereabouts and that he was settled. That made her feel better. She no longer needed to regard him as one of those missing persons whose stories sometimes feature on news bulletins. She considered that she had found some degree of happiness and she was pleased that Chris, too, was content. What she really didn't know now was whether she would prefer Chris to be content with her. He'd been an idiot in Scotland but she could forgive that. There was Andy – but for how long? Nobody knew the answer to that one.

Did she feel anger? To her amazement, she wasn't at all angry. She didn't think she could be angry now that Andy was on the scene. Andy didn't do anger. His laid back, easy going approach to life seemed to be rubbing off on her. Could she establish the same sort of semi permanence – or permanence - with Andy as Chris had with his mysterious new lady? She thought she could, and anger would only have stood in the way of optimism, so it wasn't an option.

But was a relationship with Andy what she really wanted in preference to one with Chris? She really did not know that, but what she did know was that receiving the letter still had at least the potential to make her upset and that the way to cope with this was perhaps to tell someone about it.

Mum and Dad in the Deep South? Perhaps she wouldn't tell them just yet. They weren't up to speed on recent developments and communication was sporadic at the best of times. She would tell them at some stage – probably.

She waited very patiently until later in the evening when she was fairly confident he would be home, and then she rang the one person who she really did want to know.

"Andy, it's Sarah. I want you to share my news."

"Glad you've phoned. I was going to ring you later in any case. But first – what's happening at your end?"

Sarah told him, in rather monosyllabic tones. "The big news is, I've had a letter. Chris has written. He seems to think it's all over." She conveyed the news in as phlegmatic a way as she could.

Andy listened and then said, "Sarah – I'm so sorry. How do you feel about all that?"

This wasn't an easy question to answer. If Sarah's tone of voice conveyed distress and sadness, it might burn Andy off. He might think she was desperate for Chris to return. If she went to the other extreme and said that she was really rather delighted, the implication being because it freed her and Andy up to be an item, that might frighten him off as well if he thought it was all moving too fast. A very measured response was therefore needed.

"There's not a lot I can do about it," she said. "It appears he's made his mind up. I can't influence what he thinks or does. All I can do is recognise the fact that he's not here now and move on accordingly."

Andy latched on to the word "now". Did Sarah mean that although Chris wasn't there at the moment she hoped or expected he would be sometime in the future, or did she mean "now" in the sense of "any more"? Sarah's voice didn't give much away, and without seeing her face it was impossible to tell. Why, in this day and age, were videophones not standard in every home?

In the absence of anything more deep or meaningful to say, Andy said, "I think you're right. Life is for living now. 'Carpe diem', as the Latin scholars would have it. Nobody knows what the future might bring. We might all be dead next week."

There was a silence. Andy wondered if he had said the right thing. Sarah reflected on the fact that she hadn't had a classical education. Latin had been removed from her school's curriculum shortly before her arrival. She fell to wondering, not for the first time, whether Andy was, in fact, something of a smartass rather than an all round good bloke.

Sarah decided to give him the benefit of the doubt and it was she who broke the silence. "You said you were going to ring me in any case. What can I do you for?"

Andy didn't know whether to tell her the real reason or not. He reckoned he had to make a simple decision – to press on with his original script or not. He decided he would. Everything seemed to be in his favour.

"I was wondering if you'd like to go out again soon."

It was a new restaurant – or at least new to Sarah. "Pick a good restaurant that you know," Andy had said, but every good restaurant that Sarah knew had been visited with Chris and she wanted to go somewhere different. That's why they were in a Thai restaurant Sheila had recommended. "The food's great, but the service isn't too rapid," she had said.

She was certainly right about the second point – they had been there half an hour and hadn't had a thing to eat so she couldn't yet confirm or otherwise Sheila's view on the cuisine. The restaurant had a nice ambience, with enough diners at other tables so that they didn't feel exposed yet with enough empty places so that the establishment didn't seem overcrowded.

Of course, they weren't just there to eat. Initially conversation had been a little slow but as they settled into their evening it gradually became more fluent.

They began by exchanging pleasantries, but everyday life didn't seem to provoke too much interesting chat. Sarah didn't want to discuss fruit and veg and there was clearly nothing fascinating to report from Andy's office.

Andy upped the tempo by reminiscing about their trip to the Lakes. This was the one thing they had in common apart, of course, from having lost their partners, but neither of them gave much thought to what Chris or Helen was doing at that moment. If only they knew!

Andy had thought about what he would say. He was good with words and, while he was not a natural raconteur in a crowd, on a one to one basis he could talk to some effect. He transported them effortlessly back to Cumbria. Sarah could hear the birds singing, feel the sun on her back, and smell the wet grass after one of the Lake District's showers. She felt she'd like to go back there soon, except that she now knew that Chris was there. Rather like the selection of the restaurant, she thought she should be looking for new places to see and new things to do. It wasn't that she was bothered about accidentally bumping into Chris, embarrassing though that could be; it was rather that she felt she had a clean new slate upon which to write the next chapters. Meeting her husband might cause her to revise the new sections of the story. She wondered whether that would be a bad thing or not.

At about the same time that Andy felt he should stop rattling on about what a good time they had had for fear of overdoing things, the food finally arrived. Sheila had been right about that as well. Eating provided a distraction. Andy used the opportunity to drop his suggestion into the now broken conversation in as casual fashion as he could manage.

"Do you know, or think you know, of any reasonable reason why we couldn't repeat the process of our going away?"

He thought he'd expressed that strangely. He was obviously more nervous than he thought.

"Don't you think we should get to know each other a little better first?" Sarah was testing both him and her own resolve.

Andy grimaced. He wasn't totally prepared for that. He had rather imagined that, after his colourful Cumbrian reminiscences, Sarah would easily be seduced by the idea of another expedition.

"You might be right. I was jumping the gun there, wasn't I? I'm very sorry."

"That's OK."

An awkward silence descended. Sarah looked at Andy as he ate. She found him attractive. He was not as good looking as Chris, perhaps, but his demeanour was winning her over. He was unremarkable in many ways, but polite and very considerate. If he died tomorrow (God forbid), his epitaph might read, "Here lies Andy Wilkinson. He didn't do much, but he was a thoroughly nice bloke."

Which was more important to Sarah now – dynamism or niceness?

"Did I tell you the man we rented the cottage off in Scotland sent a refund? I told him the holiday went pear shaped, and he took pity on me."

Andy smiled. "That was kind. And they say the Scots are mean. But I think that's nonsense. I've met some great people north of the border. It just goes to show you can't believe everything you read."

"No, indeed. It leaves me in a nice position. Thanks to you, I did have a holiday, and I've got some unexpected money in my pocket." She tested him again. "So will you let me pay for this meal?"

"No can do," said Andy cheerfully. "This is my treat. I thought it would be a way of thanking you for looking after me when we were away. Can you imagine how dismal it would have been searching on my own?"

Except I don't recall doing too much searching, thought Sarah. But never mind.

"If that's the case, then here's my treat," said Sarah. "I'm going to put some of my little windfall towards treating us to another trip away."

It's hard to imagine it getting any better than this, thought Andy. He feigned a protest.

"You can't do that. It's from yours and Chris' holiday. Part of the money belongs to Chris, surely? Shouldn't you send some to him and spend the rest on yourself?" "And get something like a nice dress," he nearly added, but stopped himself. It wouldn't do to appear patronising, or to give the impression he was not keen on Sarah's dress sense.

"How can I send it to Chris? I told you, although he sent me a letter, he didn't include his address."

"Sorry. I forgot."

"Apology accepted."

Sarah was touched by his reaction. "I can take us away and, what's more, I am taking us away. End of story."

"That's a brilliant idea but I'm not sure I can afford to take any more time off work."

Sarah thought fast. "You know, I'm not keen on this time of year," said Sarah. "Don't you find that when the damper weather arrives it's just a breeding ground for germs?"

Andy guessed where the conversation was going and he didn't look too comfortable but Sarah was not about to take no for an answer. "Diary out, Mr Wilkinson. We've got an illness to book."

Andy didn't like to tempt fate like that but he could see how committed Sarah was to the idea and he decided to run with it. Despite his doubts about the ethics of deceiving his work masters, he was pleased. "That's brilliant," he gushed again. He boldly raised his glass. "To us," he said.

"To us."

CHAPTER 24

At about the same time as Mr Davidson was dismissing Mr O'Neill's history class, Chris was setting out for his first day's hard graft at Mrs Jackson's. Which of the two Whiteoaks colleagues was the happier?

"By the heck," said Ray who moderated his language when he saw some of his female colleagues had already arrived for break, "what on earth has happened to those kids since the summer?"

"What year have you just had?" asked Pete.

"Year nine," replied Ray.

"You've not lost them already, Mr D?" Steve Lloyd had breezed in.

"They're not mine to lose, thank God," said Ray. "I was caught for cover."

"Caught by the deputies," said Steve. "How painful is that?"

"Mr O'Neill's darlings?" asked Pete.

"Who else? He's the only one of us who failed to come under starter's orders."

"I know what happens," said Steve. "Just after the start of the holidays, all the year eight pupils are rounded up and taken to the health centre for their naughty pupil injection, the effects of which last at least a year. For those who are particularly susceptible, of course, the effects can be longer lasting."

Peter Cropper

"Just after the start of the holidays," said Mike Prescott who had joined the little group. "Can anybody here remember that far back?"

A little later, at about the same time as Ray was embarking on one of his specialities – a wonderfully intricate and colourful diagram of a glaciated valley for the benefit of some of Whiteoaks' less academically challenged pupils - Chris pulled up outside Mrs Jackson's. It had been a pleasant drive. It was the end of the first week of term, so the sun was shining, of course, and everywhere was delightfully free of children, of course. There was a car parked outside Low Rigg. Its boot was open so Chris concluded it must belong to departing holidaymakers in no particular rush to leave. He hoped they had written something nice in the visitors' book. Mrs Jackson would like that. She was proud of her visitors' book.

Chris rang the bell and Mrs Jackson greeted him. She didn't look very happy.

"Not a great start, if you don't mind me saying so," she frowned.

"What do you mean?"

"You're supposed to ring." Mrs Jackson's face then transformed itself and a beaming smile appeared. "Otherwise I won't know to put your tea and cake out. Take a seat in the lounge. If you don't mind waiting a bit, I'm just waving last night's guests off."

A short while later she returned with a large pot of tea hidden by a vivid, bright green tea cosy, patterned china cups and a plate of cakes and biscuits big enough to feed half a dozen starving gardeners.

She smiled again. "Had you going there, didn't I?"

Such an expression seemed strange coming from Mrs Jackson but it was quite right, she had indeed "had Chris going."

"Yes you did," said Chris. "You could be an actress."

This was just the cue Mrs Jackson needed. "Well as a matter of fact, in my younger days when I lived in the Midlands, I was in an amateur dramatics society. I enjoyed that. Some of the parts they gave me to play!"

And she was off. It seemed she took at least one, sometimes two, major roles each year and there was a story attached to every one. Occasionally Chris would recognise one of the plays she mentioned but he wasn't a great theatregoer so much of what he was being told was meaningless. However, it was obvious Mrs Jackson wanted to talk so he sipped his tea, nibbled his cake and dutifully listened. Clearly Mrs Jackson got lonely when the guests weren't there and she appreciated having someone to talk to – or should that be "talk at"?

An hour passed at the end of which Chris was feeling quite waterlogged and he'd not so much as tugged at one weed or picked up a single one of the tools in the garden shed. It was money for old rope. He thought briefly about what he should have been doing back at Whiteoaks and then he smiled to himself. He was still smiling after Mrs Jackson had eventually released him and he found himself weeding the border.

At the end of his stint Chris was paid in cash, as agreed. When he calculated how much work he had actually done in the time he had been there, the reward in relative terms didn't seem substantially lower than that which he received for teaching. It was, of course, and he knew his idea was quite illusory, but if you took into account the valued added factor of his being in Cumbria on a beautiful late summer's day as opposed to being cloistered up in a suburb of questionable savouriness surrounded by company he'd rather not keep, then it seemed like a great deal.

He agreed when he would return – in a few days' time, towards the middle of next week – and made a move to go home. A cup of tea? One for the road? (Not a wee dram at that time of day, surely?). Chris wasn't sure he could physically drink any more, but it would have been rude not to, so the weary, overworked teapot was called into action yet again

Eventually, with liquid sloshing round in his stomach, he drove home. Helen managed to greet him with a smile, but it was a weak affair, and it was obvious there was a problem.

"What's wrong, love?"

"Nothing."

Chris was patient with her. "It doesn't look that way to me," he suggested as pleasantly as he could. "What's the matter?"

Helen looked unhappy.

"This can't be right, Chris. You come home from work, and I go out to work. Why don't we have a revolving door fitted?"

It was a disappointing reaction. Chris had had a good first day. If he could continue to work at that pace, it seemed there was enough work at Low Rigg to last him for ever if he wanted it. He had been very pleased with the situation as he thought it over while deadheading the roses. He could stay as long as he wanted providing he didn't cause any problems, or so it appeared to him, and he couldn't imagine what problems he would cause working alone in a garden. Now Helen was throwing the proverbial spanner in the works before he'd got into his stride.

"It's just the way it is, love. At times we are going to be out of step, but when you think about it, how often will I be out gardening? Once or twice a week? If you look at it that way, there'll still be plenty of time to spend together." He was trying to be mollifying but he came over as patronising, and Helen didn't seem in the mood to see it that way. She couldn't see past the current scenario and she seemed to think it would be that way every day.

"You don't see it, do you Chris? But if I were you I wouldn't just ignore me. In my line of work there are plenty of nice young men about, and don't think I've not noticed their admiring glances. I'll be getting some more tonight so it's time I was off to make myself look my best." She stood up and without looking at Chris made her way upstairs to the bathroom.

Bowing Out

Chris was concerned, not so much about the crowds of suitors who, as far as he could gather from his visits to the pub, only existed in Helen's head, but rather about Helen's less than secure hold on reality. He was also disturbed by Helen's tone of voice. He had never heard her talk so acerbically before and he hoped that she wouldn't again.

CHAPTER 25

Sarah asked Andy in for coffee. It was the natural thing to do, and Andy had boldly suggested that a coffee would perk him up for the drive home. Sarah found Andy's reluctance to assume that he would be asked to stay totally charming, and she provided a strong brew from Java which Andy hoped wouldn't keep him awake after he'd finished his journey. A small plate of veteran after dinner mints was produced. The mints could have been out of date, but Andy didn't know and Sarah didn't care.

"Another trip away," said Andy, with a huge grin on his face. Now that he'd convinced himself that feigning a few days' illness wasn't a crime on the scale of mass murder, he was like a little boy in a toy shop. "But can I just check again – are you sure you should be spending that money on us?"

"If I were you, I wouldn't ask again. My mind is made up but if you keep rattling on about it you might just talk me out of it." There was just enough edge in Sarah's voice to persuade Andy that she meant it, and he knew that it wouldn't do to upset a lady.

"OK," said Andy, suitably chastised. "Where do you fancy going?"

"Somewhere neither of us has been. Somewhere completely new."

Bowing Out

"That's a very good idea." A quick comparison of travel notes revealed that, between them, they had a good knowledge of the British coast and inland Britain offered more virgin territory.

"Any preferences?"

"Not really," replied Sarah. "What about the tried and tested pin – in - a - map trick?"

Andy was a gentleman and it was therefore Sarah's turn first. She shut her eyes and the pin landed on an industrial town with very limited visitor attractions fewer than twenty miles from where they were sitting,

"I think not," said Sarah. "Your go."

Andy closed his eyes and landed on Lincoln.

"Possible," said Sarah.

"Lincoln," said Andy. "It's a very pleasant city with lots to see. The cathedral is particularly impressive. But I have been there, so if we're playing strictly by the rules, then we'll have to rule it out."

"Quite right," said Sarah. She admired Andy's honesty. "My turn."

They had three more failed attempts each, two of which landed in the sea, before running out of patience.

Andy started to make a move. "Thanks for the coffee," he said. "I'd better hit the road. Time's getting on." His disappointment was palpable. "We'll just have to meet up again soon and pick a venue for our trip."

Sarah smiled sweetly at him. "Perhaps if we try the pin routine after breakfast tomorrow when we're refreshed? I'm sure we'll have better luck then."

Resistance, as they say, was useless.

Andy woke up to another of Sarah's sweet smiles and a cup of tea. He smiled back.

"Is this the way you treat all your guests?"

"Only special ones, and even then, only those who have done something exceptional to deserve it."

They recalled the events of late the previous evening, laughed together as lovers do, and reprised. When they finally started to drink their tea, it was cold.

Sarah went downstairs after showering, leaving Andy to use the bathroom. Instinctively she went to fling open the windows and noticed for the first time that there was no real need to do so. The air was fresher and Sarah, too, felt fresher. She knew why it was, of course, and gave herself a little congratulatory pat on the back as she put the kettle on and arranged the cereals on the table to give Andy the impression he was away on his holidays. Everybody had said giving up was so difficult, but right now it looked like a piece of cake even though, if she were honest, she couldn't be sure she was entirely free of the weed's clutches.

Andy strolled into the dining room when he was good and ready. He felt slightly uncomfortable wearing yesterday's dirty clothes, but apart from that he couldn't recall ever feeling as relaxed. He had fleetingly considered hiding a small overnight bag in the boot of his car – "just in case" – but he had decided it was probably better not to tempt fate like that. Would it have made a difference? He would never know. He wondered if Sarah would have offered the use of some of Chris' clothes had the two men not taken different sizes, but then he quickly decided that such speculation was completely futile. Instead he said, "Sarah, the table looks a picture." Indeed it did, because the very finest crockery was on show – the wedding present crockery. Sarah had not felt totally guiltless when she put it out but "what," she said to herself, "is the point in having fine breakfast china shut up in a cupboard?"

The sun was out, the garden looked in reasonable condition because Sarah had found the time to do a little perfunctory tidying since her return, the scrambled eggs had been done to perfection and the hot buttered toast with the extra fruit jam rounded things off perfectly.

When breakfast was over, Sarah said, "Is it time to turn our attention to the atlas and pin again?"

"Ready when you are," said Andy. "And, as should always be the case, ladies first."

"No, you go first. I think you'll find somewhere this time."

Andy closed his eyes and hit the jackpot – somewhere neither had visited, and somewhere neither had considered in the past. It was virgin territory which would fit the bill perfectly.

"Herefordshire it is, then."

Meanwhile, of the two men, Chris was less happy than Andy. He was thinking about the previous night's events. Helen had dressed differently to go to work – "dressed to kill" would just about sum it up. "How do I look?" she had barked.

"Very nice," Chris had replied, but without conviction. He was distracted because he still couldn't fathom why she seemed to be making a special effort on this occasion. His answer had not convinced Helen.

"Liar. You think I look like a tart. I can tell. Well, you're wrong. I don't. I'm off somewhere where I'm appreciated."

When she came home, somewhat later than Chris had been expecting, Helen blasted straight up the stairs and she took the non-stop route into bed where she went to sleep without saying a word.

She was still there now as Chris sat alone, drinking tea and wondering if everything was starting to unravel.

It was a while before Helen emerged. Chris thought that she had wasted half the day as she crept into the kitchen in search of breakfast at about the same time as Chris was contemplating what he might have for lunch. He could feel her behind him as he looked through the kitchen cupboard even though he had heard nothing because she had padded downstairs so quietly in her dressing gown and slippers. She did not look at her vibrant best. With unkempt hair and bleary eyes she had the appearance of someone who had spent far too long dozing in bed. Chris tried some very basic conversation.

"Hi, Helen. Sleep well?"

"Not bad." It was a start. Chris feared she might have just ignored him but at least she was talking, even though her voice was lifeless.

"Can I get you anything to eat and drink?"

"No. I'll sort something out. You get what you want and I'll get what I want."

Helen breakfasted at the same time as Chris lunched, but Helen waited until Chris sat down at the table before taking her tray through to the living room. Chris didn't know whether to join her or to leave her where she was. He decided on the latter option so he could think about what to do for the best. This was no good. Why was she brooding? Surely she wasn't sulking about the previous evening. And in any case, what had he done wrong? Surely she didn't have it in for him because he'd been out to work? Was she jealous of the time he spent at Mrs Jackson's? The more he thought about it, the more ridiculous it seemed. They would have to have a chat but, at the moment, that was a daunting prospect.

CHAPTER 26

Sarah was feeling rather pleased with life. It had taken a few phone calls but she and Andy had found a cottage willing to offer them a three night break in the depths of the Herefordshire countryside providing they could wait a little while until it became free. This was not a problem. Sarah could book her days off work and she could have the delicious anticipation of three nights – four full days – away with Andy.

Andy, too, was happy with the arrangement. He could return to work and settle back in, and after a day or two neither he nor his fellow workers would remember he had been away. Then the mystery ailment would strike and he'd be off again.

There was only one worry. Would Chris return home in the meantime and ruin everything?

Lunch – or breakfast – over, Chris tried again. He cleared his empty plates away and left them in the sink for later, made a coffee for Helen and himself and took both drinks into the living room. Helen had eaten about half of the cereal.

"Not hungry, love?"

"No."

"I've brought you a coffee."

No real response.

Peter Cropper

Chris sat down on the sofa beside Helen. He didn't go too close for fear that it wasn't safe to do so. He tried to approach her again.

"Helen, love, we can't go on like this. I can tell there's something the matter but until you explain to me what it is, I can't do a lot to help."

Helen turned to him. There was real anger in her eyes.

"You really don't know, do you?" she yelled. "Well I'll bloody well tell you what the matter is. You're on top of me all the time. You never give me my own space. I've no life. I'm totally dominated by you. I'm not prepared to stand for it any more. Things will have to change."

She spat the sentences out intermittently like machine gun fire.

Chris could not have agreed less but he kept his calm and he spoke to Helen as nicely as he could. "So what exactly do you want me to do to improve the situation?"

Helen stood up and towered over him. She looked considerably taller than her five feet four inches. For the first time in their relationship, Chris felt threatened by her. In fact, it was the first time that he could recall that he had felt threatened by any woman.

"It's obvious, isn't it?" she shouted. "Just leave me alone for a bit, will you? I need some space and I need some time." She stormed out of the room and went back upstairs. She dressed very quickly, and a few minutes later Chris heard the front door slam.

He wandered round the room, bemused, and after a short while the awful irony of the situation struck home as he realised that he was feeling like Sarah must have felt in Scotland not so very long ago. Helen had gone straight out and had not left a note like he had, so that meant she was coming back soon…didn't it?

Sarah kissed Andy goodbye. It wouldn't be long now until the Herefordshire trip but they had arranged to meet in the meantime. "Come to me," Andy had said. "I may

Bowing Out

not be the greatest in the kitchen, but I'll give it a go, if you're willing to chance it."

Oh yes, thought Sarah, I'm willing to chance it. Although you may not be the greatest in the kitchen….

CHAPTER 27

Two days after Helen's dramatic exit Chris found himself with some time on his hands. He was trying to relax in an old pub situated in a narrow street not far from the lake, having thought he should treat himself to a couple of pints. A few weeks before the pub would have been full of tourists but now there were plenty of seats and idle moments for the bar staff. Chris was still pleased by the lack of children, although he noticed a couple of boys with someone he assumed to be their father in the far corner. The conversation seemed serious and the one young face that Chris could see looked unhappy. You're supposed to be in school, thought Chris, but then again, so am I. The father left his seat to go to the bar to stock up on lemonade and crisps. He didn't look any happier than his younger son.

Helen's departure hadn't been permanent. She had returned later that evening after a "time out", but where she had been had remained a mystery.

Chris had undertaken a little simple investigation. "Hello, love. Where have you been?" he had said brightly. Helen's reply had left him in no doubt that she preferred that he didn't know. Nevertheless, Chris was pleased to see her again even though Helen didn't seem ready for any contact of any description, let alone the type of contact they had both very much enjoyed not so long ago.

Bowing Out

A lady entered the pub alone, looked round briefly, and made a beeline for Chris.

"Excuse me for asking," she said very politely, "but aren't you a friend of Helen Wilkinson?"

Chris was surprised. "I am, yes. How do you know?"

"I'm also a friend of Helen's and I've seen you with her in town a couple of times." She extended a friendly hand. "Sue Mason."

"Pleased to meet you, Sue. Sit down. Can I get you a drink?"

"Sparkling mineral water, please. It's a bit early in the day for wine."

Chris looked at his pint, two thirds finished, and wondered what Sue thought about that, but quickly decided that it was nothing to do with her. It was he, and he alone, who decided when a beer was appropriate. He wandered off to the bar where he nodded and smiled at the father who was still being served by a barman in no discernible hurry. The father returned a smile but it was unconvincing and it failed to hide an underlying sadness. He then returned to the table with the latest round of refreshments.

Chris returned to his table with the water freshly sourced from one of Britain's mineral springs. It was no doubt good for the drinker's health, but Chris preferred to turn on the tap at home where the water appeared for free. He also found water tastier when flavoured with barley and hops.

So, what was the purpose of Sue's incursion into Chris' private little world?

"I presume Helen has told you of the little incident in town the other day?"

"I'm afraid she hasn't. I'm sorry, but I've no idea what you're talking about." Chris was suddenly nervous about what he might hear next. "What happened was ridiculous really. Did you enjoy the pork chops you had for tea the other day?"

"Yes, thank you." Helen had done them really nicely in a white wine sauce. Chris had never eaten chops cooked like that before even though Sarah knew many varied and interesting recipes. He had been fortunate in that he had stumbled from one great cook to another. "How long have you known about our menus?"

"Oh, let me tell you, you were lucky to have those chops. They were the last two in the shop and Helen was behind me in the queue. We were passing the time of day, as you do, and then I asked for them. She went berserk."

"How do you mean?"

"Exactly what I say. She grabbed me by my jacket, said she'd splatter me across the shop if I took her tea, and then she threw me against the wall."

"She did what? Were you hurt?"

"Not really. It's just as well I was standing close to the wall in the first place. I didn't have far to travel. I was shocked, though. You're bound to feel a bit shaken up after something like that, aren't you? I could feel myself just staring stupidly at her as she bought the chops and then she left the shop, ignoring me totally. She brushed past an old lady on the way out. It's just as well she didn't treat her like she treated me or she would have done some serious damage. The butcher said her attack on me was assault and he was all for calling the police, but I said I didn't want to, so he left it. Helen and I are mates, after all."

Chris was shocked, too, and embarrassed. "I can't do any more at this stage than apologise for Helen's behaviour. God only knows what's come over her."

Sue's next suggestion was far too bold. "I assumed you two might have been having words, but, even so, it was a pretty violent reaction. I wouldn't have thought Helen would take it out on someone else in quite that way."

Chris wasn't happy with Sue's assumption. "No, we hadn't been 'having words' as you put it," he said sharply. He had always taken umbrage if he had been wrongly

Bowing Out

blamed for something. It was one of his pet hates, right up there with violent year ten pupils and arrogant work colleagues.

"Sorry," said Sue. "I shouldn't have said that." She had no interest in blaming or alienating Chris. She was hoping he would be able to help her solve her friend's problems.

There followed a short awkward silence, broken by a suitable cliché from Sue.

"Well, what's done is done," she said. "No use crying over spilt milk. To be honest, I'm more worried than anything. I've known Helen virtually all the time she's been living up here and I've never seen her act like that. It's just so out of character. She's just about the last person I would have expected to do that. You've not noticed anything strange about her recently, have you?"

Chris felt he could trust Sue. He was sure her apology was sincere and it was obvious she was genuinely concerned, so he put her in the picture about Helen's recent erratic behaviour.

"Listen," said Sue, "a friend of mine – a professional – knows about these things. Would you object if I picked his brains a little?"

"A professional?" asked Chris. "A shrink, you mean? Do you think Helen's a nutcase?" Sue found it hard to make out whether Chris shared her concern or whether he was deeply offended by the suggestion, although the former seemed the more likely.

"No," said Sue, "he's not a shrink exactly, but Neil is someone who can perhaps throw some light on this," and she groped around for what she deemed to be a suitable expression, "atypical behaviour."

"Well, yes, that's fine, I suppose," said Chris. He had been concerned, of course he had, and this story of high drama at the meat counter only added to the gravity of the situation. "How are we going to touch base again to compare notes? I hardly think you can ring me. What if Helen answers and you ask for me?"

"Very true," said Sue. "What's your mobile number?"

Chris wrote it down. "Would you mind if I took your number as well?"

"No, I don't mind. You can have my mobile and landline numbers." Sue tore open a beer mat and scribbled both numbers down. "Give me a ring in a few days. I'll speak to Neil as soon as I can. It's the least I can do for a friend."

Chris wasn't sure whether he or Helen was the friend in question, but he assumed she meant Helen, and in any case it didn't matter a lot. Sue got up to go, so he thanked her and followed her with his eyes as she left the pub. He returned to his drink, pensively at first, wondering about such matters as how Sue knew he'd be in that pub at that particular time, but he then decided he needed a break from all this and he looked for something or someone to distract him. A chat about the basics in life, like football, with a like minded man would help. He turned to the corner of the room but the sad father with the children had slipped out unnoticed.

Three days later, he rang Sue. He had thought a lot about what had happened. Helen's attitude towards him showed no sign of changing. "Aloof" might be the best word to describe it. One positive thing was that Helen showed no aggression towards Chris, but that was probably because they were never both in the same place for long enough. This meant that while things couldn't get much worse, neither could they improve.

Bloody answer machine! Chris decided not to leave a message, and he tried the mobile. Bloody voicemail!

He tried again a couple of hours later, and this time he had better fortune. After brief pleasantries had been dispensed with, Chris got straight to the point. "I was wondering, have you managed to speak with your friend yet?"

"Yes, I had a chat with Neil last night," replied Sue. "I told him of the butcher's shop incident. He was wondering whether Helen tended towards dramatic or emotional behaviour. Does she like to be the centre of attention?"

Chris recalled the walk at Grizedale and Helen's reaction to the simple tumble when she went down as if she'd been shot. "Well, I've not known her well for that long so I'm not sure I'm qualified to say, but there is one time I can think of which would fit the bill there."

"Neil seemed to think that, if there were a pattern of such behaviour, she might have something called a Borderline Personality Disorder," said Sue.

"And that means..?"

"I'm not sure really, but he thinks he can help her if you could persuade her to meet up with him."

"Does Neil live locally?"

"No, he lives just outside Durham."

Chris visualised a map of the north of England. It would involve a drive across the north Pennines. "In the overall scheme of things that's not too far," he said. "It would be good if we could get your friend and Helen together for a chat, don't you think?"

"Very much so," said Sue.

Chris thought about the story of the mice who wanted to attach a bell round the cat's neck so that they would know when it was coming. The mice's task seemed like child's play compared with what was being suggested now.

CHAPTER 28

It was perfectly sweet of him to go to the trouble of cooking for me, thought Sarah as she finished the main course. Most men would have bought a ready meal from the supermarket and had done with it; in and out, quick as you like, so to speak. Andy had relived his student days and cooked Spaghetti Bolognaise. "It's an old favourite of mine," he said, "and one of my specialities. Everyone likes Spag Bol."

Of course, for all Sarah knew it could have been Andy's only speciality, but he had obviously tried his best, throwing in a number of random bits from the fridge's salad crisper, and he had garnished the whole thing with what appeared to Sarah's taste buds to be a number of different herbs, some of which complemented each other well and some of which didn't. Sarah reflected that, a couple of months ago when she was a dedicated smoker, she might not have been as receptive to this subtle blend of flavours. Perhaps the taste of Andy's meal with its odd combination of seasonings was a good advert for taking up smoking properly again? No, thought Sarah, how could you ever think such a thing? That's naughty.

"More wine?" asked Andy.

"Yes please," said Sarah. She was taking a gamble here because neither of them had confirmed whether Sarah would be staying the night and, if she wasn't, driving home over the limit would not be the best idea. However,

Bowing Out

on the grounds that Andy was probably bound to ask to stay her unless the evening went horribly pear shaped, she accepted the wine. She had no intention of saying or doing anything to rock the boat, and, she suspected, neither had Andy.

"You'll take some dessert?" beamed the host.

"Yes please." Andy was gone a short while and he came back with a delicious looking pie accompanied by a large jug of cream.

"Apple pie," he announced.

"My favourite," Sarah lied. She'd never met anyone else who, like herself, was not keen on apple pie, but she wasn't about to let Andy know that. "Have you made this too?" she enthused.

"It's come from the baker's down the road," said Andy. "I cannot tell a lie, as George Washington would have said."

Why not, thought Sarah. I managed it with no trouble at all.

"Are you happy with cream, or would you like some Wensleydale with it in the old Yorkshire style?" suggested Andy with great gusto.

Was that with or instead of the cream? This wasn't a culinary tradition with which she was familiar. Apple pie and cheese seemed to Sarah to be a weird combination, but she didn't want to disappoint. "That would be lovely," she enthused again. What an actress! Some of Andy's newly acquired skills must have rubbed off on her.

After the meal they shared a pot of coffee and settled down to think about their plans for Herefordshire. It wasn't long off now and, as they both confirmed, neither of them could wait, although Sarah had wondered whether she was guilty of looking forward to it just a little too much. She had always been plagued by a pessimistic streak which usually stopped her from looking forward to good times too much but this time it was different. Although she was sure nothing would go wrong during their time away, there was always the small chance…

"Autumn is when it looks its best down there, or so I've read somewhere," said Andy. "There's fruit all over the place, and the colours..."

"Right," said Sarah, shaken out of her little daydream before the ridiculous feeling that they would be better not going because of the slight possibility that it may go wrong really took hold. She imagined their cottage with the trees around it, looking magnificent in their autumn tints. She could see the windfall apples, crispy and fresh and waiting to be enjoyed, on the lawn in the back garden and the hedgerows groaning under the weight of thousands of blackberries. There they were, the two of them, wrapped up against the cooler weather, ready to embark on a ramble with a thatched pub boasting a roaring log fire conveniently situated half way round. What could possibly go wrong?

"I'm really looking forward to this trip," said Andy. "Are you?"

"Oh, yes." Sarah successfully removed any traces of doubt from her voice. Sitting cosily with Andy after a nice meal with an impending holiday to look forward to, she should not have had a care in the world. And yet....

Chris could no longer bear the silence and Helen's evasive behaviour. He had been following a policy of leaving her alone, partly to give her space but partly because he was frightened of approaching her, but where was that getting them? At this rate, they would never have a serious conversation again and their life together would either be stuck permanently on hold or it would go into a seriously irreversible decline.

He decided he had to make some sort of move. The deadlock needed to be broken.

Helen was sitting comfortably in the sitting room. The television was on low, but Helen was browsing a magazine and not paying much attention to it. The programme looked interesting. Some trekkers were making their way very slowly up a steep slope. Chris imagined they were probably somewhere in the foothills of the Himalayas, or perhaps the Andes. It looked like hot work in the damp and humid conditions - a real challenge. It was the type of adventure that he really wanted to take part in but feared he would never get round to, and ordinarily he would have settled down to watch the efforts of the young people living his life for him. Watching others doing what he would really like to be doing was just about better than nothing. However, he had not gone to the living room to watch others realise his dream for him. He had an important project in the here and now to attend to. He was much too nervous to embark on the task of recording the programme, so he sat down on the other end of the settee in the hope that he wouldn't have his head bitten off.

He had tried – of that there was no doubt. He had brought in tea freshly brewed in the best pot accompanied by the best china in the house and there were biscuits arranged as carefully as they would have been in any of the upmarket hotels not very far from the house. If there were any more he could have done, he hadn't been able to think of it.

There was no reaction from Helen and the tray sat forlornly on the small table midway between them.

"A cup of tea?" ventured Chris bravely.

Helen looked up from her magazine. She seemed amazed to see both Chris and the teashop scene in front of her, although she must have heard Chris come in with the cups and saucers rattling on the tray.

She smiled at Chris. It was his turn to be surprised now. It had been a long time since he had seen her smile like that. The last time was weeks ago, he thought, although it hadn't actually been that long.

"Tea and biscuits. Chris, how thoughtful," gushed Helen with inordinate enthusiasm. It was if he'd brought in a diamond set in a ring on a silver salver to announce long term intentions. Chris was delighted with her reaction, of course, but also puzzled. It was, after all, nothing more than a pot of tea and a plate of digestives.

Peter Cropper

Helen switched off the television and looked closely at the tray. "That's beautifully arranged," she beamed. "We could be in that really posh hotel up the road.... what's it called again?" She then went on to explain how a friend of hers had told her she had recently been to take afternoon tea in a hotel by one of the lakes – she could remember the name of neither the lake nor the hotel – and how much her friend had enjoyed it. Perhaps it was Sue, thought Chris, though that doesn't matter now. "But this is even better," she continued, "because we're in our own little home, just the two of us," and she smiled again and moved much closer to Chris on the settee.

Between sips of tea and mouthfuls of biscuits, Helen talked almost incessantly. She asked Chris about his day and gave him just enough time to outline very sketchily what he had done. She wondered when he was next at Mrs Jackson's and told Chris how wonderful he was to go and help an old lady and keep her company for next to no reward. She then told Chris about an article on the Greek Islands which she had been reading in the magazine and how nice it looked there and would it be possible for her and Chris to go there very soon as a rest, sunshine and, most importantly, quality time together would do them a world of good? Chris was much too astonished to contribute fully to the conversation – not that he was given any time to do so.

"But before all that," said Helen, "I think we should go somewhere a bit closer and a bit more comfortable," and, without further ado, she led a silent and dazed Chris away from the tea party and up the stairs. It was like old times again.

CHAPTER 29

"So, how exactly can I help you?"

The problem of how to persuade Helen to go to see Neil Hunt had seemed insoluble. Chris had been unable to find the confidence needed to bring the subject up, so he tried another approach. He thought he would leave Helen out of the equation and go and see Neil alone.

The first difficulty was that Neil's busy diary dictated that he could only see Chris on one of Helen's days off and Helen increasingly spent free time at home reading and doing housework whether she needed to or not. He'd lost count of the number of times that the Hoover had been left lying round and the furniture polish seemed to spend as much time on the mantelpiece as the collection of ornaments which Helen had brought back as souvenirs from previous trips to France. The pledge and the miniature Eiffel Tower were developing quite a relationship. Had Helen been at work, Chris would have been to see Neil and then would have come back without her knowing it, but, as it was, he had to concoct a story.

He told Helen he had to go home to collect some important papers that he needed. He didn't want to contact Sarah to ask her to post them for all sorts of reasons that he was sure Helen could understand. He intended to sneak in and out without Sarah knowing.

"You just said you needed to go home, but this is your home," protested Helen. Oops!

"Well, yes, of course," blustered Chris. "But, you know what I mean."

Helen's pained expression said, "No, I don't know what you mean, and if you go there you'll bump into Sarah and she'll want you back and she'll keep you there and that will be the end for us."

"If I go now," Chris said quickly, anticipating what Helen was thinking, "I'll be in and out of the house while Sarah is at work. I'll be really careful not to disturb anything and she'll never know I've been there. That'll be best for everyone, don't you think?"

"Suppose," said Helen quietly.

Chris had felt surprisingly calm as he drove the forty or so miles to the café where Neil had suggested meeting. The feeling that he was doing it entirely for Helen's benefit more than counterbalanced any guilt he might have felt at deceiving her. It was actually for both their benefits, of course, but that was by the way.

The café was halfway, but in Chris' favour. This guy must think a lot of Sue if he's willing to do this for someone he hardly knows, or perhaps doesn't know at all, thought Chris. Or maybe he does know Helen through Sue? Mind you, if that's the case, it's strange Helen had never mentioned him – or Sue, come to that. If he wasn't careful, his thinking would start to confuse him, and he wanted a clear head. He relaxed into the drive. It was a pleasant, partly sunny morning, although clouds did look rather threatening over some of the hills. The weather didn't know which way to go at the moment though to Chris it seemed that the remaining clouds would soon break up, both literally and metaphorically.

When he arrived at the café, Neil was already there, sipping a large cup of coffee. He stood up immediately and shook the other man's hand.

"Chris O'Neill?"

"That's me. And you're Neil Hunt, I presume."

Bowing Out

"Correct." The two men completed the formal greeting, as befitted the seriousness of their meeting.

"Sorry I'm late. Tractors and stuff," said Chris as he sat down. Neil followed suit. Chris was embarrassed by the fact that he had not been there to greet Neil because he knew he had driven the shorter distance, so he felt a fabricated excuse was in order.

"Don't you worry about that. It's one of the hazards of country driving, but it's more than offset by the scenery round here. That view as you come down from the top of the hill on the main road! Besides, I've not been here long myself, and I have a book to keep me company, as ever." Neil waved a paperback at Chris and smiled warmly. "Tea or coffee?" he added as a young girl dressed as a Victorian waitress came over.

Chris felt at ease. First impressions are lasting impressions, and there was nothing you could say about Neil at this stage other than that he was a thoroughly nice bloke.

How could he help? Chris considered this very simple but very pertinent question very carefully. It would all have to be done second hand, so to speak.

"Sue Mason has told you about the problems Helen's having, hasn't she?"

Neil nodded, but what he said next added a distinct note of pessimism. "She has outlined them, yes, but before we start, I should point out that it's not normal practice to even attempt to treat or help someone in their absence. There's the issue of confidentiality, you understand. I think that the thing the two of us could perhaps do would be to explore ways in which *your* life with Helen could be made more palatable in the light of Helen's behaviour."

Neil picked up on Chris' tangible disappointment. The therapist's stated reluctance to talk about Helen suggested to Chris that he would just have to put up with her and adjust *his* life, behaviour and outlook accordingly. Neil could see that Chris thought that the exercise was doomed to failure from the very start.

Neil continued. "However, Sue is a good friend of mine and I know how worried she has been after the incident in the shop. You're the person who spends most time with Helen, so providing you with some insights, albeit theoretical, is, I think, the best way forward, given that Helen isn't here."

It was apparent to Chris that Neil really did want Helen to be there but, on the other hand, he had known in advance she wouldn't be and that had not prevented him from giving up his valuable time and driving over forty miles to talk to somebody he had never met. That said, the situation was surely far from hopeless and Chris wasn't wasting his time. Buoyed by this thinking, he began to feel a little better.

"Sue said you'd identified the problems as possible borderline something or other." Chris was frustrated with himself because he couldn't remember the full name of Helen's alleged problem even though he had been trying hard to do so on the way over. It was one of those things he couldn't make lodge in his memory bank, like South American capital cities.

Neil smiled. "Borderline Personality Disorder."

"That's it," said Chris. He clicked his fingers in an inappropriately exaggerated gesture. "What's all that about? I've never heard of it."

"What we'll do," said Neil, "is talk through the basic theory in layman's terms. However, I would point out that I'm giving you textbook theory and obviously all people are different. We all have Borderline traits in our personalities, actually, but it's only when these traits become exaggerated that a problem emerges. I can only describe these traits so that we can look at them and see whether they manifest themselves as a problem in this particular situation. Let's start in general terms – would you say she suffered from intense episodic dysphoria?"

Neil immediately realised he had pitched that all wrong, a feeling confirmed by the look on Chris' face. Chris was reminded of an acquaintance of his, a computer expert, who insisted in talking to him in fluent jargon

– probably to show off, Chris had always thought. He might as well have been talking Sanskrit, as might Neil now.

"Sorry," said Neil. "You don't know what I'm talking about, do you?" he added pleasantly.

"No," said Chris.

"My fault. Dysphoria is a state of unease or mental discomfort. As I say, that's something general for you to consider. Is Helen prone to that?"

"If you mean is Helen prone to bouts of unhappiness for no real apparent reason, then I think I would have to say yes."

"Fine. Let me give you something a bit more precise to focus on. Does her self image change according to the reactions she receives from other people – at work, for instance? She's a barmaid, isn't she?"

"She is, yes. She works in a small country pub. I've not seen her at work much. But I get the impression that on the shifts she does, there aren't usually enough punters there to give her conflicting reactions."

Neil nodded sagely. He thought that was a sensible, well thought out answer, but it didn't help them make a lot of progress. He introduced another idea.

"Timekeeping," said Neil. "Has that become a problem recently?"

Chris considered carefully. He recalled one or two occasions when Helen was rather slow out of the blocks for the start of her shift, but he didn't think it was a particular problem.

"Obviously it's a bit of problem because she's a woman," offered Chris. Neil looked at Chris over the top of his glasses. He clearly wasn't impressed with the attempt at humour. "But," Chris added hastily and with suitable seriousness in order to redeem himself, "I don't think her timekeeping has altered either way recently, to be honest."

Neil thought for a few moments. "Push and pull behaviour is another sign," he said.

"Pardon?"

"Sorry, my fault again. Let me explain a little more clearly. People with BPD need dependable relationships, yet they cannot always admit this need and they often push away those people who are closest to them. They pull them into a relationship, then push them away – hence push and pull."

This sounded more like it to Chris. "I do think Helen falls into this category. Her behaviour can fluctuate wildly. Sometimes she's all over me, and at other times she doesn't want to know. Push and pull – they're opposites, aren't they?"

"Exactly."

Neil paused for thought again before continuing. "Impulsive behaviour – that's another common trait. Compulsive eating, shopping, gambling – do those things ring any bells?"

"Shopping – I wouldn't know. What man in his right mind would go shopping with a woman?" Chris chuckled at his little witticism.

Neil's expression suggested again that jokes were inappropriate in the current forum and that if Chris were intending to be flippant, he would finish both his coffee and their conversation and drive straight back to County Durham. Having decided to give Chris the benefit of the doubt, he added, "Have you noticed anything unusual that Helen has brought into the house from a shopping trip, for instance? Has there been a sudden increase in the size of her wardrobe? What about her appetite? Have her eating habits changed? Alcohol intake – is that any different? Is there more food and drink in the house these days?"

It was a lot to digest, and the café fell silent. For the first time since he had arrived, Chris looked at his surroundings. The café doubled up as a gift shop and he spotted some wooden toys and a small rocking horse which, like the young waitress, seemed to have been transported from another era. He also noticed an elderly couple sitting in the far corner, and he hoped they hadn't heard anything. It was unlikely that they had as he and Neil had been talking very quietly throughout and there was a little low piped music which Chris also hadn't noticed. There was nobody else in the café and the waitress had not reappeared from the kitchen.

Chris thought for a couple of minutes but he was unable to think of examples of what Neil was suggesting. He had always thought that the nature of Helen's job could give her the opportunity to drink more, but she always drove back from the pub and you needed your wits about you on those lanes in the dark. He very much hoped she wasn't trying to drive home under the influence. Police hiding behind hedges with cameras weren't a problem, but some of the bends were sharp and there were some hefty old trees by the roadside that nobody in their right mind would argue with. He winced as he thought of horrible possibilities, and he knew that, for his own peace of mind, he would have to find some way of checking this out with Helen. That promised to be a fun conversation.

"That episode in the butcher's shop when Helen lost her temper over something really quite trivial. Would you say that's typical?"

It may be trivial to you, but that's my tea you're talking about, Chris wanted to say, but he stopped himself in time. He'd already seen what happened when needless humour was introduced. Another witticism like that and Neil would probably be straight out of the door.

"To be honest, I would say she's always got the potential for losing her temper, yes," replied Chris after a moment's thought. "When I'm with Helen, I very often feel that it's like treading on eggshells. I'm sure you know what I mean."

"Interesting. I do, yes." There was another pause, and then Neil played his trump card – the one that would really set Chris thinking.

"There is one other thing I'd like you to think about," he said. He spoke even more quietly than he had before. "Have you seen any evidence of self harm – self inflicted cuts or wounds, for instance, attempted overdoses or even," and now he lowered his voice even further so there was absolutely no chance of being overheard, "attempts at suicide?"

Chris looked startled. He was disturbed by the suggestion that what Helen allegedly "had" could manifest itself in such behaviour. He was both unwilling and unable to think of these possibilities so he said, rather too quickly, "no, nothing like that."

There was another silence, longer than before. Neil had said his piece. He had nothing more to say because he thought that Chris would not be able to provide any more useful information before he had had a chance to reflect and think at some length. He was right - Chris hadn't a clue what to say next. Neil's last revelation had rendered him speechless.

It was the therapist who broke the silence. "To be honest, Chris, I don't think we can go much further at the moment. You've given me a picture of Helen's behaviour, but, to be frank with you, it's up to her to do something about it if she's concerned. You are in charge of your behaviour and, of course, the same thing applies to Helen. As I've explained, what you need to do is consider what your problem is with the situation as it stands. How is it affecting you? After all, you're the one who's talking to me about it."

There are more questions than answers, thought Chris. "Thanks a lot for your time, Neil. That's been most helpful and I do appreciate your help. Another coffee?"

Chris found he had plenty to think about on the drive home. He tried to take a break from the seriousness of it all by distracting himself with the radio and admiring the scenery, but neither tactic worked. He could not get the conversation with Neil out of his mind. He didn't really know how to play the scene when he arrived home. Of course he couldn't tell Helen where he had been or what had been said, so he supposed that just about the only thing he could do would be to monitor Helen's behaviour to see if it fitted in with what Neil had told him. But if or when it did, what did he intend to do then?

When he arrived back, Helen was out. A note on the living room floor announced she was out with a friend. Chris assumed it might be Sue Mason, but there was no indication either way.

A thought struck him. While the issue was fresh in his mind, this could be a good opportunity to check out BPD on the internet to substantiate what he had learned during his discussion with Neil.

He went upstairs and fired up the computer, being careful to leave the bedroom door open so that if he heard Helen coming back in he could effortlessly switch to another site in the time it took her to track him down.

The first thing he noticed was the title of a book which the website recommended – "Stop walking on eggshells". He remembered that was an expression he had used earlier that day to describe his life with Helen. He settled down to study the website, convinced it would offer him invaluable information.

He read a quote from a Borderline sufferer. "Being a borderline feels like eternal hell. Nothing less. Pain, anger, confusion, hurt, never knowing how I'm gonna feel from one minute to the next. Hurting because I hurt those who I love. Feeling misunderstood. Analyzing everything. Nothing gives me pleasure."

There was more, but he felt he had read enough of that particular quote. It all sounded extremely grim and he felt very sorry for Helen if that was how she was feeling. He realised why she tried his patience and why she would continue to do so, but he knew he must be sympathetic. Surely anyone with any degree of feeling and compassion would be sympathetic towards anyone in this position, let alone their life partner.

Is that how Helen could now be described, or was that still a description of Sarah? There was that quandary again. It simply refused to go away.

He carried on and read the caveat. "Be very careful about diagnosing yourself or others. In fact, don't do it."

Peter Cropper

That was fine. He hadn't done it. He was merely backing up what the expert had told him. "These traits must be long-standing (lasting years) and persistent. And they must be intense." The last word was in italics.

Chris hadn't known Helen for years so he knew neither how long she had been suffering nor, indeed, for how long she would continue to suffer. And how intense is intense? Intense compared with what or whom? Perhaps it was time to recontact Sue to glean a little information on Helen's recent past. It would be polite to get back in touch with Sue in any case to thank her again for putting him in touch with Neil.

He decided finally to read extracts from a book used by therapists to make mental health diagnoses.

"Frantic efforts to avoid real or imagined abandonment." In the short time they had been together he had seen evidence of this. On one occasion when Chris had been going into town, Helen seemed beside herself with worry. She had physically grabbed Chris as he was about to walk out of the door. Chris had been unable to convince Helen he'd be back within the hour and she'd finished up going with him on what was a routine trawl through the streets. She had loitered and, much to Chris' frustration, the sequence of errands had taken twice as long as it should have done.

"A pattern of unstable and intense interpersonal relationships characterized by alternating between extremes of idealization and devaluation." Chris thought back to the afternoon's discussion and, again, he was almost certain that this was something which he had mentioned to Neil. "At any particular moment, one is either Good or EVIL. There is no in between; no gray area....people are idealized one day; totally devalued and dismissed the next." Again, Helen seemed to qualify.

"When the idealized person finally disappoints either the idol is banished to the dungeon, or the borderline banishes himself in order to preserve the all-good image of the other person." That fitted, too.

Chris felt his head starting to spin, so he concluded that was probably enough for one day. He glanced downstairs

Bowing Out

and outside the house outside to check he was still safe and then he printed off the relevant pages. They could provide a starting point to a fruitful discussion with Sue.

"In fact, I'll give Sue a ring now," he said to himself, but he stopped when he remembered that she might well be out with Helen. Instead he hid the printout very carefully so that it wouldn't be found on one of Helen's famous housework sprees, put everything to one side mentally, shut down the computer and went to watch something far less cerebral on the television.

CHAPTER 30

Andy, you are going to have to do something about your timekeeping, thought Sarah.

With her luggage waiting in the hall, Sarah sat in the living room, bored. She was in limbo. There was no point starting anything as Andy could arrive at any moment, and in any case she couldn't think of anything that she needed to do. She didn't want to ring him on his mobile since she was sure he was on his way and, even though she felt some annoyance, she was a little fearful of pestering him. She was rather puzzled at these two contradictory thoughts going through her head, but she decided that it was because the relationship was at that delicate early stage and she didn't want to jeopardise it. Although she told herself she shouldn't, she went upstairs to her dressing table, took out the carefully concealed packet and lit a cigarette – just the one, just to relieve the tedium, you understand.

She'd smoked about a half when she heard a car tear up the road and come to a sudden stop outside her house. Hastily, she stubbed out the offending article and disposed of it safely before popping a mint in her mouth. She wafted the air round the room as best as she could. There was no point in getting the holiday off on the wrong foot.

Andy stood at the door, full of apologies. Sarah smiled and said that it didn't really matter, but the smile

Bowing Out

was unconvincing, and it was apparent to Andy that she wasn't impressed. He wished he'd brought some flowers, but where would the logic have been in leaving a bunch of flowers in an empty house? He'd have to think of something to make it up to her on the way down south.

"Sorry, love," said Andy. "Traffic."

That old chestnut of an apology! It was exactly the sort of thing Chris would say.

Whether it was true or not, Sarah could see no mileage in allowing Andy's lateness to become an issue. She said, "No problem. You can't do much about traffic, can you?" She might have added, "It would have been courteous if you'd phoned, though," but she didn't. Instead, she asked, "Cup of tea, or do you want to be off?" with the stress definitely placed on the latter option.

Sarah was quiet as the motorway miles slipped by. Andy thought she was sulking, but he was wrong. She was thinking.

She was thinking that another trip away like this was another nail in the coffin for her marriage, and she wasn't sure that this was what she wanted. Was she "over Chris", as the saying went? Surely she couldn't be, because it was only five minutes since he had made his spectacular Scottish exit. There had been no recent contact between her and Chris, but what did that really mean? Had Chris decided that he wanted to let the relationship die a natural death, or, given his insistence of having some space and time to himself, was he leaving his options open? Sarah thought it might be a case of "no news is good news". She also fell to wondering why, or indeed how, she had let matters drift. She had never thought to take the initiative in putting things right. She could not recall ever phoning and coming straight to the point and saying, "Chris we need to talk," and now, for the first time, she wondered why she had never made that call. All this uncertainty was not what she needed as she set off on another break. The case in the boot was not the only baggage she was taking with her.

"Are you all right?" A simple question from the driver's seat interrupted her musing. Andy had never known Sarah be so quiet.

"Yes, fine."

"You're not still annoyed that I was late, are you?" Andy sounded anxious, as if he had committed a heinous crime for which he felt he could never be forgiven. Sarah gave up staring at the traffic in front and turned to look at him. He looked like a nervous young pupil in a school where being sent to stand outside the headmaster's study was still a terrifying prospect. At the same time he looked like a man very much subordinate to the woman in an established relationship. Andy's body language suggested that he knew who was boss in their partnership and this persuaded Sarah that she was in a position of some power. She was in charge.

"No, I'm not annoyed," said Sarah, but Andy didn't believe her. He felt very vulnerable. He regressed and became considerably younger. He had a vivid memory of what car journeys with his parents used to be like all those years ago, and he said something his dad might have said to him when he was about ten or eleven.

"Let's play a game."

Sarah's expression said that two intelligent adults on a car journey would not choose to play games. Their world was full of important matters to discuss. But Andy soon got into his stride.

"Look at where all these lorries have come from. Which one has come the furthest, or has the furthest to go home? Fraserburgh," he said excitedly without stopping to draw breath as a large refrigerated lorry came into view on the opposite carriageway. "That'll take some beating, don't you think? I don't think he'll be home in time for tea."

What a ridiculous game, thought Sarah, who, as well as finding it childish, also didn't know as much as Andy about where anywhere was in relation to anywhere else. Clearly Andy didn't know, or had chosen to ignore the fact, that most women didn't spend their time poring over maps like some men did. Because she didn't particularly want to show her ignorance, she said, "Fraserburgh. Yes." It sounded Scottish – Hughie Fraser and all that – but whereabouts in Scotland it was, was anybody's guess.

A couple of minutes later Andy said, "D. Stevens of Wick. That's got to be the winner. You can't go much further than that without falling off the end. It's game, set and match to Mr Stevens, I think."

Oh, that's a shame, thought Sarah. I was just starting to enjoy that.

"There's another little game we used to play with car number plates," said Andy, a couple of minutes later. "Let me explain how it works."

"Can I please pass on that one and pull all my toenails out one by one?" asked Sarah.

"Queue. Caution". Andy looked up and read the electronic message on the gantry. "You know, I'm so glad we've been given that valuable piece of information, because the fact that we've only gone about a mile in the last fifteen minutes is no indication whatsoever that we're stuck in a motorway queue. I'm so pleased to have been put in the picture." Sarah winced. Andy sounded exactly like someone else with whom she had previously enjoyed the delights of motorway congestion. Once she herself had enthusiastically practised the art of subtle sarcasm, but now she preferred not to. It had the potential to be damaging. Of course, sometimes she couldn't help herself – like if someone insisted on playing silly games to pass the time on the motorway, for instance.

Having crawled as far as the next service area, Andy, without consultation, pulled off the road.

"So you think we might take some time here to wait for the queue to subside?" asked Sarah.

"Brilliant, Einstein," replied Andy. Sarah didn't dare to suggest that taking a break and then getting back on the motorway with a whole host of other travellers who had the same idea might just be postponing the inevitable and might be more stressful in the long run than staying on the motorway and brazening it out. Instead, she ushered them both past some rather busy amusement arcades towards a possibly overpriced café. There was no need for Andy's sarcasm and every need for tea to calm frayed nerves. The café was for non smokers only, Sarah observed. One method Sarah could have used her to ease her own frayed nerves was therefore denied her.

"How's your tea?" she asked after they'd settled down at a table near the window.

"Warm and wet," replied Andy with a note of irritation in his voice. "But, when all is said and done, it is quite difficult to get tea wrong." It was déjà vu all over again.

CHAPTER 31

Chris returned from one of the local rambles he liked best. Orrest Head, a little way out of Windermere, was where Alfred Wainwright, the walker's guru and king of the Lakeland fells, came in. On his first escape to the Lakes from industrial Lancashire Mr Wainwright climbed the little hill which would many years later become one of Chris' favourites, and he was immediately captivated by the wonderful scenery and, in particular, the view. He considered it far too great a reward for the small effort needed to reach the top. The full length of Windermere, England's largest lake, dominates the scene while behind are many of Lakeland's finest mountains including Scafell Pike, the highest ground in England. Chris and Sarah had tried to climb the Pike once from Great Langdale but the miles were long and the weather closed in and even though they had completed the majority of the walk, Sarah had announced with a large degree of certainty that she could not continue. Inwardly, Chris had been very frustrated but he was a gentleman, and it was obvious there would have been no point dragging his girlfriend kicking and screaming over the final bouldery stretch in the swirling mist which would have denied them a view from the summit. They had returned to one of the pubs at the head of the valley and, over a bowl of steaming soup accompanied by a crusty roll, they had vowed to return one day and conquer the recalcitrant peak.

They never did carry out that promise. Perhaps they never would.

Mr Wainwright had never previously known that such natural beauty existed and his lifelong love affair with Westmorland, Cumberland and the far flung reaches of Lancashire began. It led to the walkers' guidebooks which had pride of place on the bookshelf in Chris' house – that is, the house he shared (or should that be used to share?) with Sarah.

Chris had two options, and today he had chosen the longer one. Rather than a quick sprint up and down, having reached the top he had carried on away from the town over the gently undulating terrain that he loved so much. The higher fells out to the east disappeared and reappeared behind the folds of the undulations but in their temporary absence there were fine trees to admire as well as the artistry involved in the dry stone walls which had withstood the ravages of the local weather for more years than anyone could remember. Chris had then returned past the farm along the narrow lane where traffic seldom, if ever, ventured before taking the well trodden path at the base of the hill. The route passed some fine residences. Chris always wondered about the lives of the people who lived there – probably retired types with no money worries who had either come to the Lakes to see out their twilight years or who had made a fortune responding to the needs of visitors over the years. Chris asked himself whether he was a visitor or a resident these days. It was not an easy question to answer.

Although the weather had clearly taken a sabbatical and it was one of those nondescript dull days where the sun had no intention of poking through the greyness but, equally, it could not be bothered raining, Chris felt very refreshed as he arrived home and went towards the kettle, stopping at Helen who looked very comfortable in the living room. She greeted him with as charming a smile as Chris had ever seen on her face. He gave her a peck on the cheek.

"Have you had a good walk?"

"Great, thanks." He nearly added, "you should have come. You would have enjoyed it," but he stopped himself. He had asked Helen if she wanted to go with him but the reception had been frosty. Helen had explained in no uncertain terms that she would go into town instead as she didn't enjoy walking at all. Chris knew that this was patent nonsense but, thanks to Sue's friend Neil, he knew a little about Helen's condition now and he had also learnt something from what he had downloaded from the internet. He didn't think making an issue out of this was the best way to continue. He just had to go and hope that Helen would have changed her mood by the time he returned. This was certainly the case. Perhaps it had something to do with what lay open on her lap.

"I've been to the travel agent," she announced in a childlike voice, looking really pleased with herself. "Look!" she said, refolding the brochure so that the front cover was visible and holding it up for Chris to see.

"Greece, Cyprus, Majorca, Gran Canaria, Lanzarote, Tenerife, The Algarve," read Chris. "No shortage of sunshine in there. Does the west coast of Scotland not get a mention?" he added, for his own amusement.

"It doesn't," smiled Helen, seemingly oblivious to Chris' attempts at humour.

"Would you like a drink?"

"I'll make one. I'll bring us some coffee, then I'd very much like you to come and sit down here with me and we'll pick somewhere we can go. We've said we'd like a trip to sunnier climes, haven't we?" Indeed they had, and Chris smiled to himself as he recalled what happened the last time the subject had been put on the agenda.

After Helen had returned from the kitchen with two mugs of coffee and the biscuit tin so that Chris could replace some of the fat that he had burned off, she looked even more delighted than before. "Look at the choice in here," she squealed. "It'd be virtually impossible not to find somewhere nice to go," and after Chris had sat down she thrust the brochure's contents page into his face.

Chris focussed on the page. There was indeed a long list of places and with the exception of one or two names, Chris had never seen any of them before. "Is there a map I can match them up to?" he asked, although he wasn't sure how much better informed he would be with a map, since this was a part of the world with which he was very unfamiliar.

"I imagine so," enthused Helen with an expression on her face that said, "but I'm far too excited to find it. Can you, please?"

Chris had realised neither that Greece was so big nor that it and its satellite islands boasted 9,000 miles of coastline. The holiday company said it wasn't surprising that, with that length of coast, they were constantly finding hitherto undiscovered locations to which they could send clients.

"It's a big country," said Chris, "which I think means we should be able to find somewhere quite quiet away from the main resorts, particularly as the kids are now back at school." The last remark made him smile. "The weather will be hot, but not blisteringly so like it is in high summer." He quickly thumbed through the brochure. "Helen, I think you may be on to a winner here."

Helen squealed with delight again, flung her arms round her boyfriend's neck and gave him a big kiss. "If that's the case, I'll just open the brochure at random and let's see where fate will take us, shall we?"

Chris didn't really do impulsiveness like this, and it made him recall the most impulsive thing he'd ever done. It suddenly seemed that leaving Sarah in Scotland had happened about twenty minutes ago, and he was about to lose himself in thoughts of whether it had been the right thing to do and what Sarah was doing at this precise moment when Helen noisily interrupted him.

"I know what we'll do." She seemed to be shouting very loudly. "Chris, you pick a number and whichever place is on that page, then that's where we'll go."

Chris would have preferred a more measured, scientific approach but, thanks to his research on Helen's condition, he knew by now that if he were to reject Helen's suggestion, she might well go off the deep end. Because he didn't want this to happen, and because the idea of a bit of sunshine before the Lakeland winter (would he still be there then?) set in was appealing, he said, "83, please Helen." He sounded as if he had been asked to pick a number on a TV game show.

If fate were allowed to take a hand in this way, they were off to the north eastern part of Crete. They looked at the page in the brochure and they both liked parts of what they saw. There were six small photographs covering five resorts, but the first two pictures looked like a "spot the difference" competition. They could have been anywhere in southern Europe. Colourful umbrellas ran the length of a golden sandy beach, and all the holidaymakers were flat out on sun beds, presumably because it was too hot to do anything else. The sky in both pictures was cloudless and Chris and Helen could almost feel the heat radiating from the page. There would be a real price to pay for any of those holidaymakers who hadn't slapped on the most powerful sun block in the universe.

It mustn't have been quite as hot in the next photograph because some people had summoned up sufficient energy to stroll along the beach. They were passing brightly coloured umbrellas and sun beds occupied by less active people frying contentedly.

So far, Chris' journey across page 83 left him with the impression that "Crete" was Greek for "sun bed city". It didn't look like the type of place that he would really enjoy, but Helen was enraptured.

"Sun, sand and sangria," she said, with great gusto.

"I think you'll find that's Spain."

"Whatever. It'll be great. I'll be taking my briefest bikini, of course."

Chris saw this in his mind's eye and then his eyes wandered further across the page.

Photo number four showed a harbour. The quayside was full of shops and tavernas, and further buildings were stacked up on the hillside behind. It looked like a white, and hot, version of one of those Cornish fishing villages of which Chris was so fond. Cafes by the sea were protected from the searing heat by ubiquitous colourful umbrellas and boats were moored nearby. One or two large palm trees completed the scene.

"Whoever owns the umbrella factory on Crete must be a very wealthy man," observed Chris.

"I think they call them parasols, love," ventured Helen. "They don't need umbrellas. It *never* rains."

Photo five was of a smaller village. It showed a fishing boat in the foreground with a harbour behind. A church stood at the water's edge. There were some low hills behind the village which might afford the chance to do some walking either early in the morning before the sun's heat got to work or in the relative coolness of the evening. The blurb for this place caught Chris' eye, mentioning a "village feel" and "low key nightlife" and "relaxing holiday in beautiful surroundings". There was a stark contrast between this and the town of Malia, a town full of tourist shops, hotels and restaurants and with, according to the brochure, more bars and discos than you could expect to visit during the course of a single holiday.

Chris thought the village of Elounda would fit the bill perfectly especially if, as he assumed it was, the quiet, curved beach with the rock pools in the photograph next to the information was somewhere nearby. It was the closest thing to his favourite beach in Scotland with added sunshine that he could envisage.

"It's quite clear to me where we should go," said Helen. "It's got to be Malia, hasn't it?"

CHAPTER 32

Martin arrived back at the caravan at the usual time, unlocked the door, glanced at the mess he had left on the floor that morning, and, having decided to ignore it, picked his way through it to the kettle. He made a cup of tea and carried it over to the window seat. With the door of the caravan open, he sat and listened to the birds – the only sound he could hear. He again thought of the difference between this life and the one he had left behind, and he was as convinced as ever that he had made the right decision. He loved the independence that living alone and undisturbed brought, and the peace and quiet. The contrast with the flat in a questionable part of town which he used to occupy was a stark one. Here he never heard wailing police sirens, intolerably loud rock music from the strange young man in the flat nearby or young drunks bawling their way home in the early hours of Saturday or Sunday. Noise pollution from traffic? He had heard the farmer's tractor pulling a trailer up the track a couple of times last weekend, if that qualified.

It was a great place to live and work – simple as that. The work in the forest was physical so he was usually tired when he got home from work, but so what? He could rest and recuperate as long as he wanted. He was answerable to nobody.

The mess on the floor which, in truth, amounted to much more than just this morning's mess, was a bit of a nuisance. He had always been a particularly untidy person, but even he thought that the lack of order in the van was becoming a problem. He thought that the only thing he was lacking was a cleaner, but in the absence of any domestics willing to find their way to his caravan, he knew he would have to do it himself. But he'd do it in his own time, and certainly not before he'd finished his tea.

After he had finally persuaded the last few drops from the pot, he resigned himself to clearing up. It probably wouldn't be as demanding as it looked.

He picked up a shirt that hadn't seen an iron for a very long time, two odd socks and a sweatshirt which he must have discarded about a week ago. Underneath were a plate and a couple of mugs which, had he left them any longer, could probably have walked to the sink. There was a ten day old newspaper which he'd bought especially because he'd heard it contained an interesting article about a conservation project in a remote part of Wales run by someone he used to know vaguely. He also found a few items of mail which he had collected from the post office a couple of days earlier. He prided himself that he had never known anyone else who had used the poste restante facility.

He looked languidly through the post, although he didn't expect to find any interesting personal mail because so few people knew where he was. He had kept a select handful of special people, such as Andrea, informed of his whereabouts, but he had put many of his casual friends and acquaintances in abeyance. Either he would surprise them one day and if they then welcomed him back it would show they were really interested in him, or he would forget about them. He couldn't see any reason to decide now.

There was nothing from Andrea. It had been a long time since she had written.

One piece of paper caught his eye. He hadn't collected it from the post office. He had found it attached to the van one day after a hard session moving wood around. He remembered reading the note very briefly at the time,

Bowing Out

then putting it down to look at again later. He hadn't done so, of course. This time he read it properly.

Martin,

Chris O'Neill here – we used to play five a side in the good old days.

I'm in the area and wonder if you fancy meeting up?

I'm staying at Low Rigg B and B in the village, or you might find me waiting to buy you a pint in the pub.

Regards

Chris

Chris O'Neill? Chris O'Neill? Martin thought for a short while, then he realised who he was. He was one of Pete James' mates, wasn't he? Wasn't he the guy who taught history at the same school as Pete? Martin thought it surprising that Chris would get in touch with him now. Chris certainly wasn't on Martin's list of "special people" and, while Martin couldn't recall there ever being any problems between the two men, he really hadn't expected to hear from Chris again once he had moved on leaving Chris, and the others, firmly stuck in the rat race.

Anyway, how the hell did Chris know this was his caravan? Had he tracked him down? Was he so desperate to find him? It was all rather mysterious, if you asked Martin.

Mind you, Martin decided, he'll be back at school by now. How long ago had he left the note? Maybe he got bored during those long holidays and it was just a flying visit. He may be back another day – otherwise, forget him.

CHAPTER 33

The tension which had built up between Sarah and Andy lasted the rest of the journey, but it evaporated as if by magic when they arrived at the cottage.

Driving through the gate, the little house with its patio and immaculately arranged garden furniture was on the left and the garden stretched away from the house on the right. The lawn had been mown sometime in the last day or two, the leaves on the trees were just beginning to turn, and sheep grazed in the field beyond the garden fence.

They stepped into their temporary home and Sarah immediately fell in love with it. The open plan hallway was bright and airy, and a door to the right led into the lounge. The walls, like those in the hallway, were painted white and there was a red settee facing a log fire. No expense had been spared, and Sarah saw a new Sony stereo as well as a wall mounted plasma TV screen. In the middle of the oatmeal coloured carpet was a glass coffee table on which stood a vase of flowers which were complemented by healthy house plants on pedestals.

Exploring further, Sarah found the kitchen. It was modern with blue gingham curtains and gleaming white units which contrasted with black granite work surfaces. The chrome kettle looked as though it had only just been taken out of its box, and the lovingly selected crockery was adorned with pictures of bluebells. Next to a large plate of custard creams covered in cling film was a welcome note with a number to contact in case of problems or queries.

The oatmeal carpet leading up the stairs matched that in the lounge. The bedroom was plainly furnished, and Sarah noticed the bluebells again, this time embroidered on the sheets. The blue and white theme was repeated on an ornamental jug and bowl, and the smell of the lavender sachets in the double wardrobe was very noticeable.

Sarah's final port of call was the bathroom. It was a bit chilly in there, but the gleaming white tiles accentuated the fact that the owners took great pride in keeping the cottage clean and spotless.

Andy brought in the box of provisions and went to weave his magic at the kettle. He made two cups of coffee and went to look for Sarah. He found her looking relaxed lying on the king sized bed. "Come here and tell me what a great time we're going to have here."

Meanwhile, Mr O'Neill was having a little less good fortune than Mrs O'Neill on the holiday front.

There had been the obvious conflict of interests regarding location. Chris led a discussion which had tried to resolve this, but very little progress had been made by bedtime. Chris suggested that each party sleep on it so that the vital decision could be made with clear heads in the morning.

Of course, Chris suspected something when he woke up a little later than usual in an empty bed. Helen had gone walkabout. That was potentially very bad news, but the uncertainty did not last, because just as Chris was contemplating a stroll into town to look for her, the door was flung open and Helen burst in.

"You'll never guess what I've done!"

Unfortunately, Chris feared that he could. "Go on, tell me what you've done," he sighed.

"Our Greek holiday is booked."

"And where exactly are we going?" asked Chris, even though he was sure he knew the answer.

"We're off to Malia, of course. Sun and fun here we come!"

Chris was unhappy, and unsure of what to say or do next. He had persuaded himself that Helen had agreed to defer a decision, but then she had gone off and booked the holiday on her own volition. Was this another sign of this BPD that she had? How should he react such that he didn't make the situation worse?

He thought that the brief chat with Sue Mason that he had promised himself might make the situation clearer. For now, he resolved to say nothing.

"Have you seen how much information we've got here?" Andy's enthusiasm was exaggerated. He was still trying to atone for the atmosphere, for which he deemed himself responsible, which had prevailed on the way down. He thought a zealous attitude would do the trick. He pulled one of the small books from the folder. "This one book alone contains 20 walks within about 15 miles of here. Look at the map – footpaths everywhere. Then there's Ross, or another small town called Ledbury or Hereford if you prefer the big city…"

"Would that be a big city with shops?"

"Not a big city with shops as you might understand it, but I'm sure there'll be people there willing to take your money off you," replied Andy, warmly. "It strikes me we've got the best of both worlds here."

Their short stay proved the point. Andy had his walking - along riverbanks, through meadows, past bushes with fruit crying out to be picked. He remembered a church sermon he had heard when he was a small boy where the vicar held up a blackberry pie and announced, "Free gift from God." Andy smiled when he recalled how he couldn't work out how the pastry had come down from heaven and how, although he had a suspicion that the vicar was just referring to the fruit, he couldn't be absolutely sure. He was pleased that he had thought it sensible not to check by asking his older brother.

Bowing Out

Sarah walked with him and enjoyed her time in the country, but she found one of Andy's routes in particular a bit long and she found time spent pottering round the shops in Hereford more enjoyable. Andy accompanied her for a while but he found he was unable to last the pace, and so he disappeared to look at the cathedral and to baulk at the price charged to see the Mappa Mundi before meeting Sir Edward Elgar who was standing quite still on his plinth nearby. Later he linked up with Sarah again for a lazy pint of local cider. The drive back to the cottage along idyllic country lanes was delightful.

It doesn't get much better than this, thought Andy.

What's the catch? thought Sarah

She's done it again, thought Chris, as Helen briefly appeared. She's got the wrong clothes on. She's not going to a society ball; she's going to stand behind a bar and serve drinks. What's that all about?

Helen disappeared back upstairs to put the finishing touches to her outfit, leaving Chris bemused in the living room. While he was busy trying to work out why she was taking so much time with her appearance, the doorbell rang. A mini tornado swept down the stairs and opened the front door before Chris had a chance to get there.

"Taxi for Wilkinson?"

"That's me. Off we go."

"Hang on!" Chris spoke sharply, and Helen stopped in response. Chris was relieved that he did not have to restrain Helen physically to have his question answered. He would have done so if necessary, but with a witness in the shape of the well built taxi driver, it would probably not have been the best course of action. "Helen, can you please tell me why you're taking a taxi instead of driving to work? You told me yesterday you thought your ankle problem had cleared up and that you were fit enough to drive again. Is that not right?" Two things were preying on Chris' mind – expense and ulterior motives.

"I don't think it's fair that every time I go to work I take the car leaving you without transport, so I thought that now and again I'd get there under my own steam and, as you realise, a bus is not an option." Helen smiled at Chris, and the taxi driver thought it must be really good to have such a thoughtful and considerate wife, and if he looked after Helen well today there could be the chance of a lot of repeat business coming his way…

He watched Helen leaving in the safe hands of Pearson's taxis and then, for the first time, it dawned on him. What had Neil said about Helen being dependent on favourable reactions from the punters? Chris was now sure that Helen was "dressing to impress". What he didn't know was whether she was out to make an impression on the group of customers as a whole or someone specific.

With Helen gone, and with Chris fortuitously in possession of the car keys, it was time to make a phone call. Unless Helen was trying to pull the wool over his eyes with respect to her whereabouts – and he didn't think she was - it was now safe to do so. He was surprised how nervous he felt as he pressed the appropriate numbers.

"Sue Mason."

"Sue, hello, it's Chris. Helen's friend."

"Helen's friend, indeed. Yes, I remember."

"Sue, I wonder if I could ask you a really big favour. Are you by any chance free now for a chat, please?"

Without hesitation, Sue said she was and she suggested a pub a few miles away. Chris didn't know it and Sue's directions sounded complicated, but he wrote them down carefully, followed them successfully and walked into an empty lounge. The only two customers in the pub were two lads playing darts in the bar. It looked like someone had made a fool of him.

"Pint of bitter, please."

The landlord soullessly pulled Chris' beer and charged him an exorbitant price. "Is there a reduction for locals?" Chris nearly asked.

"Thank you. Can I just ask, you've not seen a young lady in here obviously waiting for someone, have you?"

"No, the only other person that's been in here this evening was Greg from just across the road. Been stood up, have you?"

"No, actually." Chris wasn't surprised the pub wasn't busy if customers were treated this way. He felt disinclined to talk to the landlord who, in any case, had returned to his newspaper, so he took his drink to a table near the window and began his vigil. He would give Sue the time it took for him to drink his pint, and then he would decide that someone really had made a fool of him.

Sue cut it fine – there couldn't have been more than a couple of small mouthfuls to go when she arrived. She didn't seem concerned about her lateness and the "sorry" she muttered didn't appear to Chris to be particularly heartfelt. Chris wasn't very pleased and it was all he could do to ask Sue in a civil fashion whether she wanted a drink.

"I've a better idea," she said. "While the weather's decent, why don't we go and sit somewhere nice so that we can have a chat in the fresh air?"

"OK, if you like. Have you somewhere in mind?"

"Finish your drink, jump in your car and follow me."

Chris felt very much in Sue's hands, and he would have to do as she said if he wanted to get anywhere. Mine host winked at Chris as he left. Chris didn't return the farewell gesture.

I suppose she wants to go somewhere completely private so there's no chance of being overheard, thought Chris as he followed Sue through the narrow lanes. "So why have we not met at her house?" he said to himself. Then he realised that might have been because someone else was there who did not want to meet Chris.

Sue clearly knew where she was going, but Chris was becoming disorientated. Only the sun in the western sky gave him any idea of the direction in which they were travelling.

A few minutes later, Chris was surprised to find himself one of the benches at Bowness Pier, where the lake cruises depart. Opposite, the information boards showed the selection of trips available in the morning.

After pleasantries had been dispensed with, Chris broke the ice. He wanted to ask Sue why they had not simply met at the lakeside in the first place, but instead he said, "I had a good chat with Neil."

"I know. He told me."

"So, first, of course, I must thank you for putting me on to him. Without your help, I wouldn't now have an insight into what's up with Helen."

"And what is up with Helen?"

"She's got Borderline Personality Disorder."

"Yes, Neil did mention that."

The conversation was stilted and prospects of its going anywhere did not appear good. Sue shivered. There was a slight chill in the air, but it was a pleasant evening, with just a gentle breeze doing its job. It was the only thing which would keep the midges at bay.

"The thing is," said Chris, "I was thinking you might be able to tell me how long Helen's symptoms, for want of a better word, have been going on, because you've known her longer than I have. I've got a lot of information both from Neil and off the internet, and it says that for BPD symptoms should be intense and long lasting. The problem is, I've not known her that long really, so I can't say whether they are long lasting or not."

Sue didn't look comfortable. She could see some tricky questions coming up, and she would have to think carefully about the answers. However, she did not doubt Chris' integrity. She was sure he wanted to help to solve Helen's problems, and that he wasn't simply interested in prying into Helen's past. Chris, for his part, was keen to glean as much information as he could, but he was unsure as to exactly what he was going to do with it.

"For instance," continued Chris, "the internet spoke of good versus evil. That sounds rather drastic to me, but I suppose that perhaps equates to wildly contrasting behaviour. Can you think of any examples over time?"

Sue waited while a couple passed by with recently acquired supplies from the fish and chip shop. They smelled good.

"Well, obviously I told you about what happened in the butcher's, didn't I? I suppose that's a good example, because she wouldn't normally do that, but other than that, no. As I think I explained at the time, that episode surprised me, but whether you'd call that 'evil', I don't know."

"And you can't think of anything else?"

Sue paused. "Not off the top of my head, no."

"There's the push-pull aspect of relationships, as well," said Chris.

Keep it simple, smartass, thought Sue. "How do you mean?" she asked.

"Does she accept your friendship, and then reject it?" asked Chris. It was his turn to pause now, as a couple of large ice creams went past. "With me, sometimes she's all over me, then the next minute she can't stand being near me. Have you found that?"

Sue looked at Chris and thought it strange that Helen would ever not want to be near him. A slight tendency to pomposity was the only criticism Sue could level against Chris in the short time she had known him. She couldn't find anything to criticise in his looks. She wondered if he would be a gentleman and offer her his jacket – or a protective arm – if she shivered again.

"I suppose what I would say in that respect is that I don't see her on a very consistent basis. Some weeks she might have been round to my place three or four times, and then she'd disappear for a while, and if I tried to contact her she'd either be out, or perhaps unwilling to answer the phone. If I left a message, she wouldn't return it straight away, but she'd get back to me when she was good and ready. I wouldn't necessarily think that was a problem, though. It's just the way Helen operates, I think. Or maybe I'm wrong?"

Chris digested this for a few moments, but before he had chance to pose the next question on his list, Sue asked, "Are you hungry at all? I'm a bit peckish. Fancy a bite to eat at my place?"

Chris didn't make any further progress through his list of questions but, over a plate of cheese and pickle sandwiches, he did learn more about Sue and Sue learned more about him. As he left the pleasant, small house tucked away in a side street close to the pub where he had first met her, Sue said she'd be more than happy to discuss things further, if he'd like to give her a call sometime soon.

He had lost track of time and he returned home later than anticipated. He didn't know whether a barrage of questions or a stony silence would welcome him, but, as it happened, he found an empty house. He didn't beat Helen home by very much, however, and it wasn't long before she came through the front door. Had the same taxi driver brought her back? Chris wasn't certain whether Helen had had a little too much to drink or whether she was just in one of her moods. She might be excited or angry according to reactions she had received at work. If that were the case, Chris hoped it was the former and that she had been paid some compliments – but not the type that were too fulsome.

Helen had enjoyed her work today. It was possibly the most enjoyable job she had ever had, and now that the Bohemian looking guy had come back, the whole package was starting to look even more attractive. She had first noticed him a few weeks ago when he had called in on two separate occasions, but then he had disappeared again. He could have been a summer visitor to the area, of course, but Helen suspected he wasn't, if only because he had the same weatherbeaten complexion as the two guys who almost constantly propped up the bar. That alone was enough to convince her that he lived somewhere locally and that he possibly worked outside, or at least spent a lot of time in the fresh air.

It was just this evening that the Bohemian had reappeared, but instead of taking his drink away to ponder in silence as he had done previously, he had stayed at the bar. Helen thought he seemed to be studying her every move and, in the many quieter interludes, his flattering behaviour drove her to study him as well.

He was tall and powerful, with muscles for a girl to admire. His beard was thick and perhaps a little wilder than it should have been, although he had taken the trouble to trim it a little more carefully than he usually did. Helen wasn't a fan of beards, but this one definitely suited him. She liked his long hair which he was wearing loose tonight, whereas previously he had preferred a ponytail, and his clothes. His dark green t-shirt was tight fitting while his jeans were faded. They had seen better days, yet they suited him as well as his beard did. He had taken some care with his appearance tonight, Helen thought, although he obviously wasn't as debonair as she was.

"It doesn't seem quite as busy tonight."

Helen snapped out of her trance like state.

"Er, no, it doesn't. Sometimes we are busier than we are, but tonight we're not as busy as we are sometimes." Helen seemed to have temporarily lost the ability to construct an English sentence properly.

"Your landlord keeps a nice pint. Can I have a packet of nuts to go with it, please?"

"Salted or dry roasted?" Helen managed to construct this potentially complicated question successfully.

"Dry roasted, please. I suspect they're probably better for me. Too much salt is not good. I like to look after myself."

Good idea! Helen could feel herself trembling slightly as she pulled a packet off the piece of cardboard hanging on the wall. A little bit more of the pretty blonde lady was revealed as a result. The customer smiled as he handed his money over.

"Are you visiting our beautiful area, or do you live locally?" Helen successfully constructed another potentially complicated question. Her fluency was improving.

"I live quite locally, actually," came the reply.

"Oh, really. Whereabouts?"

"Promise not to laugh if I tell you. I live in a caravan. I'm a fully qualified dropout. I've escaped from the rat race."

Me too, thought Helen. I've done that!

"And where is this caravan of yours exactly?"

"I could tell you, but I'd then have to kill you."

"Right!" Helen laughed nervously.

"What sort of shifts do you work here?" The conversation seemed to be moving on apace. Was this man leading up to asking her out? Helen didn't know what to say.

"It varies." A nice, neutral, uninformative answer. "They keep me pretty busy."

"I guess that's because you're a very good barmaid," said the flatterer.

Helen blushed. "Could be, I suppose."

"Well, if that's the case, I'll probably be seeing more of you. I like it in here. It can get very lonely in the van sometimes." He finished his pint. "Goodnight. I'll see you soon, I hope."

"Mmm," was about all Helen could manage.

Back home, Helen seemed very excited.

"You look happy. Had a good evening down at the pub?" asked Chris.

"Yes, it was enjoyable tonight. There was a good crowd in who I've not seen before. I think they're up on a walking holiday. We had some laughs."

"Was it a big group?"

"There were about half a dozen of them. Good mates – I think they've probably known each other a long time."

"That's good," replied Chris.

Mrs Jackson's garden didn't look quite as nice the following morning. It was still very attractive and well maintained – of course – but the weather was spoiling things. It couldn't decide whether it was drizzling or just misty, although it was still warm. It was always too

Bowing Out

damp to take off his coat, and it wasn't long before Chris started to sweat.

He reminded himself that he wasn't there to admire the garden and relax, but the weather made him feel a bit languid and he worked more slowly than usual. He also had something on his mind and he was focussed on that when he heard a familiar voice.

"Chris! Tea!"

"Thanks, Mrs Jackson. That's very welcome."

"Do you want to come in out of this rain?"

"No, you're OK, thanks. It's hardly raining really, and I don't want to trail mud into your house."

Mrs Jackson noticed Chris looked a bit distant. "I hope you don't mind me asking, but is there something on your mind?"

It was nice of her to ask. Chris didn't think she was interfering. The tone of her voice made him think she was treating him like the son she'd never had.

"No, nothing. I'm just musing. But thanks for asking."

Mrs Jackson brought Chris his tea and biscuits and then returned to her chores. She didn't fully believe him, but if he didn't want to say…

When Chris returned home after the gardening, Helen looked rather agitated. "Chris, can we have a word?"

"Can it wait a bit? I'm rather hot and sweaty, and I wouldn't mind a shower."

"Well, not really."

CHAPTER 34

"Aren't you going to be late for your shift?" Chris called to Helen who was standing at the bottom of the garden looking at the low hills, which looked inviting now that the day had dried out. Chris might well have been on the hills by now had he been on his own, but he wasn't and he didn't like the way that Helen didn't look like she wanted to go to work. Timekeeping problems. Neil had mentioned those, or he'd read about them, or both. Whatever, he was aware of them.

"I'll be fine," said Helen. "What's the rush?"

Chris said, "I wouldn't think it would be a great idea to upset your boss by being late. There must be loads of other girls round here queuing up to be barmaids." He immediately wished he hadn't said that. He had found out that Helen liked to be thought of as indispensable at the pub. An atmosphere was developing between them, and saying something like that would not help to ease the tension.

"I'm going, I'm going." There was impatience in Helen's voice. It wouldn't be right to say the house shook when she slammed the door because that only happened in cartoons, but she did leave forcefully.

The atmosphere had built up as a result of what Helen had said when she diverted Chris away from the bathroom.

Bowing Out

She had told Chris she had cancelled the newly booked Greek holiday.

"You mean, you've cancelled it because it's not somewhere I really fancy?"

"No, I've cancelled it because I have decided we're not going."

"Why not?"

"Because we're not." Helen was sulky now and didn't seem to want to discuss the matter further.

Chris was very disappointed. At first he hadn't been enthusiastic about Helen's choice of resort, but the drizzle of a Cumbrian day had helped to convinced him that a week in the sun, even in a potentially noisy resort, would be just what they needed. He had further cheered himself when he realised they were, of course, going out of peak season, so it wouldn't be as busy as he had first feared and he wouldn't have to manoeuvre his way through crowds of children. By the time he had finished his shift in the garden, he was looking forward to the holiday.

Helen's announcement, therefore, came as something of a blow.

But, on a more general level, that was the second occasion in a short space of time on which Helen had made a decision without him. Chris thought they were a team, and that they would discuss matters and reach decisions together. These were holiday decisions, ultimately not life changing, but what if she applied this independent (or selfish) thinking to other areas of life?

"I'm sorry I'm a bit late, Ian. Something cropped up at home, and I just couldn't leave it." Helen was flustered by the time she arrived at the pub.

"Fortunately, we're not too busy at the moment. But this isn't the first time, is it, Helen?"

"Yes, I know I've been a bit late once or twice, but it really won't happen again."

"It'd better not." Ian wasn't moved to ask about Helen's problem at home. From his perspective he would be pleased if Helen left it there.

Peter Cropper

Ian was right when he said they weren't very busy. In fact, now that most of the holiday crowds had dispersed they seemed to be quiet for too much of the time and Helen had thought fleetingly that Ian might consider whether he could continue with just one barmaid. What she failed to realise was the obvious issue that if her punctuality didn't improve, she could well be the one to be forced out.

Come to think of it, the pub was drastically quiet. Even the two reliable, ruddy-faced regulars weren't there. Helen looked at the space where they normally stood. It looked very empty, as if a piece of furniture which had been there for years had been taken away. An elderly couple sat in the corner, he nursing a pint of mild and she a soft drink, but the pub wasn't going to prosper on the takings of customers like that. Mind you, if you removed them and the two young men in the other corner, there would be no one left. Helen was most disappointed by the non-appearance of one customer. He had praised the pub and he had praised her and he had hinted he would be back. Where the hell was he?

"Sue."

"Chris. Hi. How are you?" She seemed happy to hear from him again.

"Sue, you remember the other evening" – Sue did – "and how you said we could meet again and talk about Helen's problems? Would tonight be OK?"

"Not a problem. Cheese and pickle at my place again?"

Chris immediately put the phone down, put his jacket on and left the house. He walked quickly through the town to Sue's, making a mental list of points he wanted to raise as he did so. There was urgency in his step. He felt he had important things to discuss.

"Chris. Come in. The kettle's just boiled." Sue's bright and breezy disposition offered encouragement.

Bowing Out

"Thanks. It's good of you to see me again at such short notice."

"No problem. Any friend of Helen's is a friend of mine. I hope I can be of some assistance."

Chris sat down in the armchair. Sue, attending to the tea, called from the kitchen, "cheese and pickle again?"

"Biscuits'll do me, thanks," said Chris. He was not very hungry. He was far more interested in beginning the discussion.

Sue almost danced into the room with the tray and put it down on the table with a flourish. It reminded Chris of the time he had brought the tea in for Helen and she had been so delighted.

"So," said Chris, "can I mention some recent happenings and see if you think they relate to BPD, and perhaps also you can indicate any possible long term pointers to Helen's condition?" .

He sounded like an interviewer, and the tone was a bit too formal for Sue's liking. She expressed her preference for a more relaxed approach by kicking off her shoes and draping her long legs along the sofa. Her skirt shifted a short way up her thighs.

"Indeed," she said. "I hope I can be of some use."

"I'm sure you will be," said Chris, and an enigmatic little silence fell over the room.

Sue took a sip of her tea. "Fire at will."

"Timekeeping," said Chris. "How is Helen with timekeeping?"

"Well, I'm sure you know what we girlies are like with timekeeping," replied Sue. It was her attempt to keep the conversation light, and it saved Chris from the temptation to crack that same tired old joke. "But maybe Helen has been bad at it over the years. I remember we missed a train down to London once because she was late, and half the planned weekend was ruined. There was also that time they wouldn't let us into a concert in Carlisle till the interval. Again, that was down to Helen being late."

"And did she seem bothered when she made you late? Was she apologetic?"

Sue thought for a few moments. "No, not especially. In fact, in a strange sort of way, she almost seemed proud of the fact that her lack of punctuality had put the kibosh on everything. I think it perhaps made her feel important."

Sue swung her legs off the sofa and crossed them. The result was another little skirt movement. Chris wasn't sure whether Sue was patting the sofa to straighten out creases, or whether she was inviting him to sit next to her. He decided she was simply making things tidier, although he was far from certain. He continued with his interrogation.

"Now, I believe compulsive behaviour can be a trait of this BPD." Chris retained his composure very well. "Gambling, eating, shopping – that type of thing. Have there been any indications of that?"

"Eating – well she loves chocolate, as I'm sure you've noticed," said Sue, with the emphasis on "loves", a word she delivered very slowly; she pronounced it "lurves". "And she can hardly ever walk past that little deli in town – you know the one I mean?"

"I do know the one you mean," said Chris. "You do need a will of iron to stop yourself going in there. I don't think that's a problem exclusively for BPD sufferers."

"No, neither do I," agreed Sue. "What were the other things you mentioned?"

"Gambling was one."

"Gambling – I bet you any money she's never indulged. It's odds on she's never been inside a bookies." Sue paused to smile at her own witticism. "And shopping. Did you mention shopping?"

"Compulsive shopping, yes, not just ordinary shopping. Any sign of that?"

"I remember we went up to the Metro Centre near Newcastle one time, and you should have seen how she was loaded down. Mind you, every other woman was in the same boat, of course. It was in the papers – Next had to close down for three days due to a lack of stock. The car was so heavy with shopping that we had to have it towed out of the car park by a nice man with an enormous truck."

Sue was not taking this seriously any more.

Chris decided not to take the compulsive behaviour idea any further, so he changed tack. "Have you ever noticed Helen's mood change according to the reactions she gets from other people?" There was an element of impatience in his voice which Sue could not fail to notice, and she decided to be helpful again.

"Here I would definitely say 'yes'. I think Helen always sets great store on what people say about her, and what people think about her."

"Does she react when men look at her?"

"She does, of course. But then again, any self respecting woman would be pleased if a man looked at her in the right way." She looked at Chris and treated him to a very wide smile.

Chris continued, bravely and undeflected. "This is just a hunch," he said, "but I've noticed she really does dress up to go to work these days. Ian, her boss, thinks appearance is important, I know that, but it seems over the top to me. I'm no expert in ladies' fashion, but I think she's almost too smart."

"Really?" said Sue. "What sort of clothes does she wear to work?"

"Well, I'd have thought a smart pair of jeans and a presentable t-shirt would do the job. That's what she was wearing when I first met her, as was her mate whose name I can't remember."

"Claire?"

"It might have been, but that's not important. What might be important is the way she's changed what she wears. Now it's more likely to be her top which is a bit low cut." In fact, "conspicuously low cut" would have been a more accurate description of the embroidered, tie-dyed blue and purple top which Helen liked to wear. To this she added very smart jeans, rings on carefully chosen fingers, bangles and large earrings. The hair extensions with small plaits with the borrowed diamante hair grips, the darker than usual red lipstick and the liberal dash of perfume suggested she was making a real effort. "Does that sound to you like she's trying to impress her boss, the punters in general, or maybe a particular punter?"

"Could be," said Sue. She left the answer ambiguous because she had had enough of talking about any problems Helen might be having. Instead, she said, "Chris, you say you're no expert on ladies' fashions, but," and she stood up and moved towards him, "what do you think of what I'm wearing? I'm not too sure it shows off my best features. Do I impress you? You're a man; I'd be *very* grateful for your opinion."

Chris opened his mouth to give her his opinion, but nothing came out.

CHAPTER 35

The pub wasn't the only establishment where trade was suffering as the main holiday season drew to a close. There were three cafés in direct competition with each other within very close proximity in the town centre, and on this cool autumn morning there couldn't have been more than a total of twenty customers in all of them. One of the customers was Helen, who was sitting with a couple of bags of groceries at her side. She was staring into space, completely oblivious of anything that might have been happening around her, and she didn't notice someone slide into the chair next to her. She was startled to hear a cheery, "Good morning. Where have you drifted off to?"

"Sue. Good to see you again." The café was also one of Ms Mason's stopping off points. The two ladies had made no arrangement to meet, but, once Helen had emerged from her reverie, neither was surprised to see the other.

"Been shopping?" Sue used the obvious to break the ice.

"Yes, the deli as usual. They always have some lovely food in there. It might be a bit expensive and some of the items aren't day to day stuff, but so what?"

"Well, there's no harm in treating yourself from time to time. Have you got something in that bag that Chris likes?"

"I'm sure we can find something in there for him if we try hard enough."

Sue didn't ask how Chris was, which Helen found surprising, because she usually did, even though she didn't really know him.

"Any plans for the rest of the day?"

"Not really. I'm working later today, but I'm not sure what I'll do until then. Chris has gone off somewhere – probably for a fell walk. He didn't tell me what time he'd be back."

"Knowing you, you'll probably end up clothes shopping."

"Yes, maybe."

Helen then found out why Sue hadn't needed to ask her how Chris was.

"I bumped into Chris the other day. He asked me something about you which I thought was rather strange."

"And what was that, then?"

"He asked me about what you wear. I thought that was strange, because he can see for himself. He apparently thinks you're dressing up more these days when you go to work in the pub, and he can't seem to understand why. I think I might know, because I'm a woman and I understand these things."

"Oh, yes? And what do you make of it?" asked Helen tersely.

Sue hesitated. "Well, I can only assume there might be someone there you want to impress. To be honest, I get the impression that's probably what Chris thinks as well. Otherwise, why would he have asked?"

"I see."

"Well, spill the beans. Is there?"

"What if there is?" Helen was becoming quite angry. "Chris and I aren't married. We are perfectly free to wander off and do our own thing. I presume, for instance, that Chris is now wandering round on some mountain, but how do I know that? He could be anywhere, with anyone."

Bowing Out

Sue took Helen's failure to deny the accusation to be a "yes". If Helen wanted to preserve her relationship with Chris, she was playing rather a dangerous game. Sue thought she would not be much of a friend if she didn't point out to Helen what might happen next.

"To be honest, Helen, I think Chris has had his suspicions aroused to such an extent that he might be thinking of doing a bit of investigative work. That would be no problem for him, of course. You do work in a public house, after all. I think you may find he becomes more of a regular customer, as he is perfectly entitled to."

"And your point is..?"

"I'm just warning you, that's all. I can see this ending in tears."

"Thank you for your advice, but to be honest, Sue," and here Helen mimicked Sue's concerned and serious tone of voice from a few moments earlier, "I'm not sure it's any of your business. But if you don't mind me asking, which magazine is your agony aunt column in at the moment?"

The waitress finally shook off her lethargy and wandered over, brought Helen's coffee and looked enquiringly at the new customer. Sue looked at her watch and feigned surprise. "Is that the time?" she said unconvincingly, and she bade Helen as polite a farewell as she could manage before disappearing through the door.

Helen took a couple of sips of her coffee, clattered the cup down on the saucer which made the elderly ladies on the next table turn round, and weighed up the situation.

She drew three main conclusions.

Firstly, she was annoyed with herself for not seeing that "dressing to impress" would arouse Chris' suspicions. Did she not think she could rely on her personality to get what she wanted? Did she need the supporting crutch of fancy clothes? That was a poor reflection on her, surely? She was even more annoyed when she vaguely recollected that she had said something at some stage about going somewhere where she would be appreciated. That had been a stupid thing to say. Chris was far too clever not to suspect when she was foolishly spreading these clues out in front of him.

She was also annoyed with Chris for asking Sue for advice. Sue was her friend, not Chris'. And how likely was it that Chris would stop Sue casually in the street when he hardly knew her in order to quiz her about Helen's dress sense? That didn't add up in Helen's mind. It suggested Sue and Chris knew each other better than Helen realised.

And, of course, she was annoyed with Sue who seemed to be in cahoots with Chris. She couldn't escape from the idea that they were ganging up on her. The possibility that Chris had been discussing her with Sue for some time rapidly took shape. That was quickly followed by the notion that Chris might subsequently want more from Sue than information about what Helen was doing.

Essentially, she was one annoyed lady.

By the time she had finished her coffee, Helen had come to the conclusion that Chris was having an affair with Sue. The irony of her anger, given what she herself was planning to do, was beyond her.

"Excuse me." The waitress responded and drifted over again.

"Can you bring me another coffee, please? I'm actually just popping out for a couple of minutes so if I'm not here when you bring it, you'll know I will be back very shortly." The waitress looked a little dubious.

"You can trust me, I'm a regular. I'll leave these bags here so you know I'll be back."

Having marked her territory, Helen stormed out. She walked with some purpose to the nearest newsagents and chose the first postcard she saw on the rack in the doorway. The tranquil scene – yachts on Windermere with the wooded hills of Claife Heights beyond – couldn't have made a greater contrast with what she was feeling.

"Do you sell stamps?"

"I'm sorry, we don't, but it's not far to the post office. Would you like me to tell you where it is?"

Bowing Out

"No, thank you." Helen retained a modicum of politeness as she left the shop.

When she returned to the café with the stamped card, there was no sign of the coffee. Helen didn't appreciate that the waitress was holding it back to prevent it from going cold.

"Have you forgotten that coffee?" Helen boomed across the café. "Oh no, she's back," said the expressions on the elderly ladies' faces.

"I'll bring it right away, madam," said the waitress as politely as possible.

Helen had to change her attitude and turn on the charm after a search in her handbag proved fruitless. "Excuse me, you haven't got a pen I could borrow, have you please?"

"Certainly, madam." The customer was always right. The basic training had taught the waitress that.

Sarah would be very surprised to receive a postcard which read:

I bet you never thought Chris would shack up with me! You always reckoned you were the pretty one, but she who laughs last…

If you want to get in touch, give us a ring. Come up and we can have a cosy little threesome.

Helen

At the bottom of the card Helen had written her phone number in as large numbers as the space would allow. She had even returned to the newsagents to splash out on a bright pink highlighter pen.

Having made the critical visit to the post box and spent some time wandering round the shops, Helen returned home for a bite to eat before going to work at the pub. She was surprised to find the house empty and when she looked in the usual place where Chris tended to leave notes she found nothing. That was strange – if he had gone for a walk on the fells, as she thought he had, he always left a note saying where he was going and what

Peter Cropper

time he would be back. What if he had an accident and couldn't get a signal on his mobile? He could be lying in a gully somewhere for days and nobody would find him and if his injuries didn't kill him the unpredictable mountain weather would see him off.

She went to the phone and dialled his number. "The mobile phone you have called has been switched off." She realised she wouldn't be able to talk to him now so she made a sandwich and made sure that she looked her best for her stint behind the bar. Perhaps Chris would return home soon.

When it was time for her to go to work there was still no sign of him but she couldn't wait. It would have been a bad idea to test Ian's patience again, so she left the house in good time.

Again, the pub wasn't busy when she arrived but before she had a chance to reflect that this continuing lack of customers could have dire consequences, she noticed a man standing at the end of the bar with a half drunk pint and a bored expression on his face as if he had been waiting for too long for someone or for something to happen.

"Chris. What are you doing here?"

In view of what Sue had suggested earlier, Helen shouldn't have been surprised, but she made it sound as if seeing her man standing in a pub was the most amazing thing she had ever seen.

The question invited a sarcastic response, but instead Chris replied, "I'm enjoying an early evening beer. Your landlord keeps an excellent pint." Helen remembered hearing another customer say that recently.

"But you don't normally come in here."

"No, I don't, but I thought – why not have a change? A friend of mine recommended it, and, I have to say, it was a good recommendation. I also knew it must be a good pub because you work here."

Which friend would that be? thought Helen.

"Well, a change is as good as a rest, as they say." Helen tried to smile at Chris, but she couldn't manage it.

Bowing Out

The conversation stalled as a young couple came in and stood at the other end of the bar. Helen went to serve them. The diversion gave her the chance to think about what she might say to Chris next.

When she returned, Chris beat her to it. "Anyway, as well as my friend's recommendation, I know this pub already, of course. This is where we met, remember? This pub will always have a place in my heart." He smiled broadly at her. "And, of course, there's always the chance that the bloke I've been looking for will turn up. Remember, the guy in the caravan I was asking you about?"

The guy in the caravan! That man who was chatting Helen up mentioned a caravan. Helen thought that had to be the guy Chris was looking for when he first met her. It was too great a coincidence to be otherwise. She found it hard to understand how she had failed to make the connection before.

"The guy in the caravan," said Chris again, as Helen seemed to be enjoying one of her daydreams. After a short pause, he said, "I don't suppose you've seen him in here recently, have you?"

Helen spent the next short while wondering what would happen if caravan man came in and went straight over to her to talk to her again while Chris was keeping a watching brief at the bar. Chris didn't seem to be in the best of moods. That suggested that perhaps Sue was right and he was suspicious. If that were the case, he might not embrace caravan man like a long lost friend.

"Yes, that's right," said Helen. "That was the original purpose of your visit to this part of the world, wasn't it? No, I don't think I've seen anyone who looks like the man you're looking for."

"That's a shame," said Chris. He sounded far from convinced by what he had heard. He drained his pint glass. "Same again, please, barmaid."

Helen knew that she was pulling Chris' second pint at least and, as he had to think about making his way back home to get something to eat (she hoped), she didn't think he'd be staying much longer which, under the circumstances, was probably just as well.

"Pass the menu, please love," said Chris. "Where's the specials board tonight?"

"Be walking while you're talking, please," shouted Ian, as the half a dozen or so drinkers made their way home at the end of the evening.

"It's safe to assume you'd like a lift back, isn't it?" asked Helen.

"That's right," said Chris. About half an hour earlier he had started to slur his words. Helen thought about making him walk, but then he'd know for sure that she thought there was a problem.

It was a quiet, nervous drive home through the lanes. Chris sat very still and fixed his gaze on the road ahead. Helen could not recall having seen Chris under the influence like this before, and she found the silence ominous. She had no idea how Chris might react or what he might say back at the house.

She led the way inside and lit up the house. "Drink?"

"Perhaps the smallest of wee drams," Chris replied.

Helen hadn't really meant that type of drink. "I was thinking more in terms of a milky drink. Wouldn't you prefer one of those?"

"If I'd have preferred one of those, I'd have said so." Arguing with Chris at this stage about his choice of drink didn't seem like a good idea. There were weightier matters to address.

It was time for Helen to confront Chris. She felt as though the net were closing in, and she had to say something. Seconds out, round one.

"Chris, I believe you've been speaking to Sue."

"Yes, I've been communicating with a fellow member of the human race. I believe that's still legal, or is it a crime these days?"

"No, but I'm not very happy with what you've been saying, to be honest."

Bowing Out

"Really. And what have I been saying?"

"You've been asking her about what I've been wearing."

"You are well informed, aren't you?"

Helen sighed. "Sue thinks –"

"Does she?" interrupted Chris. "A woman who thinks for herself. I've stumbled across a right gem there, haven't I?"

Helen kept her cool. "Sue thinks that you think I'm dressing smartly to impress someone at work."

"She's right," said Chris. He turned to face her instead of the wall opposite. "I do think that. Are you? You are, aren't you?"

"In my job it's important to look smart. Ian says –"

"I know what Ian says. Ian says you should look presentable, and I like it when you make an effort, but you've been going over the top recently. I've noticed – I'm not a fool, you know."

No, you're not, thought Helen, and that's part of the problem. Fooling Chris O'Neill was no easy task.

"You've been making more of an effort to look smart for work than you have for me," continued Chris. "So what other conclusions can be drawn, eh?"

As happened during Helen's conversation with Sue in the café, her lack of an answer spoke volumes.

"Well, I know one thing," said Chris. "As long as we're together, this isn't going to continue. It's very simple, really. As long as there's any suspicion in my mind that you're playing away, then I'll get to the bottom of it and, if you are up to nonsense, I'll put a stop to it. Do you understand?"

Helen did understand. Chris had made his intentions very clear. He would stop any nonsense, and it would surely make life a lot easier if she could stop it before he did. The question was – did she want to?

Chris finished his whisky in one gulp. Thus ended an evening during which he had drunk more than he had drunk for a long time. He was out of practice and he would have got very short odds on his feeling delicate in the morning. For now, he didn't feel as though there was much more to be said.

"I'm off to bed, Helen," he said, with a calmness which she found unnerving. "I'll see you in the morning."

CHAPTER 36

There is a catch, thought Sarah, and it is clearly that this holiday was never going to last forever and that we were always going to have to return to reality.

As they made progress up the motorway the rain set in, and the evening turned grey and miserable to match Sarah's mood. The Malvern Hills disappeared into a depressing, gloomy mist. Andy didn't seem to want to talk or to play amusing games with lorries, so the journey largely passed in silence.

As they approached Birmingham, Sarah thought she would use tried and trusted English tactics in order to start a conversation. Not only did she want to break the awful silence, but she also needed to discover what might be happening next.

"I'm pleased we didn't have this weather while we were away."

"So am I," replied Andy. "Still, I won't need decent weather where I'm going tomorrow."

"And where would that be?" asked Sarah, even though she was afraid she knew the answer already.

"I've got to get back to work, obviously." There was a mixture of impatience and disappointment in Andy's voice. "I've swung the lead enough already. There's no way I can take any more time off."

"What time do you have to be in?"

"Nine o'clock at the very latest."

Sarah asked another question, the answer to which she already knew. "Does that mean you won't be stopping over tonight?"

"I'm afraid so. I'd love to, but how can I? If I did, I'd have to get up about five o'clock to beat the rush hour traffic."

"Could you not do that, as a one off? For me?" There was desperation in Sarah's voice.

"No, I don't think so."

It strikes me you're more interested in keeping hold of that job than you are in spending time with me, thought Sarah.

"So," continued Andy, "after I've dropped you off and had a quick cup of tea, I'm going to have to love you and leave you, I'm afraid."

That's assuming I offer you a quick cup of tea, thought Sarah.

It didn't take long after Andy had gone for that feeling of emptiness to seep back into the house.

"We will see each other again soon, won't we?" Sarah had said.

"Of course we will," Andy had replied, "but just let me get back into my routine first. I hardly seem to have spent any time in that office recently. When my feet have touched the ground, I'll ring you."

"So getting back into a routine at work is more important than spending more time with me?" Sarah wanted to say, but she stopped herself. She thought of advice her mother often used to offer: "Least said, soonest mended." Instead, she said, "Will you ring me tomorrow when you've got home from work?"

"I will. I promise."

Alone in the house, she inevitably reflected on her relationship with Andy. He would probably consider that he had changed beyond all recognition and become a dynamic and fascinating person. Sarah could see his outlook on life had altered to a certain extent, but he was basically not much less staid than he had always been.

Bowing Out

When it came to the crunch, his secure job and steady lifestyle were more important to him than anything else. That's his choice, thought Sarah, but it doesn't augur well for him and me long term – if there is a long term.

She, too, had a choice – she could either bring the relationship to a close because it wasn't going anywhere, or leave it be because there was nothing better on the horizon. She had always suspected that this was the situation in the real world, but she had refused to acknowledge it during their time in Cumbria and Herefordshire.

She slipped back into her old way of talking to herself. "Basically, Sarah, you're not much further on," she said to herself and the four walls. "Your husband's buggered off and left you in an empty house. Tomorrow you'll go back to work at the greengrocer's and ask yourself where you're going in life. At least you did once have a soul mate."

Where had she put that packet of cigarettes?

"Did you have a nice time?" asked Sheila.
"Yes thanks."
"Where did you go again?"
"Herefordshire."
"Where's that?"
"It's way down south, Sheila."
"Did Chris enjoy it too?"
"Yes."
"What did you get up to?"

Sheila, will you please stop this questioning, otherwise I shall probably go mad and do something completely inappropriate with that bunch of bananas.

It was back in the old routine. Cumbria and Herefordshire had been on different planets. Sarah opened the front door after a particularly unrewarding day with the fruit and the veg and Sheila's seemingly constant interrogation. The alarm bleeped its familiar ring to remind Sarah that the house was empty. She went straight to the phone and rang Andy. She wasn't prepared to wait for his call, even though she expected the answer machine to tell her he wasn't there. Sarah had told herself that he would probably be staying late at work, catching up on tasks he had missed. But did she really know what he might be doing?

As anticipated, he wasn't home yet, but he did keep his word and he rang her later on. The conversation was stilted and uncomfortable. Sarah was unsure whether he wanted to talk to her at this time.

"Andy, are we going to get together sometime soon?" She tried to ensure she sounded enthusiastic rather than desperate.

"Yes, we are," replied Andy, "but it won't be tonight, that's for sure. There are one or two things I need to sort out first. That's the snag with being away for so long." Sarah hoped he wasn't blaming her for persuading him to go away, and she wondered what could possibly have happened in Andy's life in the short time they had been away to demand his attention so fully. He had hardly been on a world tour, nor would it have taken him long to jump in the car and see Sarah. Even a couple of hours would be better than nothing, but he didn't seem willing to grant her that small request.

"I miss you, Andy." As soon as she had said it, she wished she hadn't. It made her sound like she was playing the lead in an over sentimental film.

"So do I," replied Andy, but his tone was monotonous. Sarah could detect no real feeling.

After an uncomfortable pause, she continued. "Andy, if you're so busy, perhaps I could come and see you for a bit? That way it would save you the time you'd use up driving and we'd still get to spend some time together."

Andy answered immediately. He didn't even pretend to give the suggestion any thought. "That's not going to be possible at the moment. But I'll ring you towards weekend and we'll try to sort something out."

Sarah was unimpressed. "We'll try" was completely different from "we will."

"Why is it not possible at the moment?"

"Because it's not." Sarah didn't think she had heard Andy sound so impatient before. He could feel the upset coming through the telephone wire and he softened his tone. "Sarah, look – I will phone you soon and we will get together as soon as possible. That's really all I can say at the moment. Take care." He rang off.

Sarah spoke to the four walls again. She gave them the full benefit of her opinion.

"What a bastard!"

If the phone call had been a blow, it was nothing compared to that which she experienced when she looked through the day's mail.

The postcard had arrived.

Sarah read the card and then read it again a couple of times. The message was short and easy to understand but it took three readings before it even began to sink in. She didn't know what was more incredible – the fact that her husband would "shack up" with her erstwhile best friend, or the fact that Helen felt the need to tell her about it and even provide a contact number. The whole thing was surreal, and as for the idea of having a cosy threesome…

It was if Helen was saying, "Why don't you come up and help us do something about it?" Sarah found it all quite ridiculous.

She amazed herself by what she did next. Once she would have gone berserk and probably thrown something the length of the room, but calmly and without a fuss she went to the telephone directory and ran her eyes methodically down the list of dialling codes to find out where Helen and Chris were. It didn't occur to her the number might have been false. Something - probably female intuition - told her it wasn't.

Windermere. She recalled the bed and breakfast where she'd stayed with Andy, the much coffee drinking and wandering round the town, and that boat trip. She was probably never more than a few miles from them during all the time she and Andy had been in the Lakes, but their paths had never crossed.

Helen was right – she was nowhere near as attractive as Sarah. So what exactly had driven Chris to her? It had to be something more than wet weather in Scotland.

Peter Cropper

He had been lightheartedly predicting continuous rain in the weeks before they had gone, so that would not have pushed him over the edge. Sarah could only presume it must have been something she'd done or failed to do, or perhaps what she'd said or not said at a particular time. Did she and Chris communicate as much as they could have done? She wasn't at all sure that they did. Had they been as good to each other as they should have been? Quite possibly not.

She reached the conclusion that she was as much to blame as anyone for the current situation. Equally well, she was sure she was more suited to Chris' needs than Helen was. She had to be – it was her that he'd married after all, and he couldn't possibly be as happy with Helen. She noticed with some surprise that she didn't feel angry at Chris. Instead she felt sorry for him. She looked around at her - their - lovely home. Helen would have a nice house – she wouldn't tolerate anything less - but she couldn't possibly have anything as nice as this, could she? Chris would be happier here. She could make him happy again. She would make him happy again.

Helen would probably be doing her best for Chris, but Sarah could do much better. It was only fair that everyone was aware of this.

CHAPTER 37

When Chris came back from an afternoon's work at Mrs Jackson's, Helen wasn't there. He went to look for a note to indicate where she might be, but there wasn't one.

It seemed they weren't even communicating through the written word any more. It was very different from when Chris had moved in. Then they told each other everything and they knew the other person's movements as well as they knew their own. Now it was pretty much all down to guesswork. It might have helped if Helen pinned her rota up like Sarah used to, but she'd never done that and, in view of recent discussions, she was hardly likely to start now.

They had taken breakfast together that morning but the atmosphere could hardly have been described as convivial. Chris had been pleased he had some calls to make in the town before gardening. He had welcomed the chance to be out of the house earlier than usual. He had been in no hurry to complete the errands and he had worked more slowly than usual at Low Rigg.

He did a little tour of the kitchen. Supplies were plentiful, but somehow there was nothing there that he fancied. He wanted something more basic than the food Helen had brought in from the delicatessen. After a session in the garden he was hungry even after the usual huge slab of Mrs Jackson's home made cake. Beans or poached eggs on toast would not do a job today and Chris could not face the supermarket, so the fish and chip shop in the town would have to provide the solution.

As he walked to the life saving establishment he wondered where Helen might be. The pub was an obvious possibility but he just had the feeling she wasn't there at the moment. If that were the case, she could be out with Sue or she could be anywhere with whoever it was she was trying to impress.

He didn't want to be seen to be spying on her but he needed to find out so he decided that afterwards he would ring Sue, ostensibly to find out how she was, but really to discover Helen's whereabouts.

He finished his tea, ran through the conversation he was about to have with Sue and picked up the phone. There was a message – might it be Helen giving him some sort of clue?

He was very surprised to hear a female voice which he instantly recognised. It certainly wasn't Helen's.

"Helen – what the hell do you think you're playing at? I'll be ringing again."

It was Chris' turn to be baffled by what Helen had done. He listened to the message a couple more times, although there was no doubt whose voice it was.

Just as his wife did, Chris fell into the habit of talking to himself. "How has Sarah got this number? I've not been in touch. She can only have got it from Helen, I suppose. Are they in contact? What the hell is going on?" The surprised tone in Sarah's voice suggested the two ladies had not spoken to one another, either face to face or on the phone. Helen must have written to Sarah. Elementary, my dear O'Neill.

"So," said Chris, summing it up for his own benefit, "it can only be the case that Helen has written to Sarah telling her where I am. That's bloody marvellous!"

Sarah felt better when she had made the call. She summed up the situation with her four friends, the living room walls.

"I now have a means of communicating with Chris. Nobody answered the phone then, but, if somebody had, there'd be a 50-50 chance it would have been Chris. If Helen hadn't meant me to use the number, she wouldn't have given it to me. Therefore, there'll be no problem in my ringing it until such time as Chris answers, then I'll get to talk to him."

The fact that Andy seemed reluctant to get back in touch with her suddenly didn't seem very important after all.

Chris wondered whether he should try Helen on her mobile, but he rejected the idea in favour of the original plan. He would have a word with his confidante – the lady who seemed happy to talk to him at any time.

There was no reply, so Chris left a message. "Sue, it's Chris again. I'm really sorry to pester you again, but would it be possible to have another chat? Thanks." If anyone heard that message who wasn't supposed to, then that was just tough.

He replaced the receiver and went into the kitchen to make a coffee. He sat by the window with his drink and stared out at the low hills to mull over the situation, but he hadn't got very far when the phone rang.

"Chris, Sue here. I'm sorry I missed your call. I've just stepped out of the shower. What can I do for you?"

Chris pictured the scene chez Mason. "I'm sorry to bother you, but can I have another chat with you?"

"Of course. Come round. Just give me a few minutes to dry my hair and put some nice clothes on, will you?"

Sue opened the door and smiled warmly at Chris. "Come in, come in. Tea or coffee?"

Chris politely accepted the offer of another coffee even though he didn't really want one. He waited patiently in Sue's living room. It was simply furnished with a couple of pictures on the wall. They depicted Lakeland scenes, of course. Chris wondered if there were any houses in the area without Lakeland scenes on the wall. Skiddaw viewed from the southern end of Derwentwater adorned Helen's lounge wall. Sue had views which he didn't recognise. He guessed they were probably of those less frequented lakes past Keswick on the way to the coast.

There were no photographs of people - no clues about Sue's life, no clues about who was regarded as important in it. Not that that mattered, because, he reminded himself, he was there to try to sort out the problem that was Helen Wilkinson, not discover more about Sue Mason.

"Here we go," said Sue as she brought two steaming mugs of coffee from the kitchen. "Let me just put them down here," and she leaned over close to Chris to put the drinks on the coasters on the small table next to where he was sitting. Chris noticed Sue's pink and white striped t-shirt with the low cut neckline and he smelled the newly applied perfume. He tried to remember what he wanted to say.

"Is this a social call, or do you want to talk about our mutual friend?" asked Sue.

"Well, yes, it's to do with Helen," Chris replied.

Although Sue had expected Chris to say that, it wasn't really the answer that she wanted to hear. Never mind, it couldn't be helped.

"What's up this time?" Sue looked very concerned. Chris continued, confident in his ability to deal with his confidante.

"You'll never guess what she's done? She's only gone and told my wife where I am – without my permission, of course. Why would she want to do a thing like that?"

"Your wife? You've got a wife?"

"Estranged." That sounded very grand to Chris – very formal and final, and he wasn't at all sure that he liked the sound of it. "I don't see her any more. She's out of the equation." He wasn't sure he liked that very much either.

"If she's no longer on the scene, I'm not sure of her relevance," said Sue. "Does Helen know about her? I'm presuming she must if she's contacted her."

"Oh, yes," Chris replied. "Helen knows about her."

Bowing Out

"She's contacted her because she wants you all to be friends. How's that for an idea?"

"I don't think so, no."

"Why, then?"

"Could it be as a result of what you've been saying to her?"

"Sorry?"

Chris presented his theory. "I think you've been talking to both parties in this little scenario, and as a result of that Helen thinks I am convinced she's gone off with someone else."

"What?" Sue pretended not to understand. She feigned bafflement and confusion.

Chris continued to clarify the situation for her. "But I don't think Helen's very happy at the way you and I have been talking so, for a bit of revenge, she's decided to try to drop me in it and tell Sarah where I am. Sarah could cause all sorts of mischief now, you know, and she need never have found out. If you'd been loyal to one party I don't think any of this would have happened."

"Oops," said Sue, trying out a little-girl-lost image.

"Oops, indeed. I'm not sure you don't owe me one, or maybe even more than one, so you can perhaps start by telling me where you think Helen is now, or, indeed, who she's with now."

"At work?" suggested Sue.

"Do you know that?"

"Obviously not. How do you think I can know Helen's work rota?" For the first time since they had met, Chris noticed irritation in Sue's voice.

"Let's assume she's not in the pub, but rather she's with another bloke." Chris paused momentarily. "Have you any idea who that might be?"

"No," said Sue quietly.

"So you've no idea where she is now?"

"No," repeated Sue.

Chris stood up to go. Sue straightened her t-shirt and pulled it down a little. "You're annoyed, aren't you?"

Chris looked at his hostess and concluded that he was, although it wasn't easy to be annoyed with a woman like Sue. Nevertheless, he seemed to have managed it.

"I need to talk to her," he said. "I'm going to go to the pub and see if she's there. Thanks for the coffee. I'll catch you again."

Sue didn't like the idea of an upset Chris storming off. She particularly didn't like the idea that he might storm off and never come back, so she asked him as nicely as she could, "How are you going to get to the pub?"

Good question. If Helen were there, she would probably have taken her car now that she was fit enough to drive again. Or had she rung Pearson's? Was her car at the house? Chris hadn't bothered looking – he had been too agitated to think of doing that.

"Well –"

"If you like you can borrow my car. Like you said, I probably owe you one."

Chris accepted the offer. "Now you will drive safely, won't you?" said Sue. Chris wasn't sure whether Sue meant for his sake or for the car's sake.

He managed a smile. "I will. Thank you."

Sue had only half expected a peck on the cheek, so she was only half disappointed when none was forthcoming.

CHAPTER 38

Chris drove too quickly down the country lanes, and the man in the silver car he had just avoided hitting close to one of the bends was right to curse him, although it probably wasn't necessary for his passenger to lean out of the window offering him the vee sign.

"All right, all right, don't make a meal of it," said Chris. "I was going a bit fast, but it's hardly a crime worthy of the death penalty." Nevertheless, he did slow down. He had just had one warning on a road on which it wasn't a good idea to take liberties. If he carried on at the same speed, he might not get a second.

After he had arrived at the pub and parked the car, he had a quick check round the car park. It was busier tonight, but Chris nevertheless had no difficulty in locating Helen's – or was it their? – car parked against the wall next to the road. So, she had gone to work, but if there was nothing underhand going on, Chris wondered why she hadn't just left him a note, or perhaps even told him at breakfast. Oh, yes, he remembered why the latter didn't happen; they weren't speaking, were they?

So, what was it he was intending to say again? He was going to ask Helen why she had contacted Sarah. He was doubtful as to whether such a public place was the best venue in which to ask that question, yet it could not wait. It was bound to provoke a peppery response, then Ian would come over and take issue, and that would only make Helen worse and before long Ian would suggest that there were plenty of local girls who would love to work behind the bar and how would Helen react to the threat of being sacked...?

As he walked into the pub, he couldn't recall the last time he had felt so nervous.

It was Claire, not Helen, who he saw behind the bar, which he found puzzling. She recognised him from the first time he had visited the pub. She smiled at him and Chris returned the compliment, but it was the weak smile of a preoccupied man.

"Is Helen in tonight? Her car's outside."

Claire half shrugged and turned her attention to the vital task of rearranging the pint glasses on the shelf above. It was an important job which could wait no longer.

He scanned the bar and noticed a couple by the window with their backs to the rest of the customers. Chris thought they looked as if they didn't want to be noticed. The woman's attempt at camouflage wasn't good enough to deceive Chris.

Chris' mind raced. That was the man there with Helen. That was the man who Helen liked at the pub. That was the reason why Helen dressed as if she were going to a society ball whenever she went to work. That was his rival – public enemy number one.

Chris made his way to the far end of the bar, well away from where the touching little scene was being acted out. The young couple perched on the barstools provided a barrier from behind which Chris could safely observe. Then, as further cover, two more locals appeared and positioned themselves between Chris and the barstool drinkers. Chris thought he recognised them. He was fairly sure they were the two workers who had directed him to Martin's caravan, but they didn't acknowledge him. They were much too involved in their own conversation.

"Who's next, please?" Claire spoke in an efficient, business like manner. She couldn't ignore Chris any longer.

Bowing Out

"Pint of bitter, please."

As Claire pulled the beer, Chris said, "that's her over there with her back to us, isn't it? Do you know who that is that she's with?"

Claire said, "Can't say." She didn't say, "Don't know." It didn't necessarily mean the same thing. Chris thought her choice of phrase was very significant.

"So you've not seen him before?"

Instead of answering the question, Claire told Chris the price of his drink. She took Chris' money and passed back his change in an embarrassed silence. She then quickly moved to greet the newcomers, grateful for the distraction. It was like some of those occasions when Helen wouldn't respond to his questions. Claire had given no answer, and that told him more than any verbal reply could.

The man had either invaded Helen's personal space or had been invited into it. Whichever it was, Helen seemed disinclined to remove him from it. Chris saw her toss her head back and laugh. She had obviously been amused. A few seconds later she did it again. Chris realised he had not seen her do that for some time.

Chris took a gulp from his pint and deliberated. Of course, it could all be innocent. Just because you made friends with someone of the opposite sex, it didn't mean it would necessary develop into anything, did it? There was such a thing as a platonic relationship. Chris himself had been very friendly with Kate, that art teacher who was at Whiteoaks a couple of years ago. They had enjoyed each other's company in the staff room, and sometimes Chris would visit her at the end of the day when she was tidying up. They would chat and Chris would admire the pupils' work. To his surprise, he thought much of it was very good. After Kate had left to go to another job in Nottingham, Chris rang her a couple of times to wish her well and to see if she was settling in, but then they lost touch. There was nothing in it – it was a platonic relationship.

Sarah never knew of Kate's existence. Why was that? Chris asked himself. It was, of course, because he didn't believe that Sarah would think there was "nothing in it." Perhaps it was only men who could acknowledge a platonic relationship.

Now the boot was perhaps on the other foot.

Chris' thought process continued. Sarah, level headed and sensible, would not have bought into the idea that there was nothing between Chris and Kate. In other words, she would not have accepted the existence of platonic relationships. Chris therefore found it very logical to believe that Helen, far from level headed, could not possibly view her own relationship with pub guy as platonic. Look how close together they are sitting!

He could only see the back of Helen's friend's head so he didn't really know what he looked like, but Chris did notice his hair was quite long. It looked unfashionable, and his outfit of jeans, lumberjack shirt and well worn trainers contrasted with that of Helen, making the two of them look ill matched. Chris felt frustrated, and annoyed that the other man was not showing himself. He wanted to see his face, to know exactly what he was up against.

Helen stood up, turned and went to the ladies. Chris wondered whether this was his chance to confront Helen's new man, but he decided against it and he opted to stay where he was. Just in time, he looked down and tried to conceal himself in his beer. He did not want Helen to see him. There was nobody nearby available to engage in conversation, so he stared into his drink as if it would provide some revealing answers to some difficult questions.

Out of the corner of his eye he saw Helen return to her seat. Her friend leaned over and whispered something in her ear. "Do you know that bloke at the bar is watching us?" Chris imagined he might have said, but Helen's reaction suggested otherwise. She laughed again and, unless Chris' eyes were deceiving him, the man moved closer to Helen. Helen took his hand and squeezed it momentarily.

Bowing Out

That was enough. Chris finished his beer and moved over to the happy couple.

"Good evening, Helen," he said. He sounded very polite.

"Chris. What are you doing here?" Helen looked very unsure of herself. There was a note of panic in her voice.

"I've come to enjoy a drink in a public house," replied Chris, "although I've ended up watching what seems to be a very public affair. What I've seen hasn't made the evening out very enjoyable, to be perfectly honest."

Martin hadn't yet turned round. If he had, Chris would have noticed the amused expression on his face. Helen hoped he intended to remove it if he were thinking of looking at Chris.

"I see you've got some company," Chris continued. "Aren't you going to introduce us?"

Before Helen had the chance to speak, Martin turned round and looked at Chris. "Who are you?" he said.

He looked to Chris as though he'd just wandered out of a forest clearing. A complementary beard matched the long hair. Surely this wasn't the gorilla Helen was trying to impress? Yet here she was, dressed in her finery, obviously enjoying his company so much.

"I'm sorry," said Chris, pleasantly. "I have a little bit of a problem with my hearing. It's not all it used to be. If we're going to have a chat, I'm going to have to ask you to stand up. I just can't hear you properly when you're down there."

Astonishingly, Martin fell into the trap. As soon as he was in position, Chris didn't hesitate. He hit him.

Chris wasn't in the habit of hitting people; in fact, if he had had the time to reflect, he would have struggled to think of the last time he had done so. Because this punch was special, something of a one off, he put as much effort into it as he could. If Jason Farrell and his friends had been there, they would have stood and applauded.

But it wasn't so much the strength of the punch, it was more the way in which Martin fell which caused the damage. He tottered backwards over the stool he had been sitting on, but hitting his head on the corner of the table proved decisive. He came to rest on the floor and lay still.

Silence descended on the bar. It was broken by one of the two forest workers.

"I thought Martin Cooper was a friend of yours. Bill and I would never have told you where he lived if we'd known you were going to do something like that to the poor bugger."

Martin Cooper! The penny hadn't dropped when Chris had faced him and even if it had, the penny would have disappeared into the red mist swirling around it. Now the man who was supposed to help him lay the foundations for a new life was lying motionless at his feet.

Helen was next to speak, although "speak" hardly did justice to what everyone in the pub, and probably everyone in the village, heard. "Chris," she screamed, "what have you done? You've killed Martin." She took hysteria to new level. While Chris stood rooted to the spot, Claire came out from behind the bar, looked at Chris with disgust, and went to try to calm Helen down.

"Where's Ian?" someone asked. Ian had gone into the back to make the all important phone call, but not before he had gestured to one of his bigger regulars to take up a position near the door.

Chris thought that, despite the imposing figure of Paul barring his way, he really should make a run for it, but even though his brain sent down very clear orders, his legs failed to obey.

As the police entered the pub, quickly followed by the ambulance men, Chris told himself that at least he had succeeded in finding Martin, but he did not enjoy the irony of the situation. It wasn't long before the two friends were both leaving the pub, in contrasting states of health, under the auspices of the local emergency services.

CHAPTER 39

It was the talk of the Whiteoaks staff room shortly after Mr James had held court with the little group who, he considered, should hear the news first.

"Our absent friend is in some trouble then, isn't he?" Ray Davidson contributed something very obvious to the discussion.

"You could say that," replied Pete.

"I think it's only fair his departmental colleagues should know what's been going on," said Steve. "Jane," he called across the staffroom, "come over here and listen to Mr James' news."

Jane Foster came over. She was a rare visitor to Pete's enclave. In fact, Mr James couldn't recall ever having seen her there before. It wasn't that he disliked Jane - nor, as far as he was aware, did Jane dislike him - but rather she was one of those colleagues he never spoke to simply because they had nothing in common.

"Have you heard what Chris has done?"

Jane shook her head. Before Pete had a chance to speak, Steve told her his version of the story.

Jane looked at Pete, Ray and Steve in amazement. "I wouldn't have believed Chris was capable of behaviour like that," she said and then, shaking her head, she wandered back to her place to talk with Jo Matthews in an area of the room with which she was more familiar.

"I have to say, I tend to agree with her," said Ray.

"But I don't think we necessarily know all the ins and outs." Pete sprang to his friend's defence. "Chris didn't leave a very detailed message, and I'm not sure we're getting the full story. Something must have wound him up, don't you think?"

"Full story or not, provocation or not, you can't go beating people to a pulp in a pub until they're carried out unconscious." The observation came from Jim Lewis who had been sitting opposite Ray. He hadn't said a word, but he had taken everything in. "I can't say I'm overly surprised. Do you remember the way he behaved at the meal in summer?"

"He was pissed!" said Pete. "I don't think you can equate talking nonsense when you've had a few to beating someone up."

"Maybe he was pissed when he knocked this chap out. Perhaps his aggression moved on from the verbal to the physical?"

"At least he didn't kill the bloke, did he?" Steve Lloyd made his positive contribution.

"No," said Pete, "but, according to what Chris said, he wasn't feeling too great when he left the pub."

"So what state is he in now?" asked Mike Prescott.

"Don't know," said Pete.

"I think we could do with a bit more information. Pete, why don't you give Chris a ring when you've a bit more time?" asked Ray.

"I might do," said Pete. "I've got a free period just after break." The others could see he had no real intention of doing so.

"Knowing Chris, he'll come up smelling of roses, as usual," said Steve.

"I'm not so sure about that," said Ray.

"Well, he managed to get away with it when Sarah didn't find out about Kate Newton, and if he could get away with that, he can get away with anything." The little group of men laughed. "He'll get away with this as well. Just wait and see."

Alistair Johnson, who had caught the tail end of the conversation as he was passing with his tea, sat down and asked, "What's going on? Am I right in thinking I'm going to have to work with that supply guy for a little while longer?"

At Blake's, three workmen were also discussing a message that one of them had recently received.

"Chris O'Neill," said Phil. "I thought he'd disappeared up his own arse. Where did you say he was, Dave?"

"The Lakes. I met him over summer and he was really pissed off, moaning about teaching and whatever. He should be back in school now, shouldn't he? He must have done a runner. I'm not surprised he's gone to the Lakes. He's always liked it up there, I think."

"What, he's left the ever lovely Sarah behind?" said Jim. "I don't think that's something I would have done. I wonder if she needs anyone to look after her – you know, a rugged bloke to keep an eye on her."

"I don't think I'd have left her either," agreed Phil. "I'll fight you for that job, Jim." The three men chuckled at Phil's witticism before he continued. "So what exactly did this message say again, Dave?"

"It's all kicked off in the Lake District. It sounds like he's given another bloke in a pub somewhere a real pasting. I wonder what he did to deserve that."

Jim frowned. "From what I remember of Chris, to beat someone up like that…I wouldn't have expected him to do it."

Phil put forward his theory. "Somebody must have wound him up, big style. It's my betting there was a woman involved," he said. He turned to the page of greatest interest in the newspaper. "Talking of women, just take a look at those," said Jim, looking over Phil's shoulder. Chris O'Neill was forgotten.

Claire was finding the task of offering complete consolation too demanding, and as a result Helen was still crying. The policeman took statements in turn from each of the witnesses. None of the drinkers was in any doubt as to what had happened. They were all in agreement that the guy who was standing on his own at the bar had knocked out the hippy type man sitting by the window. There was no immediate provocation. Claire, who knew more about the personalities involved, was able to provide a little more information.

"If you ask me," said Claire, making herself heard between Helen's sobs, "it could be a crime of passion."

"Thank you, madam," replied the police officer in a tone which suggested he thought Claire might have seen too many courtroom dramas on television.

"Claire might be right, officer," offered Ian. "I don't want to tell you your job, but it sounds as if she might know something?"

The officer felt duty bound to ask Claire to expand on what she had said. She spoke of the eternal triangle, but the policeman didn't seem thrilled or excited by what he heard. It was nothing he hadn't heard before, and it didn't alter what had happened.

When it came to Helen's turn to make a statement, the policeman made very little progress. It wasn't easy getting sense out of her in this distraught state.

After the police and the customers had finally left, Claire and Ian looked helplessly at each other, while Helen sat at a table. She had temporarily stopped crying and was sitting motionless, staring into space.

"Can you take her home, Claire?" Ian had no intention of leaving the pub, and he knew he would have no chance of handling Helen in her current state. "I know I can leave her in your capable hands."

Thanks, Ian.

"OK," said Claire. She could see it was her responsibility to rescue the situation. "Helen, shall we make a move?"

"I don't want to go home," cried Helen. "I don't want to be on my own."

Claire looked at Ian, as if he could provide some advice. Ian looked blankly at Claire. He couldn't, and, thanks to his delegation skills, it wasn't his problem, he was pleased to say.

"You'll be all right when you get there," suggested Claire.

"No I won't," screamed Helen. Ian winced, relieved there were no overnight guests.

Someone had to take charge of the situation. "Come on then," said Claire. "It's back to mine tonight." And that's just for tonight, she thought. Claire hoped Helen would have calmed down by the time she had got her to her house. The kids would both be in bed, as, almost certainly, would Mick. It could be potentially disastrous if Helen were to wake anybody up.

Claire opened the front door as quietly as she could and led Helen inside. The wailing and crying had been replaced by occasional sobbing. Claire thought Helen was actually handling the situation quite well, but she realised she would have to be extremely careful regarding what she said to her. One misplaced word could result in Helen's flaring up again.

"Cup of tea?" There couldn't be anything wrong in suggesting that. A cup of tea provides an instant solution to any problem.

Helen managed a faint smile. "I'd love one," she sniffed.

"Would you like anything to eat?"

"No, thank you."

"Are you sure?"

"Positive."

While Claire was making the tea, Helen looked round at Claire's simply furnished home. She felt suddenly extremely grateful that Claire had been prepared to take her in. Her gratitude was very quickly accompanied by sadness as she realised that, if Claire hadn't been kind like this, there would have been very few other people to whom she could have turned. There was Sue, of course, but it would have been unfair to phone her at this time of night.

"Claire," she said, as her hostess returned with two mugs of tea, "it's very kind of you to look after me like this."

"No problem. That's what friends are for." That set Helen off and she started crying again. Claire realised that tonight was definitely not the time to be talking things through. She feared that if Mick, who was due out early to work, heard a commotion, he would be down those stairs and there would be a different type of discussion.

"Now listen, Helen. I'm going to have to make this bed up here for you. It's a sofa bed, but it's perfectly comfortable, according to the people who've slept on it. Will that be OK?" She didn't wait for a reply, and yawned for Helen's benefit. "I think I'll have to turn in myself soon. I'm knackered. It's very late."

"Don't leave me!" Helen wanted to shout, but she composed herself in time. Don't be so pathetic, she thought. Be strong. She released Claire from her late evening's work, and settled down as best she could with so many different thoughts whizzing round in her head.

They all boiled down to one thing. At the start of the evening she had had two men. At the end of the evening she had seen them both taken away by the emergency services. Could it get any worse?

She buried her head in the pillow in case she made any noise and disturbed anybody upstairs.

The following morning, Helen woke late. It had taken her a long time to fall asleep, and even though it was now not far short of ten o'clock, the lack of sleep was acute. She sat up and looked around, bleary eyed. There was a vague smell of tobacco smoke left, presumably, by Mick. The house was peaceful. The only sound she could hear was that of plates clinking as they were being put away. She quickly dressed and made her way towards the activity.

"Claire. Hi." Helen managed the briefest of greetings. Claire turned round and looked at the exhausted figure in the kitchen doorway.

"Helen. How are you?" The question didn't need an answer.

"Not too great."

"Sit down, please, and I'll sort you out some breakfast." Claire's authoritarian tone left Helen with no option.

Over a bowl of porridge, through which Helen worked her way very slowly, and a pot of coffee, the two women attempted to put some shape into the day. Claire thought she needed to provide some sort of distraction for her ailing friend. She felt sorry for Helen, but domestic obligations and pressures meant she could not be lenient. One thing was certain - Helen would not be spending a second night there. Claire imagined what Mick would say if she suggested it, and she shuddered at the thought.

"Helen, you can stay for a few hours, but not really any longer. I'll need to pick up the kids from school and Mick will be back later. He told me this morning he didn't mind you staying last night, but I don't think he'll be happy if you are still here when he gets back tonight. If he comes home tired and ratty from work as usual, then I don't think you'll particularly want to know him."

Helen had never met Mick, and Claire's tone of voice made it sound as though she didn't really want to. Come late afternoon, Claire would have her hands full with the children. Helen sighed and looked pathetically at her saviour of the night before.

"OK," she managed.

"I'll tell you what," said Claire, "when we've finished breakfast, how about some fresh air? I don't want to sit round here. What would you say to a walk by the lake and then I'll drop you off at home? Or, if you're hungry after the walk, we can have a bite to eat in town."

Helen recognised that she wasn't being given much option. Claire was telling her as kindly as she could that her time in the house was up. "OK," she said again, looking through the window. At least it wasn't raining.

Inevitably, Chris spent a night in the cells. Usually he was keen to try new experiences, but not this time.

Peter Cropper

The upshot of Chris' short stay at the police station was that he was released on bail. The following morning he stood outside the police station and he felt completely alone. He had very little idea as to what he should do next. He presumed he had to tell someone what had happened. He wandered across to a nearby bench and took out his mobile.

He rang Pete. It was voicemail, but Chris was undeterred. Perhaps, under the circumstances, that was for the best. He felt he had to unburden himself. He left a message, mentioning in as casual a fashion as he could manage that he was probably the first person that Pete had known to have been placed on police bail. He wondered if Pete would ring him back soon, then he ended the call, hoping he hadn't sounded too pleading or pathetic.

He tried Dave Sullivan. Bloody voicemail again. People invested in mobile phones but never had them switched on. He explained what had happened, and ended, as he had on Pete's message, by asking Dave if he would send his regards to his colleagues.

If the messages were picked up, the news would percolate quickly through two networks and a number of people would get to know of Chris' unfortunate predicament. This, of course, meant that a number of people could potentially phone him. He sat and thought for a few minutes, wondering who else he should tell about what had happened. Who else could he turn to in his hour of need?

Helen? Under the circumstances, he really didn't think so.

Bob? It might have been an idea to have kept in touch with him. When it had become apparent that Sarah didn't really want to associate with him, Chris went along with what she had wanted. There was no good reason why Chris couldn't have stayed in contact with Bob, of course; he was supposed to be his own man, and Sarah could have had no complaints about Chris keeping in touch with his brother. But he hadn't kept in touch with him, so that was that.

Sue Mason? She was Helen's friend. You're being silly now, Chris.

Sarah? Sarah?

Sarah, unbelievably, seemed to be the least implausible possibility. He had upset her, of course, but he had written her a nicely worded letter explaining the position and he was sure that she had understood. She had seen the stress he had been under. He had explained reasonably that what he had done was the best way forward for both of them. He had, in effect, given her a car, for goodness sake. They were still married. "For better or for worse," was what they had said all those years ago. If Sarah was blazing mad at him she would have rung and said so now that, courtesy of Helen, she knew where he was living. There had been no such phone call.

Sarah was his best hope. Sarah was perhaps his only hope.

Sarah accepted the call.

"What are you going to do?" asked Claire.

"I don't know," said Helen. "Something. Nothing."

The barmaids were by the lake. The weather had held, but the clouds had been building for a while on the fells. Dry weather much further into the afternoon could not be guaranteed.

"What are you going to do when Chris comes back?"

"Don't know."

"Are you going to ring the hospital to see how Martin is?"

Helen gave an identical answer. Questions like these were much too difficult.

Helen was clueless. Claire took her to a pub. Conveniently ignoring the fact that alcohol acts as a depressant, she thought it might be more suitable than caffeine.

Conversation was stilted at best. Helen was distracted as her mind was again rerunning the events of the night before, and Claire didn't know Helen well enough to introduce topics of interest to make her think pleasant thoughts.

"I'm going to have a sandwich. Let me treat you to something."

Helen was touched, really. There was no doubt that Claire seemed to be going the extra mile to help her although, as Helen reminded herself, the time constraints placed on Claire's kindness meant that it would soon run out.

"That's very kind. I'll have some soup. Thank you."

The waitress brought over cream of chicken soup with a crusty roll. Helen was surprised to discover how hungry she was and she tucked in with some gusto while Claire enjoyed her cheese sandwich. With a couple of glasses of white wine on the table it would have been easy for Helen to be deluded into thinking all was well, but all too soon the party was over. After they had eaten, Claire stood up. "Helen, I really am going to have to go. The kids'll go wild if I'm not there to meet them from school."

"I understand." Helen's voice was barely audible even though the pub was quiet.

"Claire, I'm so grateful to you for looking after me."

"That's what friends are for. Now promise me you'll ring me if you need anything." With that, Claire stood up and left the pub quickly. She had changed her mind about taking Helen home. This sudden departure was the best way.

Helen stayed out as long as she could. She browsed in her favourite clothes shops, bought a couple of paperbacks from the charity shop, walked back to the lake and then back into town as slowly as she could to use up unwanted time, and finally she called into the small supermarket. Absentmindedly she bought some margarine, bread and milk even though she had no recollection of how much she had at home. When she left the shop she could think of nowhere else to go so she went home. She told herself that everything would be as it was before Chris and Martin appeared on the scene. She knew she was fooling herself.

Bowing Out

She opened the door, half expecting Chris to be there. Or was he in fact still at the police station? She had absolutely no idea what had happened to him and she had the right to know. They were partners, weren't they? That was the current terminology, wasn't it?

She supposed she could ring the police station, but instantly nerves overcame her. She would have to rehearse the conversation while she made a cup of tea. "Hello, I'm enquiring about Chris O'Neill. Yes, I'm Helen, his… partner. He got himself in a bit of trouble last night. Can you tell me what has happened to him?"

When she had perfected her lines she went to the phone. She would just see who had left a message before making the call.

"Helen – what the hell did you do to Chris to make him behave like that? He would never have done that while he was with me. I can only put it down to your evil influence. I'm going to bail him out. You can leave it all to me. I will rescue him!"

Helen didn't phone the police station. Instead she shouted at the top of her voice, "Chris O'Neill, you can go to blazes. If you never set foot in this house again, it will be too soon. And you can go with him, Mrs O'Neill!"

Sarah lit a cigarette to calm her nerves and set off at speed. She knew she was probably driving too fast but she didn't seem able to stop herself. "Shut up!" she shouted to the man in the small red van who had not unreasonably blasted his horn at her after she had cut him up. "I'm in a rush. I've no time to wait for amateurs on the road. If you can't drive properly, then bloody well stay at home."

She roared onto the motorway and headed north. The road was surprisingly quiet and Sarah was able to put herself onto automatic pilot. She had some thinking to do and some questions to put to herself.

She cut to the chase and posed the key question, "Why do I want to rescue Chris and get him out of his predicament?" She asked the question out loud. She thought that hearing it would help her focus on the issue.

The answer was not immediately apparent. Was envy behind it? Was she jealous of Helen and the fact that she had taken possession of her husband? Was it therefore to gain revenge over Helen? She thought of the times they had spent together as teenagers and young adults. Sarah had been the pretty one. Sarah had had the more attractive personality. How had she managed to lose him like this? When Chris saw her again, he'd realise what a mistake he had made and exactly what he was missing.

Did she think she had something to make up to Chris? Perhaps she could have been more sympathetic to the stresses and strains he talked about at the end of long days in school. Except days in school aren't particularly long, she thought. But then again, he does work in the evenings, doesn't he? On reflection, she conceded that she could have been more understanding. Chris must have felt sometimes as if he were banging his head against a brick wall, and you can only do that for so long before your head caves in. He had been stupid bailing out of the Scottish holiday, that much was true, but perhaps he had been driven to it. Perhaps if she had tried harder to bring him back to the holiday, everything might have been OK. Had she ever said she was sorry for driving him to take such drastic action? She was sure that she hadn't. Why had she seemingly just let him run away instead of asking him to return to the cottage? He must have been sad to want to run so far. And whose fault might that have been?

She then considered a more practical matter. Was the house too big without him? It seemed more than twice the size with one fewer resident. There was no life in it. It was a house, but it was not a home. Even on the occasions when Andy had stayed, that feeling of cosy domesticity was never approached. She smiled as she realised she even missed Chris' complaining about her smoking.

She missed his tuneless singing as he occasionally took his turn to tidy the kitchen. She missed having to pick up his dirty socks at the end of the day. He used to leave them anywhere and everywhere. She missed having to put his empty beer cans in the bin because he had thought it perfectly acceptable to leave them lying round. She missed having to tolerate endless tedious sports programmes on the television. Most of all, she missed having someone there all the time to cuddle up to in bed at the end of the day.

She then drew what was without doubt the most important conclusion. She almost certainly still loved him.

That was the reason why she was going to bring him home, but there would have to be changes.

"Sarah, hi."
"Hello, Chris."
"Thanks for coming."

During their phone conversation they had arranged to meet outside the tourist office in the town. There was so much more to say, but Chris couldn't think past the initial pleasantries and formalities at that moment. He, too, had had time to do some thinking. Even though he could see Sarah and he had spoken to her, he could still hardly believe she was there. After all he had put her through! It was Chris, not Sarah, who had written the letter saying it was over. It was Chris, not Sarah, who had fallen straight into someone else's arms. And when he considered that the "someone else" was Sarah's best friend of some years ago, he would have thought that would have been sufficient for Sarah to block him out of her life for ever. Yet here she was.

He had envisaged standing outside the tourist office way after the appointed hour wondering if his wife was going to appear, but that had not happened. Sarah's saying she would come was not, as he had suspected it might be, a trick to get back at him.

There was not to be a sting in the tale, was there? Sarah wasn't going to say, "You didn't really think I was going to come and help you in your hour of need, did you?" before bidding him a Jason Farrell – style farewell, turning on her heels and heading straight back down the motorway, was she? He looked at Sarah's impassive face. He had no idea what was going to happen next. He said the first stupid thing that came into his head. "Sarah, I knew you'd come." The slightest trace of a smile appeared on his wife's face.

It was raining, but the weather couldn't dampen Chris' mood. Never mind the fact that he would have to appear in court at a later date – he was free now. He was not being held in custody. He also felt strangely optimistic that he would not receive such a severe punishment. People hit others in temper all the time. It was no big deal. What was the punishment? Chris didn't know, but you didn't read of people receiving years in jail for a provoked attack. Yes, he had been severely provoked by Martin. That could be proved beyond any doubt. Anybody in a position of authority would be able to see he had had it coming to him. He wondered how Martin was.

After a silence which seemed to last for hours rather than seconds, Sarah said, "Drink to celebrate?" It was the first thing, apart from "Hello Chris", that Sarah had said.

"Great idea!" said Chris. He couldn't believe what he had just heard.

"I don't think so, actually," retorted Sarah. She looked Chris. "You've been stupid. I don't think stupidity is something to celebrate, do you?"

"No." Chris spoke quietly, like a chastised schoolboy. His reaction to what he thought was Sarah's excellent suggestion had been both silly and wholly inappropriate. He could not remember ever feeling so embarrassed in front of her.

"Let's consider the important things first. How's the guy you beat up?"

"I don't know," said Chris, meekly. "They've not told me."

"I don't suppose you've thought to ask, have you?"

Chris didn't reply.

"Well, the first thing you're going to do is take out your mobile, ring the hospital and find out. What are you waiting for?"

"It's a bit wet out here, don't you think?" Chris ventured. "Any chance of doing it in the car?"

"Fine. Come to my car." Sarah put the emphasis on the word "my".

The news was not as bad as it might have been. Martin Cooper was as well as could be expected. He had regained consciousness shortly after arriving at the hospital, but he was still battered and bruised. He would be staying in hospital, but not for too long. "Martin will be pleased to know someone has been asking after him. Can I tell him who called?" asked the nurse.

"Tell him it's a friend wishing him well," said Chris, before hurriedly clipping the phone shut.

Chris summoned up his courage and asked, "Do you think we should go to Helen's and pick up my stuff? I have a key, and I don't think she'll be there now." Sarah's facial expression said that was one of the daftest suggestions she had ever heard. "I'll just put a bit more petrol in my car, and then we'll be off."

"Any chance of a bite to eat first?"

"I've plenty of food in my fridge in my kitchen," replied Sarah as they set off. She emphasised the same word as she had before.

It would not have taken Chris very long to pack up if Sarah had let him go to Helen's – there were only his clothes from the holiday and a few additional items he had bought since arriving in the Lakes. Had he been allowed back to the house, he would have discovered that packing would actually have taken no time at all. Helen's ruthless filling of bin bags would have ensured that. She had worked quickly and efficiently. It had only taken her about ten minutes to remove all traces of Chris from her life. A visit from the locksmith would complete the process, and Mr Adams said he would be round later that afternoon to do the job.

Helen was more interested in the welfare of another man now, and that's why she was at the reception desk of the hospital finding out which ward to go to.

Martin was sitting up in bed. He was not looking his best and his face was less attractive than Helen had remembered it, but there was a magazine open in front of him. The fact that Martin was able to read suggested not too much damage had been done.

"Hello." Martin looked up. He was clearly surprised to see her.

"Hello." He smiled, as best he could. A couple of teeth were missing. "Thanks for coming. I really appreciate that. And thanks for ringing to ask how I was."

Helen was puzzled, but she didn't show it. "I wanted to come and see if you were OK. You took quite a battering."

"I did, yes." He paused to think. "What was it all about?"

"I'm not sure really." Helen could not see the point of telling him.

"Sit down, won't you. I'm afraid I can't offer you any grapes. It's traditional for hospital visitors to eat the patient's grapes, isn't it? But nobody's been and I haven't got any. They'll be taking away my membership of the in patients' club, if I'm not very careful."

He had retained a sense of humour. Helen liked that.

"Am I the first visitor you've had, then?"

"I'm afraid so. That must be why I don't have any grapes. If you turn your back on people, you can't really expect them to come running back just because you're in hospital, can you?"

Martin was delighted that Helen had taken the trouble to come and talk to him. It was a pity the conversation had only just got into its stride when the nurse rang the bell.

"I suppose that's time up," said Helen.

"I think it is."

Bowing Out

"Would you mind if I came to see you again? I'll find out when visiting starts and try to spend longer here tomorrow."

"When most people say that they'll try to do something, that usually means they've no intention of doing it," said Martin.

Helen smiled. "But I'm not like most people."

Martin treated Helen to another viewing of the spaces where his teeth had been. "I'd love it if you came to see me again tomorrow," he said.

CHAPTER 40

Sarah and Chris sped back home down the motorway. Chris was surprised how quickly the journey passed. He didn't remember his wife liking to drive so fast.

On two occasions in quick succession Sarah lit a cigarette. "It helps me stay calm while I'm driving," she explained as she zoomed along in the outside lane, leaving every other vehicle on the road in her wake. Chris raised no objection. He played it safe, and said nothing. Before, in a previous life, he might have said something like, "Do you have to stink the car out like that?" before adding, "What a ride! You'd pay a fortune for a ride like this at Blackpool Pleasure Beach." He didn't dare to think about dictating terms in the car now, nor did he think flippancy would go down well at this time.

It wasn't a very lively journey, unless a steady 90 miles per hour in the fast lane could be classed as "lively". Chris would have preferred some conversation but he didn't know how to initiate it. Sarah looked confident behind the wheel as she screamed past half a dozen lorries with large letters on their sides. She smiled to herself as she recalled the ridiculous game Andy had insisted on trying to play with her.

Those adventures with Andy seemed a lifetime ago. What was he doing now? The same as he always did in his little world, she reckoned. He had not been in touch. The blossoming relationship between Sarah and Andy had withered and died. She wondered if she would ever see him again, but that didn't matter because she had some work to do on her husband.

Andy never did ring back. The short sabbatical with Sarah had opened his eyes to the possibility of living life a little more to the full. It had helped him to recognise the rut he had been in with Helen and, if he were honest with himself, he couldn't really blame her for leaving. She must have been bored to tears much of the time. But that was then, and this was now. It was time to spread his wings and create a new life for himself, and he felt the need to sever all ties with his past life. That meant severing ties with Sarah. After careful consideration, Andy had concluded that the relationship had met a need, and that it had been pleasant and good fun while it lasted, but there was no future in it.

At the time when he was still considering what he really wanted to do, he found himself talking to Becky in the wine bar after work one evening. He had gone in there with two male colleagues, but fate had decreed that they be whisked away leaving Andy alone with an attractive young lady. Not long out of a crumbling relationship, Becky seemed very interested in Andy and his new goals for a more stimulating life. What a coincidence that she should be in exactly the same boat.

They arrived home, and Sarah opened the door. Chris hesitated. Sarah had done an excellent job of making him feel as if he should wait to be invited into his own house.

She let him stand on the doorstep for a few seconds before encouraging him in. Her tone appeared warm, but Chris thought there might be irony in it. He knew his wife was not averse to using irony. He entered the house warily.

"Now you said you were hungry, didn't you? What can I get you?"

"What is there?" asked Chris. He wanted to say, "I'll sort myself out," but he didn't feel able. He was frightened of wandering into his own kitchen.

"Take your coat off," said Sarah. "Unless you're not stopping."

"I am, aren't I?" Chris had never felt so anxious in his own home.

Sarah smiled. It was a warm smile which thawed the frosty atmosphere which had built up during the car journey. "Of course you are – if you want to."

I don't have much bloody option at the moment, thought Chris. He smiled back. "I want to stop, yes, of course I do."

"Then let me go and get you something to eat," said Sarah. She pretended to be puzzled. "Let me see if I can remember what you like best."

Sarah could remember, and a little later, over a salmon sandwich with salad at the dining table, she laid down the conditions. Chris suspected something momentous might be on its way. In former times they generally took snacks in the living room, either watching television or listening to music. Sitting very quietly at the table gave an air of seriousness and formality to the situation.

"Now listen, Chris." Chris sat up straight, as a Victorian schoolboy would have done. "I've been doing a lot of thinking. I'd love to have you back, I really would, but I think there'll have to be some changes."

"Changes?" Chris tried to conceal a note of panic in his voice.

"Firstly, in the wonderful world of work. Do you think I've been happy at the Fruit Bowl?"

Chris didn't know how to reply. "Well, you've never really complained –"

"Maybe not, but I've hardly been realising my potential, have I? You're not the only one who's been to university. It's time I used my brain. It's still in there somewhere."

To Chris, this represented a huge U-turn. Sarah had always been happy just pottering along, hadn't she? He had always considered her to be rather lazy, and easily content, but he chose not to voice that opinion at this stage.

"Have you any plans?" Chris asked.

"I've nothing particular in mind," said Sarah, "but what I do know is that to make myself more marketable in the modern world of work, I'll be needing to develop I.T. skills. They're absolutely hopeless, as you know, but they won't be when I've finished the intensive course I've enrolled on. That'll take up quite a lot of time, both in college and doing follow up work at home. You'll be marking homework, and I'll be doing homework. That'll be nice and ironic, won't it?"

Chris just had time to nod his head before Sarah continued.

"So, I'll be developing I.T. skills. Tell me, have you developed any more domestic skills while you've been away gallivanting? I hope so, because you're going to need them while you're here. I won't have huge swathes of time to dedicate to household chores, as you will probably appreciate."

"Right." That non entity of a response was all Chris could manage.

"What are you going to do about work, by the way?" asked Sarah.

"I have a sick note, so I needn't go back to teaching just yet." Chris looked worried, as one aspect of his situation dawned on him for the first time. "In fact, given that I'm out on bail, I don't even know if they would be able to or would be prepared to have me back at Whiteoaks at the moment." He thought about what the Headmaster would think about what Chris had done and his obvious fear that any publicity would be bad for his school. He also remembered the acrimonious way in which he had stormed out of the restaurant. Would the Headmaster welcome him back? Would his colleagues welcome him back? "I'm also not too sure if I want to go back there, even if they would have me. I'm going to need a while to settle back in here as well, I suppose."

"So, what are your intentions? Are they honourable?"

"I'm not too sure," was the mumbled response.

After a short pause, Sarah said, "How would you feel if I said we don't need to find out about whether you could get back in at your old school?"

"Pardon?"

"If you can do your full whack – and I mean full whack - round the house and offer me support while I'm moving on, that'd be most helpful – as would your salary which you could still get while you were on the sick."

Another visit to Doctor Brooker would soon be necessary. A more experienced Doctor Brooker might not be as gullible now. Chris was not sure what he would do if Doctor Brooker decided to no longer play the game.

Chris could see very few options. He nevertheless put together some sort of a protest, but he knew it would never stand up. "But, Sarah, you're a much better cook than me. You're much tidier than me. Is that going to work?"

"As you may or may not know, the cookery books are on the shelf in the kitchen, and, just to show how much I care, I promise I'll show you the on-off switch on the vacuum cleaner. I appreciate you're only a man, but if you're really up to it, I'll show you how the washing machine works."

"You're not actually giving me much of a choice, are you?"

"Your time away has not diminished your ability to see things clearly, has it? But you're back now. It's just that there are going to be some changes. You'll cope – I know you will." Sarah smiled at him. Chris smiled back a little ruefully, but there was relief in the smile, too.

Sarah had thought the situation through very carefully. "And if it proves impossible for you to go back to Whiteoaks," she continued, "you could go on the supply list. Think of the number of schools in this part of town alone, and then add the other suburbs and neighbouring towns. There'll be loads of schools looking for supply teachers although," she added with a smile, "some of the schools might not be as pleasant as Whiteoaks. But I don't think it would be a great idea to mention your adventures when you register at the supply agencies."

Chris tried not to wince. He had seen the reception supply teachers had received. They were people who knew neither the children nor the systems in place in the school, and they were fair game for some of the nastier pupils. Chris had often thought that was a position he'd hate to find himself in, but now…

Sarah stood behind Chris as he remained sitting at the table. She leant over and put her arms round him. "It will be very different in many ways, yes, but I hope that some things will be the same as they were before you surrendered to your pioneering spirit." Much to Chris' amazement, she gave him a kiss. "Come with me, you stupid bugger – I think we have a bit of catching up to do, don't you?"

ABOUT THE AUTHOR

Peter Cropper was born in St Helens, Lancashire in 1956 and was educated at Prescot Grammar School and Newcastle University, gaining an Honours Degree in German in 1979. After a short period working for the civil service in London, he qualified as a language teacher in 1983. He subsequently taught for 19 years at a school in Salford. He now enjoys his working life as a writer and part time driver.

His first book was an authorised biography - "From Great Broughton to Great Britain - Peter Gorley, Rugby League forward" which was published in 2004. He regularly contributes to the St Helens RLFC match day programme and he has had many articles published in "Lancashire Today" magazine. "Bowing Out" is his first novel.

He lives in Horwich near Bolton with his wife Josephine, who is a psychotherapist and who runs the " Rekindle your Dreams" course (www.healthyhorizons.gb.com), while his daughter Hanne has qualified as a pharmacist at the University of East Anglia. In his spare time Pete enjoys watching rugby league, cricket and football as well as walking and playing in the local quiz league.